THE GILDED FLEECE

THE GILDED FLEECE

NIGEL TRANTER

B & W PUBLISHING

EDINBURGH

Copyright © Nigel Tranter
First published 1942
by Ward Lock & Co Ltd
This edition published 1993
by B&W Publishing
Edinburgh
ISBN 1 873631 13 8

A CIP record for this book is available from
the British Library

Cover illustration by Brigid Collins
Cover design by *Harry Palmer* **Design** *Consultants*

Printed by The Cromwell Press

B & W PUBLISHING
7 SCIENNES • EDINBURGH
031-667 6679

1

ADAM METCALFE took a hasty glance in the mirror, ran a hand over his hair, and pulled down his coat. His boots could have done with a polish and his cravat might have been neater, but the groom had said he was to come at once. Anyway, he was no town dandy to prink himself up even if it wasn't everyday that his lordship expressed a desire for his company. Clapping rakishly on his head a rather shaggy beaver, and then heedfully adjusting it to an angle more suitable to the occasion, he strode out, and down the stairs two at a time. Passing a half-opened door in the hallway, he paused and thrust his head inside.

"Humphrey Augustus wants me over at the Court for something—Lord knows what," he called. "Keep me a bite, Charles—I'll not get much more than good advice out of the noble lord!"

"Adam . . . !" a voice protested coldly, but the younger man did not wait for his brother's reproof, but left him to his books and his righteousness.

Walking along the path that led pleasantly through fields and parkland from the Vicarage to Lakingham Court, Adam Metcalfe pondered the wherefore of this summons to the presence. He had not done anything sufficiently heinous lately to call for a personal wigging from Authority—at least, not that he could recollect off-hand. Still less could he claim to have risen to any such heights of virtue as to merit so great condescension. And it was not a sudden rush of affection, an urgent desire to look upon his fair countenance, the very day of his lordship's arrival from London or Bath or wherever it was the fellow passed his aristocratic time—that he could swear. He had managed to get along without hob-nobbing with his assistant-steward for some considerable time—even if they had been inseparable as boys. Well, then, it must be his Commission, the Ensignship he had been trying to land for months. This possibility had leapt to his mind, of course, the moment he had received the message from the groom, but had not to be considered till others less pleasant had been disposed of. He had asked Lady Alice to get her nephew to use his influence, and Lady Alice had a weakness for young men. Yes, it must be the Commission—though the off-chance of a slating couldn't be overlooked entirely. Considerably cheered, he proceeded between the sprouting March hedgerows; Bonaparte's days were numbered.

Presently he left the road by a wicket gate through the hedge, and cut across the wide green spread of the deer-park, direct to the Court. Old Cramb would not have approved—neither would his brother; Cramb because, in his menial soul, he considered the deer-park sacrosanct when his lordship was in residence, Charles because he was a snob and a stickler for correctness. Charles, with clerical dignity, always stuck to the Road, and the centre of the Road, on principle; who knows, his road might one day lead him to a deanery or even a bishopric if he walked it circumspectly. Well, every man to his taste.

Adam Metcalfe waved his hat at a group of wide-eyed slender deer, and laughed at their graceful bounding panic. Lord Alcaster was very proud of his fallow deer.

Skirting the mullions and fretted buttresses of the chapel wing, he passed through the mellow orderliness of the walled garden and slipped into the great house through the garden door. A serving girl, encountered, smiled a welcome and did not object to a squeeze and a slapped buttock—he was not a bad-looking young fellow, and built to fill the eye—before passing him on to a resplendent footman, under whose powder and velvet Adam was astonished to discover the embarrassed person of one Tom Rooke, a forester's son and companion of a ferreting expedition of only a few days before. Sharing the joke together, they mounted the stairs towards his lordship's library, into which, with a knock and a pause and a valedictory wink, Adam was ceremoniously ushered.

Two men shared the great sombre apartment, one lounging at ease in a wide wing-chair near the flickering fire of logs that was the cheerfullest feature of the room, the other standing stiffly beyond and close to the window. On a table between them lay a litter of papers, a decanter, and glasses.

The sitter, Humphrey Augustus, fourth Earl of Alcaster though barely three years senior to Metcalfe, at thirty-two looked a decade older at least. A slightly-made man and darkly handsome, he had a peculiar breadth of shoulder, which, allied to a short neck and a pronounced stoop, might have branded as an incipient hunchback anyone less exalted. Dressed in the height of fashion, a height dizzy for the country, his moulded frock-coat, snowy ruffles, spotless moleskins, and gleaming Hessians, did nothing to hide a puffiness, which, fashionable as it might be, sat unnaturally on a slender figure.

He glanced up as Metcalfe was announced, and the hand that automatically raised the quizzing-glass to inspect the visitor, dropped it again as if on second thoughts. "Ah, Adam, there y'are," he greeted casually. "Come in, man. Ye look devilish fit and hearty."

The voice was languid and weary, the whole attitude was languid and weary, but the eyes belied it, keen dark eyes beneath heavy lids that searched the newcomer up and down in a cool stare that brought its own hot reaction to the recipient—till he remembered that he had been spared the quizzing-glass, and summoned a modicum of thankfulness. "I'm very well, sir, thank you." Briefly, feeling positively bucolic, Adam answered him. "You sent for me, I understand?"

Lord Alcaster looked amused without sounding it. "Still the same abrupt Adam," he commented, caressing sleek whiskers. "Ye wouldn't do for the Court, b'Gad. Your brother would have greeted me with quite a speech of welcome, I'll wager."

"Isn't that what Charles is paid for, making speeches?" Adam enquired reasonably.

"Whereas *you* are paid to act." The other took him up quickly. "My faithful assistant land-steward, quietly devoted to my interests!"

"Precisely, sir."

". . . but not over-worked—eh, Cramb!"

From over by the window, his companion, a small wizened

grey man, meticulously dressed, coughed and bowed in the one peculiar gesture. "No, indeed, my lord," he agreed, to add a brief doubtful apology for a laugh, in case a joke was intended. Ezra Cramb, steward of the Alcaster estates, never knew just how to take his master; that his assistant was not similarly perplexed was one of the things that was apt to rankle.

"I've had no faults found with my work," Adam protested warmly. "If Mr Cramb had any complaints, he . . ."

"Tush, man—don't be so deuced thin-skinned," Lord Alcaster cut in. "Nobody's talking about complaints. B'Gad, the boot's on the other foot. It's good news I've got for you, not complaints. Isn't that so, Cramb?"

Adam Metcalfe's hopes of his Commission, which had been fading, rose again, but only moderately. He was suspicious of this second appeal to Cramb. He knew his man, and if the news was really so good, Humphrey Augustus would not be inviting his steward to help him out with it. He waited then, attentive.

The Earl picked up his glass again, but only to turn it over in his hands. "I gather from my aunt that you are anxious to serve your country rather more . . . actively than you are doing at present, Adam," he began. "Quite right too, highly commendable . . . but there are more ways of serving your country than by jumping into uniform and imagining yourself a hero. Any fool can do that. The country's got plenty of swaggering soldiers. What it needs is brains and enterprise and, ah, industry."

He paused for a moment, and the younger man gazed at him, astonished. Patriotism—from Humphrey Augustus! Lord, what next!

Alcaster leaned forward. "You may not be aware of the fact that food is getting scarce in this country, in the towns—God knows why! The fault of Bonaparte and those damned manufacturers, I believe. Anyway, the country needs meat, the Army needs meat, and if they don't get it Boney'll have us, soldiers or none. The Government is getting anxious, food prices are mounting, and our duty is plain—we must produce food . . . meat."

4

Sitting back in his chair, the speaker yawned, as though exhausted by his effort, but Metcalfe, watching, knew the yawn for a sham. Alcaster was not bored, this time; there was more behind this than new-found patriotism—more for Alcaster. "And my good fortune, sir?" he enquired.

"I'm going to send you up to my estate in the North of Scotland as Deputy-Commissioner!"

Adam stared. "I'm afraid I don't understand . . ."

"It's quite simple." Alcaster felt for his snuff-box. "I'm going to convert large areas of what is at present practically waste land into sheep-runs. I am assured that the ground is admirably suitable for sheep, though meantime little more than a wilderness inhabited by a few illiterate aborigines, practically savages. John Dunn, my Commissioner, has already got the work in hand, but it is a huge task and he needs assistance. So here's your chance to serve your country, yourself, and all concerned." No outburst of gratitude intervening, he went on, with obvious patience. "I'm giving you a chance, a very big chance. Strathmoraig's a big place—these Highland properties run to enormous acreages. What's the size of it, Cramb—some absurd figure?"

"One hundred and forty-seven thousand acres, my lord."

"Half the size of Worcestershire, b'Gad—and never a damned bit of use up till now. You'll be the master of all that, under Dunn, Adam. We'll get you appointed a Justice—you'll need it, by all accounts. Better than an insignificant Ensignship, eh?"

"Apparently, sir." Metcalfe was cautious. "And my duties?"

"Dunn will tell you that. I've never been near the place myself—too devilish far away. Would have sold it long ago if anybody would have bought it. You will do as Dunn directs. Good man, Dunn. Says the land should carry a hundred thousand head. Think of it, b'Gad—a hundred thousand sheep!"

"And mutton and wool prices rising monthly!" Ezra Cramb put in gleefully. He was not so subtle as his master.

"I believe they are," Lord Alcaster conceded indifferently.

So that was it. Humphrey Augustus had good solid grounds for his sudden patriotism. He would have, of course. There was a shrewd acquisitive brain behind that mask of indolence. However much he tried to hide it, his efforts to be the complete Corinthian, the irresponsible Buck that his rank and position demanded, a strain of hard-headed astuteness would out. He got it, no doubt, from the same source as he got the lands that he was now going to develop for the benefit of his war-tried country and the earldom of Alcaster, from his grandmother, heiress of the last of the Chiefs of MacVarish, who, from all accounts, after the manner of the Scots, had never found business incompatible with aristocracy.

Adam Metcalfe listened while Alcaster and Mr Cramb enlarged on the potentialities of the Highlands as sheep-runs. Apparently they had been formed entirely for this end—they were good for nothing else, as everyone was aware. Other Highland proprietors were moving the same way; Stafford had already cleared tens of thousands of acres in Sutherland, and the Chisholm in Inverness: a beneficial process that was going to set the desert blossoming as the rose and usher in an era of prosperity undreamed-of amongst those barren wastes . . . or barren but for the sheep-pasture, that is. Adam Metcalfe should consider himself fortunate indeed to be identified with a project so praiseworthy.

Adam Metcalfe reserved his judgment—rather a habit he had. He was disappointed about the Commission, of course— something he had set his heart on. Then there was young Selina Purcell, the doctor's daughter—he had not exactly set his heart on *her*, but they had been getting on rather well together; a pity to interrupt so pleasant a practice . . . though, for that matter, joining the Army would have had the same consequence, only with rather more romance about it. And Wester Ross was a long way off in the wrong direction, a howling waste of rock and heather peopled by a race of barbarians whose outlandish gibberish was apparently now to be drowned in a flood of baa-ing . . .

Still, it would be a change, quite a noticeable change from rich, fat Worcestershire, of which he was young enough to be getting vaguely tired, jaded. It would be pioneering, trailblazing, with a spice of adventure—better than life, existence, with smug brother Charles and Ezra Cramb. And Deputy-Commissioner . . . Magistrate . . . ! Names only—but not to be dismissed unconsidered by a penniless vicar's son. Not that there was any choice, of course; if the Right Honourable Humphrey Augustus said he was to go, who was Adam Metcalfe to say otherwise?

". . . and it won't do to waste any time," Alcaster was saying. "Expedition is, ah, essential. It's a devilish long journey, and Dunn needs assistance at once, he says. A couple of days should do for you, eh? Cramb here will make all the arrangements—I've got to get back to Town by tomorrow night." He waved a gracious hand toward the decanter. "A glass of claret before you go," he decreed. "We'll drink to the occasion. Gentlemen, I give you Strathmoraig—may its fleece be golden!"

Adam Metcalfe raised his glass. "Say gilded, sir," he suggested.

2

THE schooner's bows swinging westwards, dipped deeply into the long Atlantic swell that bore down on her from beyond the great breakwater of Arran. A smirr of rain, thin and cold, drifted across the grey water from the lowering clouds that capped the sullen hills of long Kintyre. A single gull in disillusioned attendance mocked the plunging mast-heads with its level sailing.

Adam Metcalfe turned up the collar of his travelling-cloak and crossed to the vessel's leeward side where he sought shelter behind the deck-house, and considered the stern mountains of Arran. This was his first sight of the Highland hills, after eight days of travelling, and he was not sure that he liked what he saw. He had sailed up the Clyde estuary three days ago in the Liverpool packet, but that had been at night and he had seen nothing. He stared, now, doubtfully.

Presently he was joined by the younger of his two fellow passengers, a dashing Lieutenant of Highlanders, the gallant panoply of whose uniform had attracted attention when he had embarked early that morning at the port of Greenock. His splendour was now hidden beneath the amplitude of a many-caped coat, and his bonnet had lost its fine jauntiness through being pulled down as far as it would go over its wearer's head. He came stamping along the heaving deck, damning the cold, but swearing that, if anything, the atmosphere and general amenity of the cabin below was worse than the weather, all with linguistic emphasis.

To him Adam indicated the bastions of Arran and all the scowling ramparts of Kintyre. "A wild country, your Highlands," he suggested. "Rather . . . grim!"

"Grim!" the other snorted. "Grim is mild, sir, grim is not the word at all. They're barbarous and dreary and depressing, a God-forsaken desolation—with population to match."

Adam was surprised at his vehemence. He gestured vaguely towards the bonnet. "But . . . you're Scotch, a Highlander, yourself, aren't you . . . ?"

His companion drew himself up and would have achieved a fair show of dignity had it not been for the lie of his head-gear. "A Scot, yes—but no gibbering Hie'landman!" he proclaimed stiffly. "Sir, my name is Seton, Lieutenant Alexander Seton, of as good a family as any in Scotland!"

"I have no doubt—I beg your pardon." Adam bowed, but doubtfully. "It was your uniform, your tartan trousers . . ."

"One can be an officer in the Highland Brigade without having the heather between one's toes," Lieutenant Seton pointed out starchily. "Good God, where would the country be if the Highland Brigade had to get its officers out of the heather!" and he laughed at the very thought of it, and forgot his ruffled pride. "You are new to this country then sir, I take it?"

"Very," Adam agreed, ". . . but interested. I'm from Worcestershire, and travelling north to Strathmoraig in Wester Ross—perhaps you know it?"

"Lord, yes—and a forlorn stretch of the back of beyond, too. You're right off the map up there . . . er—you don't own it, I hope, sir?" Reassured, he went on, "I'll probably be up as far as that myself, later on. We're on a recruiting drive." He waved a hand down towards the cabin. "My uncle, Colonel Dunbar, is on General Abernethy's staff, and the Brigade needs a lot more men. We've had devilish heavy casualties lately, y'know. My lot, the 91st, practically decimated at Vimiera and Corunna."

"But you escaped . . . ?"

"I was with the Staff," Seton explained sharply.

"Ah—of course. So you're recruiting!" Adam was interested. "Where do you get the men? I had an idea that the Highlands were largely uninhabited."

The other laughed. "Uninhabited my foot! There's plenty of men in the heather . . . except where these damned improvements are being carried out."

"Improvements . . . ?"

"Improvements." The other nodded fiercely. "All this damned

sheep-rearing nonsense. By God, sir, it's a scandal! There are estates I could take you to that were good for half a Company of men any time, where now you won't get a single recruit—there's nobody there but a shepherd or two and a thousand bawling sheep. And where will the country be, sir, if it can't get men for the Highland Brigade?"

Adam had a notion that perhaps the country might still struggle along somehow with the remainder of its armed forces, but of course he had no authoritative information. "Then these Highlanders are of some use, after all?" he suggested. The lieutenant did not seem altogether consistent.

Seton glanced at him sharply. He was not a man that was going to be played with. "Trained and disciplined they make good soldiers—when properly officered, of course," he asserted briefly. This Englishman had to be kept in his place, obviously. "Never heard of any other use for them, myself," and with a curt nod, he strode aft again, and disappeared below.

Adam Metcalfe turned to stare again at the distant forbidding line of the upheaved land, uncertain now behind a driving rainstorm, and to ponder a number of things. And still the solitary gull sailed above, without effort and untiring, till, with the schooner's plunging bows rounding the jutting Mull of Kintyre and turning northward, it slanted off, heedless and remote, and the grey Atlantic swallowed it up.

All that day and the next and the next again, they sailed up into the Western ocean, through squalls and wind and sleet and patches of brilliant sunshine that revealed in breath-taking glimpses the magic beauty of the isle-studded sea. They called at a number of ports, at rocky havens on rugged coasts, at the sandy bays of green islands, at the mouths of narrow sea-lochs that pierced deep into the heart of stern mountains, small isolated townships in the wilderness, whose names sang a strange wild refrain of their own, Machrihanish, Askaig of Islay, Colonsay, Tobermory of Mull, Arisaig. It was at Arisaig, small and scattered at the head of its loch and loud with the smell of seaweed, that they picked up two more passengers, two ministers of the Scottish Kirk returning to their remote parishes from a Synod meeting at Fort William. Watching them as they came down the little pier, Lieutenant Seton strolled forward. "Mr Metcalfe," he observed. "You are always anxious to increase your knowledge of things Scottish. You will now see approaching what looks to me like two promising specimens of the genus corbie, or black crow, a bird that caws devilish loud in Scotland . . . damn the breed!"

Nevertheless, with the schooner standing out once more into the tossing waters of the Sound of Sleat, the Army lost no time in making itself pleasant to the Church, the Army on this occasion including the Colonel Dunbar, a lofty and resplendent personage who had not felt called upon to so unbend to an assistant-factor designate. In his role of diligent searcher after information, Adam sought explanation, a process he was finding quite enjoyable.

Mr Seton explained with commendable patience. The Kirk carried a lot of weight. Its assistance in the matter of recruiting was invaluable. Those potential warriors that the Army failed to convince, threaten, or cajole into the firing line, the Kirk could advise in no uncertain voice, with the choice between hell-fire and a martyr's crown. It paid to be on good terms with the ministers; Metcalfe in his own sphere would appreciate that in due course.

The Reverend Mr Spence was tall and spare, and the Reverend Mr Hardie was taller and sparer. Both were stern, almost grim, though, if anything, Mr Hardie was the grimmer. Obviously they represented the Church Militant. Adam, accustomed to the comfortable sporting parsons of the English shires, perceived that he would have to adjust his attitude to religion.

That night they anchored off the little harbour of Isle Oronsay in the Aird of Sleat, under the fearsome mountains of Skye. In the long dark evening, out of an urgent desire to avoid for once the inevitable panegyric on the fighting qualities of the Highland Brigade, Adam Metcalfe rashly entered into a theological discussion with the divines and was therein comprehensively and pitilessly routed—as indeed his temerity deserved. In extenuation, it must be conceded that he laboured under a handicap, since it became apparent that their respective theologies concerned two very different codes of belief, even two distinct deities. Before Jehovah the Terrible, jealous God of Battles and of the Reverends Hardie and Spence, Adam's milder benevolent Episcopalian God retreated, vanquished and abashed. The young man retired to his bunk considerably chastened.

At Portree next day, the military party and Mr Spence disembarked, he to his manse amongst the braes of Trotternish, they to the house of Macdonald of Dalinish from thence to conduct their campaign amongst his island clansmen. Mr Seton took his leave quite reluctantly; despite the Englishman's tactless questions, he seemed to find him better company than his decorative uncle. Assuring Adam that he would make every effort to get as far as Strathmoraig later on, when he would expect a fine drove of stalwart recruits awaiting him, he departed in a swirl of mist to enlist Skye for the English king.

The Reverend Andrew Hardie was standing by as the goodbyes were said. As Metcalfe turned away it was to find himself under the minister's keen regard. "Did I overhear your friend mention Strathmoraig as your destination, sir?" he enquired. He had a harsh voice that went curiously with the sing-song Lowland accent that he had carried with him from his native Fifeshire.

"You overheard correctly, sir."

The other's grey eyes narrowed slightly. "Then you must be the new assistant-factor I've heard about," he said. "My parish of Menard lies in the centre of the estate. We will be neighbours, Mr Metcalfe . . . and colleagues, I hope."

"I am glad to hear it, sir." Adam lied politely. "But colleagues? Do you mean in relation to *my* master's four-footed sheep, or *your* Master's two-footed ones?"

From his expression, it was obvious that the older man considered this to be a jest in the worst of taste. "Young man," he indicted severely, "it is my duty, just as much as it is yours, to improve and cultivate these barren neglected stretches of the Most High's vineyard. The barren places of the earth shall rejoice and the desert shall yet praise God!"

12

"Ah . . . undoubtedly."

"It is a great work that Mr Dunn is doing, a great and noble work. Industry shall banish sloth. Instead of the thorn shall come up the fir tree, and instead of the briar shall come up the myrtle tree," he intoned. "And it shall be to the Lord for an everlasting sign that shall not be cut off. Lord Alcaster is a far-sighted man, Mr Metcalfe. Posterity shall call him blessed."

Adam swallowed. For so young a man he was something of a cynic.

With Skye only a jagged memory behind them, lost in its eternal mists, the *Harebell* raced up between the mountain walls of Loch Ardoch sped by a freshening breeze that came to them out of the westering sun. The loch was long and narrow and on its dark waters the wind, sweeping as up a funnel, raised angry combers that gleamed starkly white against the black shadows that already filled that gut of the hills. Ahead lay Kinlochardoch, journey's end for the *Harebell*, and the edge of the world for her skipper, beyond which he would not venture any vessel of his; if any of his passengers must go farther, then let them go on their own two feet, and God have mercy upon them. The skipper was a well-doing man from Glasgow, with a wife and family.

As, shortening sail, they came, from round a shoulder of hill, within sight of the head of the loch, Adam was surprised to see the masts and outline of another ship towering above the huddle of low white-washed houses that crouched at the water's edge. The skipper had seen it, too; from his vantage point in the bows, Adam heard him curse forcibly, and give orders to dowse all sails. Apparently the little port had berthage for only one ship at a time, and with the ebbing tide it would be necessary to lie off for the night at anchor. Losing way, the schooner slipped forward, the noise of the water under the bows sank from a swish to a gurgle, to a slap-slap, till with a rattle and a splash the anchor ran out and the *Harebell* swung-to and so lay, two or three cables' lengths off-shore.

Adam Metcalfe was examining the other vessel with interest. She was quite a big ship, twice the size of the *Harebell*, and brigantine-rigged. But it was not her size in that small outlandish haven that attracted his attention so much as the strange sound that came out of her, weakly against the rising wind, a sobbing wail infinitely forlorn, that rose and rose and fell and died away and rose again, rhythmic, persistent, and hopeless. Enquiringly Adam turned to a nearby sailor. "What is that . . . that noise?"

"Yon's one o' thae emigrant boats," he was told. "An awfu' row thae Hielant women make wi' their keening—you'd think they was being massacred."

Emigrant boat! Adam turned back to that dark ship under the darkening hills, and as the woeful lament came again across the black water, he knew a tingling sensation beneath his scalp and a strange shiver of unease. Other sounds came from the vessel too, faintly, for she was a quarter-of-a-mile away, bangings and the creak of pulleys, shouting and coarse laughter, that went ill with the wailing. There were noises from the direction of the shore, too, sounding intermittently above the sigh of the breakers, commands and cries and the high voices of children. Kinlochardoch was busy tonight.

"The old order changeth . . . and yonder you see the sign and symbol of the new, Mr Metcalfe." Adam turned to find Mr Hardie at his elbow. "Yon ship is going to take these poor folk from their miserable squalid bits of crofts and wretched holdings to the brave new lands of the Canadas, or it may be Australasia, where there is room for all and to spare, work for every hand, and the wilderness to be claimed for God."

The younger man glanced around him. "Plenty of room here, isn't there . . . and any amount of wilderness to be reclaimed?" he suggested reasonably.

"Room, yes—heather and bog and peat, but you would not condemn a people to fruitless toil on that, with the wide granaries of the New World crying to be delivered from the heathen blackamoor?"

"But haven't they lived here for centuries . . . ?"

"Lived, after a fashion—yes." The minister's wiry eye-brows bristled fiercely. "In primitive squalor and cut-throat savagery, without manners, learning, or ambition. Ye'll not tell me that

14

sort of existence is to be preferred to the fine free life overseas that the Almighty in his Providence has opened up for them?"

"And yet, from the sound of them, would they not seem to prefer it . . . ?"

"Man, that's just women's easy tears; the least thing will set them off at it, these Hieland women. What they need is a bit faith in God—and trust in the good judgment of their betters. But all that yowling will stop when they set sail—it always does."

His companion nodded slowly. "I see," he said.

The skipper approached his passengers. He was going ashore to find out when that damned brig—he begged pardon—would be sailing and he could get berthed and unloaded. If the gentlemen cared to come with him and stretch their legs . . . ? They could stop the night at the inn there, of course, but he had a notion that they might be having a disturbed night of it, with those seamen at their last night ashore. He expected that the brig would be sailing with the flood in the small hours of the morning, and drunk sailors were apt to make something of a noise.

The passengers took this advice as good, and agreed that their cabins, though cramped, might have advantages for another night. Adam was glad of the chance of a little exercise, and Mr Hardie announced that, since those were probably Glenbruach people embarking, his friend the Reverend Mr Henderson would be sure to be bidding them God-speed, he would take the chance of a word with him.

"Is it Glenbruach being cleared now . . . poor devils?" the skipper commented. "The new man hasn't taken long about it!"

"Major Parkinson's motives are of the highest—he is taking the long-sighted view, for the benefit of all concerned."

"Oh aye, I daresay."

As the rowing-boat neared the pier a scream from above turned all eyes up to the ship. A bundle of chattels, in the act of being hoisted aboard, had come apart in mid-air and a shower of miscellaneous plenishings cascaded down, some on the deck, some on the pier, some in the water, amid shouts of laughter. One of the seamen did not laugh, however; a soot-blackened pot, falling, struck him a blow, light enough, but streaking face and arm with black. With a curse he took a couple of steps and kicked that pot, so that it came flying overboard, to splash into the sea only a yard or so from the oncoming boat, spraying its occupants with water. The cheers and laughter from the ship were thereafter quelled to sniggers, to due gravity, by the resultant outburst from the *Harebell's* captain, objecting fluently to having cooking-pots or chamber-pots or any other kind of pots thrown at him, and being soaked into the bargain. Above, the cries of the woman who had owned the bundle sank to a moan, that blended and was absorbed into the general wailing and the crying of children. "What a rammy, what a devilish row!" the skipper snorted. "Worse than Glasgow Green on a Setterday night!"

On the pier they found a stout man, whose broad-cloth and riding boots stood out from amongst the hoddens and ragged tartans of the emigrants, directing the embarkation. Mr Hardie introduced him as Mr Bone, factor to Major Parkinson of Glenbruach, and enquired from him the whereabouts of the Reverend Henderson, the skipper likewise seeking the person of the brig's captain. Mr Bone directed them both vaguely along the shore to the northwards, where apparently they would find both gentlemen assisting at the rounding-up of certain misguided emigrées whose reluctance to travel was such that they had made a dash for it at the last moment. The factor's language was carefully restrained for the sake of the minister.

While his companions set off as directed, Adam stayed where he was for a little, to watch the proceedings—wasn't he to be a factor himself! But there was little to see, just the steady hoisting aboard of supplies, reed-straw for mattresses, and multi-shaped bundles of humble household goods, all pitifully inadequate in Adam's eyes to found a home in a strange land. He mentioned this general paucity of gear to Mr Bone, to be informed briefly that that was all the ship had room for them to take.

Apart from two soberly-clad individuals whose long batons stamped them as officers of the law, and who prowled about hopefully truculent, everybody on the rough pier seemed to accept the position with hopeless, if vocal, resignation—the protesters, of course, would be even now dodging the minister and the captain amongst the rocks of the loch-shore. Adam had a good look at these dejected people; these, then, were the Highlanders he'd heard so much about. Not a very fearsome-looking lot, nor noticeably wild or backward; just cowed and unhappy and apprehensive. The women, and they appeared to be mainly women and children, were mostly dark-haired and high-complexioned and well-built, many of them with good features. Their clothing was simple to a degree, obviously home-spun, but serviceable and generally clean, with only a tithe of the tartan that he had looked to see. The majority were barefooted, and their short skirts showed strong muscular legs, even amongst the older women. The seamen appeared to appreciate those legs, too. The men were all lean and in the main bent and grizzled, and old, all of them; looking around him, he could see never a youngish man among the whole company, barring a mouthing idiot and one or two cripples. Once again he enquired of Mr Bone. "Where are the young men?" he wondered. "Are they not going, too?"

"They're all away at the war," the factor explained, to add grimly: "... apart from one or two down in the hold with broken heads!"

The younger man stared. "And do they know about . . . this, the soldiers, I mean?"

"I have no idea." Mr Bone frowned testily. He was a busy man with much depending on his efforts.

Adam turned away. He moved amongst the waiting people, spoke to two women who shrank away from him as though they had been struck, and to a child that crouched against its mother, wild-eyed. Worse still, he said a few words in a kindly tone to another woman, who answered with a stream of Gaelic, her hand on his arm, supplication in every line of her. When he shook his head the babble of entreaty rose almost to a scream, and one of the constables came forward threateningly. Unhappily Adam sighed, and putting her from him, hurried away from her, from that pier, down toward the beach and the village.

17

It was not long before he saw a party approaching, three constables and perhaps half a dozen sailors, half-carrying, half-dragging between them a middle-aged man, two young women, and a lad in his teens. The man was blood-stained and only semi-conscious, the women were dishevelled and bruised, their clothes torn, and torn suggestively, baring breasts and thighs, the boy, his arms twisted behind his back, sobbed convulsively. Adam started forward, and then paused, helplessly. Immobile he watched them pass. Some distance behind came another group, respectable people these, led by two ministers. Adam, not just ready yet for further instruction on the ultimate benefits of emigration, swung off the road and plunged into the dead bracken of the hillside. Ahead of him rose a small bare hill. He went at it bull-headed. The climbing of it helped him.

Later that night, or rather, early next morning, Adam Metcalfe tossed on his narrow bunk. Hour after hour he had lain listening to the creak and groan of timbers and ropes, the lapping of water, and all the persistent uneasy sounds of shipboard, listening, and hearing not them, but the lost hopeless wailing of keening women. Try as he would he could not get the pain of it out of his head. For some time, hours now, there had been silence from that dolorous ship, but what respite that when every moan of straining wood and cordage, every whine of wind in the rigging, sang for him the same sad refrain?

And then he heard shouted commands, the clank of anchor chains, and the shake and slap of canvas, and growing out of it and through it and above it, that weary dirge of the quite forsaken. Rising and falling, swelling and declining, but never dying, the wailing approached them and passed them and went on, on down the black loch to the open sea, till its ache was only a memory among the sleeping hills. And the man, listening, threw himself over in his bunk, and heard a corresponding creak from through the thin partition that divided the cabins. "They have sailed ... and the, the yowling has not stopped," he called hoarsely.

"But it will ..." the harsh voice answered him. "Weeping may endure for a night, but joy cometh in the morning."

3

WALKING beside a pair of garrons carrying the baggage, shaggy small beasts, sure-footed and tough, Adam and the minister and an attendant gillie commenced their fifteen-mile journey to Strathmoraig. The morning mists still clung heavily to all the hill-sides and sent their chill fingers down every glen and corrie. The wind of the night had dropped, and the waters of the loch had levelled quickly and now lay grey and sullen and inert. Unseen but unceasing the curlews called mournfully, and no other sound save the sibilant whisper of a thousand burns came out of the heather.

The trudging men added little to dispel the hush. Adam, scowling back at the land, felt disinclined for talk, and showed it, keeping well to the edge of the rough track. The Reverend Hardie had a gift for silence, unless the occasion demanded otherwise; tight-lipped and purposeful he strode half-a-pace ahead, and his stride could have been that of a man twenty years his junior. In the rear, the gillie, a sallow stooping man with inscrutable eyes, spoke no English, and, meantime, no Gaelic either. The scuffling clop-clop of the ponies' unshod hooves was the company's sole contribution to the morning.

For something like five miles their course ran north-west along the loch-shore, through a desolate country of bare rock and heather and little else, devoid of man or the works of man. There was no road, only the vaguest suggestion of a track, that the party appeared to come across intermittently rather than to follow continuously, no bridges over the innumerable burns, small and great, that scored the braes with their stony scars, and no signposts. Travelling in this country seemed to demand a combination of divination, muscle, and faith.

About mid-forenoon, after fording a brawling river, Mr Hardie turned his back on Loch Ardoch and led his party right-handed up the alder-lined bank of this stream. Ahead of them it rose, fall upon fall, mile after mile, plain for all to see, up and up, scoring a green weal through the rolling brown waves of heather that lifted remorselessly in great swelling folds ultimately to lose themselves in the pall of the mist. And up there, close to the clouds, their braggart river dwindled and diminished to its humble genesis in the wedge of a green corrie. Thence, apparently, went their route. Adam looked askance, but bent to the task.

Two hours of steady inexorable climbing, and they neared the summit of the long ascent that, for some time, seemed to have been receding from them as the mists lifted. Somewhere, not so very far above them, a laggard sun was struggling to penetrate and dispel the layers of cloud that covered the land. Already the shroud was thinned and lightened, and through its sombre folds a pale radiance was filtering. It was just as they relaxed to the ease of level ground, bare rock and quartz grit and black moss, that a single narrow beam of light broke through, a sharp-edged golden sword that pierced the cloud and stabbed the earth, and hurt the eyes with its dazzling brilliance. And once pierced, the sullen mists, revealing their poor unsubstantial fabric, surrendered at once and completely, wilted and gathered up their skirts and departed, and left the world of the hills to the thin sunlight of a March noon.

Adam, a plainsman always, was unprepared for what he saw. They were not at the summit of a peak or ridge as he had assumed, but only at the head of a wide pass between two great mountains that towered hugely on either hand, austere, terrible. Behind and below, Ardoch had shrunk to a trough, sun-rimmed but sombre still, backed by an endless succession of hills that challenged the eye and confounded the imagination. Only to the west did the hills falter, before the glitter of the illimitable sea, whose age-long warfare was witnessed to by the wrack of a hundred hills, proud once, islands now, thrusting only their heads above the hungry tide. But it was what lay ahead that surprised Adam Metcalfe; before them a glen opened, narrow at first but ever widening till it sank into a broad distant valley. And that valley was like nothing that he had seen, a smiling fair place of open woods and quiet slopes, of scattered fields and small white-washed houses, of dotted cattle along green haughs, through which a sizeable river wound its way, its links gleaming in the sunlight. And beyond it the mountains rose again to all infinity, higher than ever, patched with the stark white of eternal snow.

Mr Hardie's arm described a wide sweep. "Strathmoraig!" he threw back briefly, without pausing in his stride, and down toward that goodly land they took their way.

It was further than it seemed, that pleasant place, and even when they reached it, Adam found that their walking was not finished, not by miles. Strathmoraig was a long valley, stretching fully sixteen miles from its rock-bound entrance on The Minch to its lofty head amongst the mountains of Menard, and it was up at that far end, hub to the spokes of half a dozen lesser glens, that Menardmore, the factor's house, represented the seat of authority for all that land. On his footsore way thither, Adam Metcalfe had opportunity and to spare for observation of his new surroundings.

Though judged by Southern standards it was still a wild bare country, compared with what else he had seen of the Highlands; it lived up to that first distant impression from the pass above Ardoch, a kindly open fertile place, and populous. There appeared to be nothing in the nature of a village, but small primitive stone houses thatched with reeds and turf were scattered haphazard everywhere along the valley floor and up the lower flanks of the hill-sides, each surrounded by its two or three tiny fields of tilth, doubtfully enclosed, and its few small rough-coated cattle. The people, warned by shy-eyed darting children, stood in their doorways and plots to watch the travellers pass and to make quiet salutation to the minister, unintelligible but obviously respectful; a salutation that was not always returned—Mr Hardie mentioned sternly that some of these people were Papists. Here, as at Kinlochardoch, the general absence of young men was very evident; Adam forbore to comment.

21

And so, through the pale afternoon sun, that brought out all the washen colours of a land no longer dun and grim, they tramped along the lush haughs of the swift-flowing Moraig River, through the silver and black of birch-woods and the sombre green shadows of pines, till, at a bend of the river, they came upon a long single-storeyed white-washed building set on a knoll above the stream.

"My church," Hardie indicated. "The Manse lies just behind the knowie, there. If you would care for some small refreshment, sir . . . ?"

"Thank you—but I think I will just carry on now, having got so far. Once I stop tonight I have a feeling that I will want to stay stopped . . ."

"As you will . . . but you have still another couple of miles to Menardmore."

This was the first conversational exchange for at least half an hour.

The Manse, when it came in view, proved to be a substantial two-storeyed building obviously of recent construction, an imposing raw place quite outshining the old barn-like church on its hillock. Its tenant eyed it with satisfaction. "A goodly house, Mr Metcalfe," he pointed out. "Two floors and an attic above, all mortared and slated. You will not see many of its like north of Tay. A manifestation, sir, of the enlightened direction of this estate."

At the Manse door, monument to Lord Alcaster's far-sightedness, they parted politely. Adam noted that the minister made no attempt to remunerate the gillie for his services; he had not so much baggage as the younger man, of course. The journey was resumed with no unnecessary delay.

They had not gone more than a few hundred yards, when beyond a thick clump of pines, they came upon a small group of cattle, half a dozen milch-cows and last season's calves, on a bridge that spanned a fair-sized burn. The beasts were standing, occupying all the bridge and the road; yet they appeared to be in process of being driven, and driven in no uncertain fashion. From the rear came sounds of scuffling and whacking and of a woman's voice upraised in wrath—unavailing wrath; the cattle did not move, they could not; in front, and sideways on, a large and particularly massive brown cow stood solidly, plumb in the middle of the bridge, head down, legs wide-planted, eyeing with stolid hostility the oncoming cavalcade, and effectually blocking the narrow passage to all comers.

Adam, after a few paces, turned inquiringly round to the gillie. That self-contained individual had taken in the situation at a glance, brought the garrons to a halt and was now considering the infinite with complete detachment. The younger man, without any Gaelic to counter a policy of prudent inactivity, motioned vaguely toward the bridge, a gesture that produced neither move nor sign that it had been observed. He turned back dubiously to the whacking and the shouting.

The quality and tenor of the hubbub was interesting; the voice was definitely that of a young woman, and the objurgation was in fluent if colloquial English. The significance of this he had not appreciated till he had recognised his inability to communicate with the gillie. He sought to catch a glimpse of the drover, but without success; the bridge was one of those humpbacked constructions, witnessing to the volatile habits of its burn, and the jammed cattle at its apex quite blocked the view beyond. Intrigued, Adam moved down the bank of the stream a few yards, to see what was to be seen.

What he saw was a young woman, a girl, tall and strongly made, with a great mop of unruly bronze hair, clutching a straining calf's tail in one hand, and, with a stick held in the other, belabouring the rumps of all the cattle she could reach, at the same time apostrophising them all, individually and collectively. It seemed that they were the most stupid, contrary, and feckless humbugs that ever passed themselves off as cows, that the calves were worse—just what could be expected from a union between their silly dams and Dougal Mor MacDougal's ridiculous bull—that the bridge was a pest and the burn a plague, and if only her stick was a wee thing longer she'd hit that Clara where Clara wouldn't like it, she would so. It was Clara that was the prime offender, obviously.

23

Clara was a great fat stubborn whale of a cow, Clara was a mule. Damn Clara, damn, damn, damn, Clara!

Adam Metcalfe looked on admiringly. She was a fine-looking girl, pretty as a picture . . . with a notable turn of speech. He was glad he was not one of those cows. As she paused for breath for a moment, he seized his chance. "Ma'am," he called. "Can I be of any assistance—anything I can do?"

Surprised, she left off beating her charges to look down across the burn—but she did not loose her calf's tail. For a moment or two she stared at him, frowning, then, as her captive made another dash for freedom and she was jerked right round, she shouted, "Yes—move those horses of yours back into the trees, will you . . . anywhere, out of sight . . . or we'll never get anywhere."

Adam did not quite follow her reasoning since the ponies were standing quietly fully fifty yards back from the bridge, as disinterested as their attendant, but he was not going to argue the case with that young woman—not him. Waving an affirmative hand he turned back towards the horses, and, dispensing with any involved explanations, took the leading beast by the halter and led it back into the cover of the pines, followed by its partner and the gillie, indifferent as ever. Leaving them there, he returned to the vicinity of the bridge.

The position did not appear to have altered. The large cow still blocked the road, insulated from the wrath behind by the jam of its fellows. Adam moved down the bank again, for further instructions.

"It's Clara that's doing it," the girl yelled. "It's those horses. She's always like this with horses." She had to yell very loudly, for her calf had started lowing at the pitch of its excellent young lungs. "She won't move. And I can't let go of this wretched calf—it's bolted three times already and the others just follow it."

The man nodded his head. It was easier than competing vocally with the calf.

"Get hold of Clara, will you," the girl went on, "and try to lead her off the bridge. Grab her ear and pull . . ."

24

Doubtfully Adam turned to do as he was bid. Clara, equally doubtful and very bovine, regarded his approach with extreme suspicion, and edged back a little into the press of beasts behind her. Uttering a few indeterminate noises that were meant to be both soothing and authoritative, he reached out to grasp the large ear, which was immediately jerked out of his hand by a prodigious flick. He grabbed it again, and pulled. Clara stood. He pulled harder, and tugged. He used his other hand as well, dug in his heels, and pulled with all his might. Clara remained immovable, staring at him with one great mildly-resentful eye, dribbling saliva from both corners of her mouth and regularly darting up a long pink tongue deep into either nostril, with obvious relish. The man straightened up and began slapping a broad flank with open palm, still pulling with the other hand, and shouting too, not soothingly. Presently he desisted. Had the brute no weak spot . . . what were a cow's weak spots? Lifting up his voice, he bawled, "Wait—how about backing out a bit—making a fresh start?"

Perhaps she did not hear him; all the calves had now taken up their leader's protest, and the clamour was appalling. Anyway, she beckoned him to come over to her side of the bridge, which perforce he had to do via the burn, and there she wordlessly but eloquently held out to him the black calf's tail; they were to exchange roles. But that calf had initiative as well as a tail; just as the transference was made, it put down its square shaggy head, threw up its hindquarters, and jerked its tail right out of Adam's uncertain grasp. Awkward but active, it made its stiff-legged bid for liberty.

The man dashed one way, the girl another, shouting to him to watch the rest—not to leave them; they were the sort of cattle that would take advantage of a man, evidently. The black calf was headed back this way and that till it darted down the bank, stumbled, and halted, facing the burn. The young woman made a grab at it, the beast shied, side-stepped, and plunged into the water, missed its footing but recovered, and so stood, in mid-stream, just out of reach, lowing lustily.

The girl stamped her foot at that calf. She ordered it to come, to go, she shooed it, coaxed it, but without effect. The ridiculous animal, neck outstretched, ears back, filled the afternoon with its complaint, but made no move. Undoubtedly it was a relative of Clara.

Adam had a feeling that something was expected of him, something effective. He marched down the bank—at which the lady promptly dived back to replace him at the bridge-end—strode boldly into the water, grasped that calf round the neck with a wrestler's grip, and heaved. The beast, on its long spindly legs, overbalanced and collapsed into the burn, nearly taking the man with it. The ice-cold water altered its attitude altogether. Scrambling up, it splashed frantically for the farther bank, clambered out and scurried, dripping and chastened, to the road ... where it was just in time to join its advancing companions. Clara, moving serenely in front, had got tired of standing. The road-block and the crisis had dissolved.

The man in the middle of the burn stared at the girl on the bridge, and she at him, and the absurdity of the situation overcame both. They began to laugh, and went on laughing.

Adam got himself out of the water and up to the road again, where he raised his hat to the lady with something of a flourish, and set her laughing again. "Good afternoon, ma'am," he pronounced. "I apologise for producing the horses, for failing to shift Clara, and for letting go the calf's tail."

"Not at all," she gurgled. "It was all Clara's fault ... she's a wicked beast, isn't she?"

"Wicked!" Adam agreed. He had a good look at her now. His first hasty impressions were not disappointed; she was exceedingly pleasant to look at, from the exuberant glory of her hair downwards. Her wide-open brown eyes held a soft light, but the good firm chin below a generous mouth testified that that light could be other than soft on occasion—had she been soft on Clara back there! Her dress was of the same coarsish woollen handspun stuff of the other Highland women, dyed a deep olive green, and caught round her waist with a scarlet girdle, but with it she wore a white linen blouse, spotless—or spotless enough for any man—the open collar of which served to emphasise the warm golden-brown of face and neck. The dress was longer too, than those others he had seen, but still short by southern standards—and no fault that, either—and though the legs were bare she wore good leather shoes. Altogether, a fine wholesome, straight-backed piece of young-womanhood, tall as himself and adequately made . . . and apparently not just a crofter-wench, for all her cattle. "If I can be of any further assistance to you," he went on, then, "Clara might start her tricks again . . . I will be most happy—honoured . . . ?" Considering the weariness engendered by much walking, he was very gallant.

"Oh, I've no distance to go now, at all," she assured him. "The Manse—my house—is just behind those trees, there."

"The Manse!" Though it was what he had suspected, it hardly seemed feasible. That vivid girl . . . ! "You are not Mr Hardie's daughter. . . ?"

She shook her head. "His niece," she informed. "Niece, housekeeper . . . and cowherd. Do you know him—my uncle?"

"I've just left him. We travelled up from Arisaig together."

"He's here . . . ?" Almost automatically a hand went up to smooth the fine disorder of her hair, to touch collar and dress. Smiling, Adam thought that he understood. "I . . . I hadn't expected him back for a day or two yet. You came by boat, then—to Kinlochardoch, and over the hill?"

Over the hill! That was one way of describing what they had done that day. "To Kinlochardoch . . . and over the hill," he agreed. "Your uncle is something of a walker, ma'am."

They had been moving back in the wake of the cattle, and were now level with the garrons amongst the trees. Her brow wore a small frown. "Yes—he will be tired, hungry. I will have to get back—he will be wanting his food. You, too . . . if you would care to join us?"

This second invitation took more refusing than the first, but he had his manners to consider. "I would like to, very much, very much indeed . . . but I think perhaps I should finish my journey now I'm so near the end of it. Another day, if you would be so kind . . . soon, I hope?"

27

She smiled. "You are staying hereabouts then, sir?"

He nodded. "I am glad to say so. I am Adam Metcalfe, the new assistant factor, making for Menardmore."

"Oh!" she said. "Oh—indeed!" and her smile faded. "I'm afraid I must go and attend to my uncle. I am sorry to have delayed you, sir," and with only a brief curtsey she turned and left him standing.

He stared after her, surprisingly rueful, till she had herded her beasts into the quite substantial farmery at the rear of the Manse. Then, thoughtfully, he made his way back to the ponies and their attendant. It was time this journey was finished.

Menardmore had been the house of MacVarish when Strathmoraig had had a chief, not a proprietor. For all that, it was little larger than the minister's new Manse, and of considerably less formidable an aspect. A long, low, unpretentious building, it was constructed part of stone, part of wood, and white-washed like its neighbours. Pleasantly situated, at the very head of the strath, on a green shelf above a smallish loch, Adam had noticed the place on its hill-side for some time without special interest, before his guide's direction made it apparent that this was their destination. Approaching it across the pine-needles of its guardian wood, he found it hard to believe that this was the Menardmore that Hardie had mentioned with such obvious respect, the manor-place of an estate as big as many an English shire. Without a demesne or a park or even an enclosing wall, with two crofts so close to it as to be almost on its doorstep, it seemed to boast none of the refinements of a gentleman's residence. "Menardmore . . . ?" he shouted inquiringly to the gillie, foolishly, for he had no reason to believe the man was deaf.

The other turned and said something, at length and with great rapidity, which Adam took to be affirmatory, before stopping suddenly, with a glance of fine scorn, and resuming the march.

Adam looked apologetic, and followed on.

At the doorway within a timbered porch, the travellers were met by such a hullabaloo from two great tawny mastiffs, that there was no need to knock or ring—and little opportunity, with the dog's menacing advances to be countered and the frightened shelts to be pacified. The gillie had actually produced a wicked-looking knife and was eyeing one of the leaping slobbering brutes warily, when the din brought forth, firstly another Highlandman, who, hopping from one foot to another, shouted ineffectually to dogs and men in a hopeless mixture of Gaelic and peculiar English, and secondly, a squat heavy man who strode out, uttered a bull-like roar that drowned every other sound, and at the same time hurled with great force and accuracy, a heavy-handled dog-whip which struck the gillie's wrist, causing him to drop the knife, yelling with pain. Then, bellowing a single curt command to the mastiffs and reaching one of them a savage kick as they slunk back to the porch, the newcomer pointed to the whip, which the servant from the house hurried to retrieve for him, and turned to Adam. "Well, sir, and what can I do for *you*?" he said.

Still holding and soothing one of the ponies, Adam swung round. "You could keep your damned dogs under better control, for a start," he exclaimed hotly. Stepping over to the gillie, who was clutching his arm and moaning, he reached out a hand to examine the damaged wrist, and found it limp and lifeless. "And it looks to me as if you've broken this man's arm, into the bargain!"

"Well!"

Adam turned to consider him. He was a short stocky man of middle age, enormously broad in the shoulder and long of arm, thick-necked and round-headed, with a fleshy face that did not hide the strong line of jaw and chin. Dressed in an old stained wide-skirted coat, cord breeches and great square-toed riding boots, he stood on feet wide-planted, arms folded and the whip dangling, an aggressive formidable figure of a man. "I am seeking Mr John Dunn," Adam announced.

"Ye're speaking to him."

He had been afraid of that. "My name is Metcalfe," he said then, coldly, "and I have been sent here by Lord Alcaster to assist in the management of this estate."

The other's bullet-head came forward, and his little pig's eyes gleamed. "Ha—so that's who ye are," he growled. He looked the younger man over from the crown of his beaver to his travel-stained boots, and his full lower lip was out-thrust. "So ye're the parson's son," he jerked. "Well, ye'll not find Menardmore a parsonage, b'God. I'm nothing so fine as that, myself—just a plain farmer's son, John Dunn, but I'm master up here, lad, and I'll thank ye to keep it in mind." He had the broad deep voice of the north-country English. "If ye're going to work for John Dunn, it'll pay ye to keep a civil tongue in your head."

"I was under the impression that it was Lord Alcaster I was to work for," Adam gave back.

"Aye, maybe—but Alcaster is a long way away, and I'm his representative, and don't ye forget it."

"I don't suppose I'll get much chance to forget it!"

The older man grunted. "Happen you're right there, lad. As long as you mind who's master, we'll get on champion . . . maybe! Now, get rid of that sniftering cateran, and come inside and get some meat into your belly—ye look as though ye could do with it . . . if my table's good enough for the vicar's son!"

Adam turned to the gillie, handed him a guinea, pointing towards the shelts, and then another, indicating the injured wrist. The man took the first, touching his bonnet, but shook his head at the second, and throwing up his shoulders, bowed with a courtesy that was natural as it was unexpected, and reached for the halters of the ponies which the servant had been unloading.

A single hoot of laughter came from the rear. "That's right—pile it on, fall on the bastard's neck, call down a blessing on his head . . ."

The younger man called to the servant who was gathering up some of his baggage, and signed to him curtly to put it down. Then he swung on the factor. "John Dunn," he said tensely, "before we go any further there's something that's got to be settled. Either you agree to behave to me with some degree of civility, if ordinary good manners are beyond you, or else I put my things back on those ponies and go back the way I've come—

now!"

"And whose loss would that be, my young cock?"

"Yours. Because Lord Alcaster is my friend as well as my employer,"—God forgive him that lie—"and if I returned and told him what I could well tell him, he'd probably sell this place out of hand—he's already talked about selling, being in need of money, as always. Your sheep schemes already strike him as something expensive in the outlay ... and he's not what I'd call an open-handed man, as perhaps you've noticed!" The man's small eyes flickered, and Adam plunged on. "And my godmother, Lady Alice, is doubtful about the whole business, and you know her influence—it's just as big as her fortune. And where would you be, Mr John Dunn, if Strathmoraig was to change hands suddenly? The new owner might well have a factor of his own ...!"

The other stared at him, his brows down, his great jaws working round and round in a strange slow rhythmic motion, as though masticating what he had heard, testing whether it was all bluff—as indeed it was—or whether there was truth at the back of it. But there was uncertainty behind those eyes, and that was itself an uncomfortable strange experience for John Dunn, and presently he spat, and spoke. "All right," he said shortly, and pivoting round, stumped short-legged into the house.

Adam Metcalfe, letting the breath come out in a long quiet sigh, followed. In the doorway, the crouching mastiffs rumbled deeply in their throats as he passed them. The man in front turned round and grinned, wide-mouthed, and said nothing.

WITH the screen of the pine-wood between him and the House, Adam Metcalfe strode downhill, breathing deeply of the sharp resin-laden morning air, as though to drive out and banish from his lungs the last trace of that air he had been forced to breathe for the past eighteen or so hours. And as he went, a strong conviction was upon him; having spent an evening, a night and a forenoon within the House of Menardmore, he was quite decided that, if he must work in the company of the man Dunn, he would not live in it—he would not. He would find another house to live in, be it only a humble cot-house, where he would be free of the man's heavy glower, his leering grin, his sarcastic laboured politenesses, his unspeakable habits. The fellow might be as able a factor and efficient an administrator as Alcaster thought he was, but he was an oaf and a boor and one or two other things besides.

At a birch-knoll above the sparkling loch he paused to consider the land and his course. He had told John Dunn what he was going to do, even asked him the name of any likely party near at hand who might be willing to accept a lodger, to be flung the fleeting information that if he disliked his, John Dunn's, company so much that he preferred to live in a mud-and-turf black-house amongst a rabble of pigs and poultry and jabbering heatherny, then let him go where he liked, choose any hovel that caught his eye—or his nose—and instal himself; no tenant dare say him nay. There was no call to *ask* anybody . . . ! That had been his answer. He looked out across the water uncertainly, at the scattered crofts of Menard each under its blue plume of peat-smoke; there were not a few of them, fully a score he could count dotting the valley and the farther slopes, not all just primitive cabins—but which of them would be anxious to extend hospitality to John Dunn's assistant? . . . and into no one of them would he instal himself, unwelcome. And then he noticed, at the far side of the loch, another larger house that had escaped his first glance in that it was not whitewashed as was the general rule. A grey house, partly two-storeyed, it sat quietly amongst open birch woods above the water-side, and at its back a hill rose gently to a tree-crowned summit. That looked the sort of place to make a start with, anyway, and pleasantly isolated from Menardmore by its clean sheet of water. He would try that grey house, surely.

Walking round the loch-shore, where the whispering reeds bowed their welcome to the lapping wavelets, Adam found the morning wholesome and vital, and good for a man who, out of urgent coping with immediate circumstances, might be beginning to see things just a little out of proportion. This hill country had something virile and challenging in its wild beauty, an unsettling, stirring quality that he had not known in scenery heretofore, emanating from towering peaks and flashing water, from frowning rock and shadow-filled valley, from the sheer sweep of rolling moors and the slashed white of distant snow-caps. Loch Menard was the brimming bowl that collected and disciplined the strident brown waters of five different glens, to discharge them, duly blended and sobered, from its western end into the broad stream of the Moraig River. Around this wide basin, then, the five glens yawned, and ridge and valley drew a wild pattern in greens and browns stained with the black of sharp shadows, under great sailing clouds of white. In the crisp air that came on a north-easterly breeze, tinged lightly with the tangy scents of a score of leagues of heather, the man knew it all to be good, and his spirits rose accordingly.

On his road, Adam passed two of the croft-houses, one on either side of a ford and foot-bridge that spanned the river, new-issued from the loch. At the first, he made salutations to a nobly-bearded elderly man a-lean against an isolated piece of fencing, who watched with some concentration an equally elderly woman industriously digging peats from a black patch of bog-land; a salutation that produced a reply of much dignity from the man and a brief hand-wave from the woman. At the second, a word or two spoken to a child at play by the river bank sent it homewards in such hasty alarm that it fell headlong into a damp ditch, smashing a little wooden sword it had been playing with, and there lay, bawling. Picking up the small fellow, mud-spattered—but not all new mud from the ditch—and the toy sword as well, the man carried him, sobbing, to the black doorway of the cot-house, where a mild-eyed strapping young-ish woman came to them, head ashake, a naked baby sucking placidly at her vein-lined breast.

Adam bowed hurriedly. "The young man thought I was the devil, and near broke his neck getting away from me," he explained, but not hopefully, since probably the woman knew no English. He set down the child, which ran to clutch its mother's legs, and from that fine place, turned, tearfully defiant. "I think the most serious damage is to this sword, here," and he held it out.

The woman smiled. "*Wheesht, Ian Beg, mo graidh*," she soothed. "'*De tha tigh'n riut, 'ille?*" And to the man, "Never be heeding him, sir. Is he not the noisy one, and him his father's son!"

Her soft sibilant English was strange in his ears, but Adam found no fault with it. Relieved that some at least of the natives could speak his language, he was able to ignore the suckling infant—almost. "He has a good pair of lungs, to be sure," he agreed. "I'm sorry about the little sword, but maybe this will help to make up for it," and he produced a penny from his pocket.

"No, no, there is no need, at all," the woman objected, but the youngster thought otherwise. Reaching out a grubby hand he grabbed the penny, and bolted into the dark of the house, his sobbing forgotten. His mother shook her head "Och, Ian Beg!" she reproved, "Just a wild *borach* he is, whatever," as he laughed pleasantly. "If you will step inside, sir, I will be giving you a cup of milk for the road."

He was for refusing this good offer, but the woman had already turned. Somewhat dubiously, he followed her within.

This was his first experience of a crofter's cottage, or black-house as Dunn had named it—and named it well. Black it was, indeed, partly through lack of light, but more noticeably through prevailing soot. There were no windows, so that such light as infiltrated must come through the open doorway or through a circular hole in the thatched roof, where it had to strive valiantly with the out-going smoke from a peat-fire in the centre of the room, that, chimney-less, must necessarily use the same apertures for egress. The floor of beaten earth was black, as were the walls and roof, yet strangely, the place had some aspect of cleanliness; the soot all appeared to have been rubbed in and polished, the few rough furnishings, a long bench, a stool or two and a plank table, were scrubbed white, and the skin and wool rugs on the uneven floor were reasonably clean. Blinking in the smoke and sudden dark, the man coughed and waited.

Presently she came out from behind a partition that divided the cottage—the sleeping quarters, presumably—carrying a piggin of milk and a thick oatcake on a wooden platter. "For the road, sir," she said simply.

Adam was surprised at this spontaneous hospitality to a stranger, and said so.

She shook her head, smiling. "The custom it is, whatever. Just for the road—and it long, maybe . . . ?"

There was frank enquiry there, and Adam smiled, too. "Not long at all—I hope." He sipped, and bit into the oatcake. It tasted crumbly and rather pleasant, and went well with the milk. "I'm just making for that grey house round the lake . . . in the first instance. What house is that?"

"Achroy? That is Ewan MacVarish's house."

"MacVarish . . . ! Is that not the name of the people who used to own this place?"

She nodded. "Always it was Clan Eachann land, this country, and MacVarish of Strathmoraig, Chief of the clan—Achroy is just a sept."

"A sept . . . ? You mean a sort of branch, junior to the main house?" He frowned. "Then this Mr MacVarish will be a man of some substance and standing . . . not likely to offer house-room to a factor seeking lodging?" Scrupulously he said it, and waited.

It was as he anticipated. He saw the woman's whole attitude change, stiffen. "Factor, is it?" she exclaimed, and her brow clouded and an arm pressed the baby closer to her breast. "I cannot say, at all . . . but you could be trying, surely," she said, warily.

Adam Metcalfe was a somewhat sensitive man, especially where women were concerned, and that instinctive protective gesture of her arm hurt. He started to speak, to protest and explain, but changed his mind, and took an ostentatious bite of oatcake and a drink of milk. "You make an excellent oatcake, ma'am," he said.

She nodded an acceptance of that, but said nothing.

"I will take the road again, now," he said then, handing back the cup and platter. "Thank you for your kindness to a stranger, and . . ." he paused, ". . . perhaps there may be more than one kind of factor."

"There could be, too . . ." she was admitting, but that was as far as she got. A man's voice broke in, and a shadow darkened the doorway. "Indeed there could not," the voice stated, a strong and vehement voice. "Only the one kind of factor is in it, at all—and them the curse of us. If you are a factor, sir, will you kindly be stepping out from under my roof!"

"Ian More . . . !" the woman began, but the man ignored her.

"You can be claiming the land for your master, maybe, and you with the law at your back, but my own father built this bit house with his own two hands, and it is no lord's house, whatever. It is my own house, and I will have no factor in it, my God!"

That voice was an angry voice, and Adam Metcalfe stepped outside as directed.

The man at the door was a well-built strapping fellow, dressed more in keeping with the Highland tradition than anyone Adam had so far encountered. Over an open shirt he wore what appeared to be a single length of faded and stained tartan cloth, wound twice round his middle to form a simple kilt, held in place by a belt, and the loose end carried up across his chest and over his shoulder to tuck into the belt again at the back. Apart from rough-made shoes of untanned hide, that was his entire costume. It left his lean masculinity very evident. Adam, eyeing him and his hot eyes and his tight jaw, could appreciate the wisdom for a decent caution.

"I would be the last to disregard your feelings in the matter," he said, "more especially as I have just been receiving of your wife's hospitality." The cunning man he was. "My name is Metcalfe, and I am the new Deputy Commissioner, seeking lodging." He used his full title for the benefit of a man who apparently did not like factors.

"Then I'm sorry—but it is not under Ian MacErlich's roof you'll be finding it," and he bowed stiffly, all at once frigidly, ludicrously, polite.

Mrs MacErlich intervened. "Shame on you, Ian More, with the gentleman just after fetching in Ian Beg and him fallen . . . and giving him the money to be quieting him, too!"

"Hold your tongue, woman, and let a man be speaking!" the other cried. He was a fine swack fellow, and knew his own mind. Then, suddenly, he seemed to catch hold of something that she had said. "Money, is it!" he demanded. "Is he for buying us now, the creature, with his money! He will not buy Ian, 'ic Ian 'ic Ailean MacErlich, nor a stick nor a stone of his house, not . . ."

"Och Ian man, wheesht you . . . a terrible great noise you make about nothing at all, just like Ian Beg," the woman reproved. Her voice was quiet as ever, and she hitched the baby more comfortably within her arm. "Achroy it is that the gentleman is seeking—what would himself be wanting with your little small croft-house of Roybeg?"

The man drew himself up. "It is a good house, a very fine good house. My own father built it, Ian 'ic Ailean . . ." And then, "Achroy, is it!" he shouted, almost laughed. "A factor seeking lodging from Ewan MacVarish, my God!" He turned again to Adam, as deadly polite as before. "You will be finding Achroy round the loch a mile, sir—easy it is to find."

"I see . . . thank you," Adam acknowledged rather grimly.

37

"And thank you, Mrs. MacErlich, for the refreshment."

"It was nothing at all, sir . . . and don't be paying any heed to himself there," she advised placidly. "Come away inside, Ian More . . ."

Adam Metcalfe turned and slipped away, and left that fierce wild Highlandman to his mild-eyed wife.

More than once on that mile round the loch to Achroy, Adam nearly turned to retrace his steps. It seemed as though his errand was foredoomed to failure, and he was far from anxious for further unpleasantness, but the thought of John Dunn's jeering grin kept him going. He would go to some lengths before he was prepared to report failure to that man.

Achroy was approached pleasantly through small ill-defined fields climbing the gentle hill above the loch, past a farm-steading where hens and ducks squattered about a generous midden, and through the aisles of a wood where the silver stems of the naked birches were gleaming pillars upholding a slender vault of finest filigree in their branches. In a wide glade amongst the knowes and thickets, the house stood and looked out across the water, and the fragrance of wood-smoke lingered there and the peace of the wood rested upon it like a halo. Approving it all, Adam crossed to the door.

He did not have to knock. A man stood in the doorway awaiting him, a grey-haired man, tall and very thin, who stroked a small pointed beard and bowed courteously. "It is a very fine day indeed for the time of the year," he stated positively, as though in answer to a question.

"Indeed it is," Adam agreed heartily. "Exceedingly fine. Er . . . am I speaking to Mr MacVarish?"

"The man himself," the other acknowledged, "at your service, sir."

It was Adam's not very confident hope that he might adhere to these sentiments. "Then I come to you as a suppliant, sir," he said. "I am seeking lodging hereabouts, and I wondered if perhaps you might be able to help me?"

"Lodging, you say?" He looked surprised. "There are

lodgings and lodgings, sir. What kind is it you seek, and for how long?"

"For quite a time, I'm afraid—where, does not matter so much . . ." he paused, and took a chance, ". . . so long as it is not in John Dunn's house of Menardmore!"

The other's grey eyes were keen suddenly. "Your own reasons you will have for that saying, no doubt."

"I have," Adam nodded. "You see, I am the new deputy-factor appointed by Lord Alcaster."

Ewan MacVarish's hand went up to his beard again. "So!" he mused. "You are John Dunn's assistant . . . and you do not want to live in John Dunn's house!"

"Exactly, sir!"

There could have been just the suggestion of a twinkle below those grizzled brows. "You might have reason in that, too," he allowed. "The same man did not recommend you to Achroy, I'm thinking?"

"No indeed, I came on my own, directed doubtfully by a young woman back there with two Ians to keep down."

"Ah—Mairi MacErlich! And what had Mairi to say of me, Mr . . . ?"

"Metcalfe—Adam Metcalfe. She said I could be trying you, surely . . . and she produced milk and oatcake to sustain a flagging spirit!"

The older man laughed outright, a cheerful bark of a laugh. "Mairi MacErlich did that, did she! Then Ewan MacVarish can be doing no less. Will you step inside, Mr Metcalfe . . . ?"

Wielding an inexpert oar, Adam pulled the squat sturdy Achroy boat back across the loch to Menardmore, and considered what he had done. He had deliberately arranged to remove himself, save for the duration of his working hours, from the company and proximity of his immediate superior, to that of a man whose relations with the said superior were anything but cordial—and that, on an acquaintanceship of less than one day. He had made a demonstration of calculated defiance, or at least of aggressive independence, to the man whom his employer had sent him five hundred miles to assist, before even starting that assistance. For there was no doubt that John Dunn would disapprove of his junior's association with Achroy; Adam had guessed something of the sort on his way to that place, but his subsequent conversation with Ewan MacVarish had confirmed it rather forcefully. MacVarish of Achroy was evidently a somewhat especial enemy of the factor's, the last representative of the old natural leaders of the people, a discomfort—though never a danger—to the new order, and a man who might be pestered but not bullied in the interests of the proprietor, the factor, and the estate in general. Assuredly John Dunn would disapprove, and in his own fashion. But then, he had known that from the start, and yet he had gone through with it . . .

Throwing a glance over his shoulder, Adam Metcalfe pulled the prow of MacVarish's boat round a point or two so that it headed for the little wooden jetty that projected from the Menardmore shore. The declining afternoon sun caught his eyes with its oblique yellow glare, and he returned to the contemplation of the quiet woods of Achroy.

Why had he done it, then, this thing that could only worsen relations with his chief, and could be called disloyalty and folly and other things as well? Intense dislike of the man, of course, was the primary reason, but was that reason enough—was that sufficient to account for his drastic action? He had, he decided, done it as a gesture, not merely of defiance, but of something deeper, of warning that he considered that the domineering and browbeating of those in his charge was no part of a factor's duty and prerogative, and that Lord Alcaster's interests could be equally well, and probably better, served—for served they must be, since he was taking the man's money as wage—by a more liberal and benevolent attitude. That was it—Lord Alcaster's best interests. Adam Metcalfe smiled to himself, a trifle sardonically, and shipped his oars as the boat grounded.

Up at the house, past the restive mastiffs, he sought out Colin the serving man, and instructed him to have all his baggage taken down to the boat. He had to repeat his order twice to a man whose apprehension was not to be hid. Then, swallowing his own, he went in search of John Dunn.

He found him in the wide, low dining-room of the house, in loud-voiced conversation with a big, bulky, red-faced man who stood wide-legged, his back to the fire, his hands clasped under the skirts of his coat, his shoulders against the mantel-piece. Dunn, who sprawled in a chair, legs outstretched, coat and waistcoat open, appeared to be in high good humour, and his guest likewise.

"Ah—there y'are, Metcalfe," he greeted, almost shouted. "Where the devil ha' ye been all this time? Come here and meet Henry Bullough from Northumberland. Harry—this is the lad Alcaster's sent up to give us a hand wi' the place," and he ended his introduction with something between a snort and a chuckle.

Adam bowed stiffly, but the big man thrust out a great hand. "Pleased to meet you, m'lad," he announced jovially, and shook hands with much vigour. "We need all the help we can get with this place—there's plenty to be done, eh John? Young blood, that's what's wanted. Poor old John here's nigh worked off his feet!" and his laughter shook the room.

The younger man inclined his head warily, and considered the man, his size and his girth, his large, flushed, grinning face, and all the careless easy might of him. "Thank you," he said briefly. "Are you another factor, sir?"

"A factor! Lord bless you, no—nothing so grand as that, lad. Just a poor sheep-farmer that rents an acre or two from your lord and gives John a hand now and then . . . isn't that right, squire?"

Dunn nodded. "That's right, Harry—just a poor sheep farmer." And the other joined him in his laughing. They were in the best of spirits. "How many sheep did ye buy at Dingwall Fair t'other day, again . . . ?"

"All there were, squire, all there were—I took the lot. Only four hundred gimmers and a few tups—but as many as Glen Druim'll carry!"

The factor turned to Adam. "You're meeting one of the men that's going to make something out of this God-forsaken country—not just talking about it, but doing something. A few more tenants like Henry Bullough and Alcaster wouldn't talk any more damned nonsense about selling . . ."

"What are you wanting with more tenants, John, blast you?" the other shouted. "Henry Bullough will do for you fine, and Alcaster too." He slapped a massive thigh, a blow that would have felled a man. "Just give me time, I say, and I'll show you sheep-farming . . . D'you know anything about sheep, boy?"

Dunn answered for him. "He's a parson's son, didn't I tell you. What would a parson's son know about sheep?" He caught Adam's eye, and gestured towards him with mock deference. "He's a friend of the noble earl, and he's come here to show us how an estate should be run!"

The young man did not answer. Dunn was making it easier for him to say what had to be said. He spoke to Bullough, quietly. "You mentioned Glen Druim just now, I believe. Is that not the ground behind Achroy, tenanted by Mr Ewan MacVarish?"

Again it was Dunn that answered. "It is—why?"

"Just that Mr MacVarish mentioned to me that the estate had . . . resumed possession of that land, and without his agreement."

"And what of it?" The factor's voice was sharp now.

Adam met his glare. "He appears to consider that his rights have been infringed!"

"Rights, b'God!" John Dunn's clenched fist crashed down on the table, making a bottle and glasses jump. "Every damned poverty-stricken rascal in this blasted country rants about his rights, and without so much as a title or a statement or a scrap of paper to back them up. MacVarish had no lease or title to that ground, he paid little or no rent for it, and he did precious little with it. When ye've been a bit longer in the Highlands, young fellow, ye'll be ready to spew at the sound of a Highlander's rights!" Suddenly he leaned forward. "And why so interested in MacVarish, anyway—what's your game, eh?"

"I have arranged to lodge in Mr MacVarish's house of Achroy." Calmly it was said, and the hat and cane laid down on the table helped to keep up the illusion.

Slowly, deliberately, the factor rose to his feet. He took a step forward, and his groping hands searched for and found the back of a chair drawn in to the table. "Ye've arranged . . . to lodge . . . at Achroy!" he said, almost whispered. He was a much smaller man than Bullough, but standing there, broad and squat and tense, his sheer dominant strength made of the other's massiveness mere bulk.

Nevertheless, it was the big man who asserted himself. "Damme," he cried heartily, "that's fine—that's grand!" His hand thumped down on the other's great shoulder, and Adam saw his fingers tighten twice. "What could suit us better than having a representative of the estate billeted on friend MacVarish—the only man who's caused you the least bit of trouble, John? Metcalfe, here, has a wise head on young shoulders—he'll look after the best interests of the estate, I'll be bound. Eh, lad?"

"Exactly," Adam repeated slowly. "The best interests of the estate . . . !"

"That's right . . . and what's good for the estate's good for you, Mister—isn't it, John?" That was cheerfully said, but his fingers still gripped his companion's shoulder.

Dunn stood motionless and silent for an appreciable time, while a clock ticked steadily on the mantelpiece and the birch logs hissed and sizzled on the hearth. Then, he nodded shortly, tossed off Bullough's hand, and turned back to the fire—from whence he twisted round suddenly and looked at the younger man intently. "Aye," he said, "so be it," and bent to reach for an ember for his pipe.

Bullough reached over to the table and picked up the bottle. "A glass of brandy, Mister . . . ?" he suggested.

It was as easy as that—for the time being.

Later that evening, amid a rising wind of night that troubled the darkling loch, Adam rowed splashily back to Achroy, his luggage beside him and his soul his own. But he frowned as he rowed.

5

THE day following was Sunday, and Adam had an order to attend church as representative of the estate—what was the use of having a parson's son as deputy if not to make use of him on tiresome tasks of this sort? This was a God-fearing country and the conventions should be observed, for the Kirk had its uses. By the same token, he was to bring back the minister to dinner at Menardmore; an enquiry as to whether Mr Hardie alone was included in the invitation met with a demand as to whether he expected them to entertain the whole cursed congregation . . . ?

So, on a blustering morning of wind and showers and scudding clouds, Adam Metcalfe strode through groaning woods and sodden haughs, by slippery paths, the three boisterous miles to the Kirkton of Menardbeg and his duty. Ewan MacVarish, a Catholic himself, saw him off and wished him good of the worship, mentioning handsomely that there were good men of every creed.

Down in the floor of the strath, where the winds rioted out of all the branching glens, he passed the croft of Roybeg and got a handwave and a good morning from Mairi MacErlich, and felt the better for it. The neighbouring croft, across the river, was deserted today, but presently he overtook the venerable owners on the road, church-bound obviously, the splendidly-bearded one fully a hundred yards ahead of his frail-seeming wife, and going strongly. To Adam's observation that the weather was miserable, he received an affable rejoinder that it was himself had taken the words out of his own mouth whatever, and him speaking the truth into the bargain, my God. Digesting which abstrusity, he pressed on.

A more than cursory glance at the Manse revealed only staring windows and a few clucking hens; he had passed the cattle in a haugh further back, recognising them without much difficulty. Breasting the needle-carpeted track up the knoll to the plain stone building under its straining pines, he ran into a huddle of men sheltering within the church's wooden porch. Prominent amongst them was MacErlich, a resplendent Ian More this, in jacket and breeches of rust-coloured homespun, a tartan waistcoat, and a bonnet bearing a silver brooch. He greeted Adam with haughty condescension, and cast a scornful seeming glance at the less reserved salutations of his companions, older men all, who stood aside decently to let the newcomer pass.

He paused, just inside the church door, and looked about him. He saw a place bare within as without, stone-floored and unceiled. A long expanse of wooden seats, mere backless forms, divided by a narrow central passage that it would have been an extravagance to name an aisle, led up to a plain table backed by a chair and flanked by a reading desk. That was all. The seats were well-filled, and from the waiting congregation arose an odour compounded of the varied scents of damp clothes, peat smoke, and humanity, tinged with domestic animal generally. A heavy and complete silence prevailed.

Adam was making for a vacant seat near the door, when a soberly-dressed aged man hobbled forward authoritatively and took him in hand, leading him forward up the passage-way to the very front seat. After glaring his resentment at the patriarch's back all the way up, he suddenly changed his expression. The entire front seat was unoccupied, save for one person—the young woman that was Mr Hardie's niece. He strode along and sat down beside her. "Good morning," he said cheerfully, and his voice, only moderate as it was, shattered the silence of the place as effectively as though he had shouted.

She inclined her head almost imperceptibly, and looked straight ahead of her.

"Miserable day . . ." he went on unabashed. The people of these parts were all very strong on the subject of the weather, it seemed. "Disappointing after yesterday, is it not!"

Another brief nod, followed by a tiny headshake. Still the forward gaze.

45

Adam Metcalfe was not going to be spurned in this fashion, not after the good work he had put in that time by the bridge. He came a little closer. "Miss Alison," he whispered—he had discovered her name, judiciously, from Ewan MacVarish. ". . . how's Clara?"

This time she turned, and her look, undoubtedly intended to be reproving, he found quite charming. She had flushed delightfully, her small frown had pushed up one eyebrow as though in surprise at itself, and the pursing of her lips to say "Ssh-ssh-ssh" produced two pronounced dimples, symmetrically placed and fascinating. "Ssh-ssh-ssh!" she whispered, then, "Mind you're in church, Mr Metcalfe."

"But the service hasn't started . . ." he protested.

"Doesn't matter . . . You can't talk in church."

"Why ever not?"

"Well—you just can't." And to clinch the matter: "All the folk will be staring."

He turned round and looked. They were. He sighed. "I can still use my eyes, I hope?" he enquired significantly and moved away slightly along the seat, the better to use them.

Perhaps she misinterpreted his action, or was thinking of the starers behind, or just wished, woman-like, to convey the impression that she did not like being looked at. Anyway, her chin rose just a little and she resumed her frontal stare. Adam was left to debate the strange practices of Presbyterianism, in between wondering whether he preferred her dressed as he had last seen her or as she was today, demurely, her hair constrained to order under a poke-bonnet, and a dark cloak trimmed with fur covering a deep blue gown that came some inches nearer her feet than she had worn two days ago; also, whether she could keep up her present pose of aloof piety till the service started, and if she had dimples only when she ssh-ssh-ed—he had not noticed them previously and there were none in evidence now. He was distinctly partial to dimples. Selina Purcell had had rather fine ones, especially when she smiled . . .

A shuffling commotion at the back as the porch loiterers trooped in, coincided with the entry of the minister by a small

46

door near the front of the church, preceded by the ancient who had shown Adam to his seat, carrying a large and weighty Bible. Adam was about to rise to his feet, when the slightest motion of Alison Hardie's hand stayed him. Everyone sat still. The man smiled. So she was not quite so remotely disinterested as she seemed! He had a good excuse now for watching her; she would have to save him from the pitfalls of a cast-iron ritual.

Andrew Hardie, vested in a black gown that was relieved only at the neck by two narrow white linen bands, was even sterner within his church than without, stern and very forceful. There were no doubts, no hesitancies and no short-cuts in his conducting of the service. In a two hour succession of psalms and prayers, psalms and prayers, interspersed with occasional readings from the great Bible, all but one out of the Old Testament, he never paused nor faltered. He led the psalm-singing in a harsh, tuneless tenor, he prayed, on his two feet, strongly, impassionedly, with a voice that sometimes shook the bare rafters, and he read with a conviction and emphasis that did not flag.

But all this was but an introduction, a preamble, for the sermon that followed. After a blood-curdling psalm that quite eclipsed all its predecessors, the man made his first pause in two hours. He lifted himself to his full height, turned his face upward, his eyes closed, and his lips moved soundlessly. A long sigh came from the congregation, and Adam, cramped and weary, stretched circumspectly and glanced about him. All waited, tense, expectant. The girl at his side stared at the stone-flagged floor, and what went on behind the brooding melancholy of her expression, no man might assert. Outside, the pines creaked and sighed in tired protest at the wind's urgency.

Then Andrew Hardie began, really began. It was not a sermon or a homily that he gave them, it was a harangue, a denunciation, a general indictment of the incredible wickedness of man, and the inevitability of the judgement that must follow, even as night follows day. There was fury and fear in it, anguish and tears, retribution was its theme and expiation its refrain. There was no hope in it, no loophole of escape, no comfortable

47

dalliance with the soft and pernicious doctrines of charity and tolerance, and precious little even with the efficacy of repentance. Suffering was the fore-ordained lot of man, the only gate through which the refuge of ultimate bliss could be gained; Christ had led the way in suffering—men must follow, painfully, or be damned eternally to further suffering unimaginable. It was in the description and portrayal of this last immeasurable agony that the man excelled himself, buffeting and bludgeoning the wilting, shrinking people, with a zeal, even a relish, that he made no attempt to hide. Adam, sitting in extreme discomfort, physical and mental, right beneath him, could not meet his flaming eyes, though he found them frequently enough bent upon him.

It seemed as though it was only sheer exhaustion that eventually stopped him, after some forty minutes of unbroken effort. With his fists clenched above his head he was invoking Divine vengeance on all idolaters, blasphemers, evil-speakers, fornicators, whore-mongers, and transgressors generally, at the very pitch and apex of his fervour, when his voice faltered, broke, and he stood thus, silent for a moment, to sit down suddenly, collapse almost, into his chair, and his hands covered his face.

The people relaxed. There were coughs and the creaking of wooden forms. Alison Hardie looked up, and her eyes met Adam's and she shook her head slowly, in a gesture that was tired and hopeless and infinitely sad, and not to be understood by the man who saw it. He grieved for her then, sorely, and knew not why.

Then Andrew Hardie rose to his feet again, his face calm and stern as ever, and announced the closing psalm. But it was sung without feeling or zest. The service had finished with the sermon. The Benediction was brief, perfunctory, and turning, the minister paced to his side door and out. Breathing its relief, Protestant Strathmoraig followed his example.

Among the leaning gravestones that shared the knoll with the squat white church, Adam spoke with the girl. She was polite, but nothing more; the lively friendliness of their first meeting was quite gone. He ventured no remark on the service, remarkable as undoubtedly it had been, and she appeared to expect none. "I have been charged to invite Mr Hardie to dinner at Menardmore," he told her, uncertainly. "It is my sorrow that the invitation I was to bring did not include Mr Hardie's niece."

She nodded her head composedly. "Why would it?"

"Good manners, if nothing else, might suggest it."

"What would they want with a woman . . . or good manners . . . at the factor's house?" That was evenly said. "My uncle goes frequently to Menardmore on a Sunday."

"I see." They were moving down the slope in the direction of the Manse. He glanced at her face thoughtfully. "Your uncle expresses a great regard for the management of this estate," he remarked.

"He will have cause, no doubt."

"Cause not shared by his niece . . . ?"

"I did not say that, Mr Metcalfe."

"No—I beg your pardon." She worried him, this girl. Her quiet, fateful calm, so different from the warm liveliness of the other day, was like armour about her, armour which he could not pierce. This could well be Andrew Hardie's effect on her. Living with that man might demand such a shield, lest herself, her inmost soul's integrity, be beaten down and lost. On Friday he had seen her free, barriers down; Hardie had been away, and she had not known that he was back. When he had told her, had he not noted her change, her whole bearing alter? She must get back, she had said—back into the armour that she had been able temporarily to discard . . . ?

Just so, just so. Adam Metcalfe shook a sorrowful head at himself and his devising. A fine edifice he was building out of scant material, with plenty of architraves and elaboration, in the romantic tradition. It but remained to insert something in the way of foundation under the erection! Here he had conceived a hapless maid set about by forces too strong for her, defending a soul inviolate within the grip of a tyrant uncle, the Kirk Militant, and dominant authority in the person of the factor—all on dimples and damnation. He held his tongue for the few remaining yards to the Manse, which was not difficult since the path was narrow and Miss Hardie showed no inclination to conduct a conversation over her shoulder.

She showed him into a small, bright room where a cheerful fire burned, a pleasant room with comfortable chairs and a good carpet; only the sober rows of books, the heavy desk, and the absence of any ornaments proclaimed it a man's room, the minister's study. Adam was surprised, not for the first time that day. He would have expected something austere and grim, in keeping with his bearing and address. If this was Andrew Hardie's room, then that strange man was a more complex character than he had realised. He would have to do some revising . . .

When, presently, the minister entered, however, he was as severe and formal as ever. He greeted Adam stiffly polite, hoped that he had fully recovered from the rigours of his journey, and expressed his readiness to accept the kind invitation to Menardmore which he understood Mr Metcalfe to have brought.

His niece had come in behind him. Now she laid a hand on his arm. "Must you go . . . there?" she asked, and there was appeal in her voice.

He did not turn to look at her. "Of course I shall go. Is it not my duty, as well as my pleasure, to do so . . ."

"Duty!" she repeated quietly. "I see!" There was no mistaking her scorn, and the accompanying glance, which included the younger man in its sweep, was hostile and indignant. "I bid you good-day, then, Mr Metcalfe," she said, and with the briefest curtsey she left them.

Andrew Hardie bowed. "My hat and coat are in the lobby— I am ready when you are, sir . . ."

Thoughtfully Adam preceded him to the door. It looked as though his imagining might not have been so far out, after all. The pity of it that he seemed to be on the wrong side in this warfare.

On the walk back to Menardmore the two men had not much to say to each other—anyway, the wind left them little breath for conversation. Walking appeared to be the only mode of travel in this country; there were no roads fit for any sort of carriage, and though there were a few horses, they were all the short, broad-backed, shaggy ponies on which panniers could be slung but on which a saddle would sit strangely and a rider stranger still.

At the factor's house the minister was received with some show of welcome, out of fairly apparent effort on Dunn's part, and the utmost heartiness from the man Bullough, who, it appeared, was a permanent resident—a heartiness of which Adam perforce had his share. It was nearly mid-afternoon and dinner was waiting; the factor and his friend, no doubt conversant with Mr Hardie's protracted ritual, had evidently been fortifying the inner man during their waiting, in the only way that would not interfere with their appetites. It was a strangely-assorted company that sat down to the well-plenished table.

John Dunn, like most of his kind, enjoyed his food, and was in a position to indulge his taste. After ill-concealing his impatience at the length of the Grace, he bent to the task, eating with a dour, steady concentration that was typical of the man, and almost fascinating, putting away as much, and more, than any two of his guests. And no one of them was a poor trencherman. The big man ate noisily and with obvious enjoyment, but owing to the fact that he took upon himself the main burden of conversation, he nothing like rivalled his fellow-countryman. Andrew Hardie, despite his leanness, proved to be no ascetic as regards his feeding, and without displaying any marked enjoyment, did no injustice to his meal; at least, he left nothing on any of his plates. Adam, hungry as he was with all his walking, probably ate least of them all. He satisfied his hunger, but did not thereafter proceed methodically toward entire repletion, which seemed to be the goal of the older men. Perhaps the fact that it was John Dunn's food that he was eating may have had its effects.

There was nothing wrong with that food. There was soup and fish and fowl and beef, with appropriate vegetables and sauces, there were pastries and cream and conserves, and there was a good dry sherry to help it over. Of each there was no lack, and of each little went back to the kitchen.

As has been said, Henry Bullough did most of the talking. He was affable, expansive even, if not always tactful, and he was very concerned for the entertainment of the guests—much more noticeably so than was the host. In fact, Adam became increasingly curious as to the relationship between these two men. Bullough, though only a tenant on the estate, seemed to have become practically a coadjutor to the factor, almost the factor's mouthpiece. And yet it was obviously not a case of a strong man imposing on and superceding a weak one; even on the slightest acquaintance any man could tell that, though Bullough might be a strong man, John Dunn was a stronger. It was an unusual situation and meat for speculation.

The big man was insistent as a victualler. "Come on, man—pass in your plate," he urged Adam. "You'll not see fare like this at Achroy—eh, Mr Hardie?"

The minister raised his head, his fork half-way to his lips. "Achroy . . . ?"

"For sure—didn't you know our young friend here's, ah, elected . . ." he nodded, and repeated the word with something like satisfaction, ". . . elected to bide with MacVarish of Achroy?"

Hardie looked straight at the younger man. "Why?"

John Dunn made one of his few remarks, proceeded by a laugh that was practically a hoot. "As my assistant, happen he thought it would be helpful!"

The other set down his fork. "Ewan MacVarish is a Papist," he stated harshly.

"And a very courteous gentleman." That was Adam Metcalfe.

Hardie's eyes were steely. "A Papist," he repeated, "a smooth-tongued heretic, and a sower of disaffection."

Adam met his stare. "And one of the principal tenants on this estate, I understand," he returned steadily.

"He's the principal reactionary on this estate, sir—and hand-in-glove with the man O'Brien, I make no doubt."

"If by reactionary, you mean he represents the previous order in this place, then surely he is a man that the . . . administration would be wise to enlist on its side in these projected improvements, rather than to antagonise, a link between the old and the new. His influence with the people could be invaluable . . ."

"Would you nurse a viper to your bosom? There can be no compromise with the forces of evil . . ."

"Evil . . .!" Adam cried. "Would you name a man evil because he worships his God something more cheerfully than you do!"

"Do not mock, young man. God is not mocked!" Andrew Hardie, half-risen from his chair, recollected himself, and glanced over at his host.

Dunn, crouching forward over his food, eyed them with grim interest, enjoyment even, but did not let it interrupt his eating. Bullough, too, looked on intently, but on seeing the minister give pause, smiled genially and resumed his role of open-handed bonhomie. "Another glass of sherry, Mr Hardie?" he suggested, and stretched over with the decanter.

John Dunn tossed the picked carcase of his chicken to one of the waiting mastiffs, and drew a toothpick out of his pocket. "Happen ye're a bit hard on t'lad, Hardie," he said casually. "He'll be able to keep an eye on MacVarish there, fine. He's got the estate rarely at heart he has, my new assistant." His little eyes suddenly stared hard at the minister, and then at the younger man, hard and unbelievably vicious.

Hardie sank back into his chair, and the prominent adam's-apple in his skinny neck rose and fell twice. "Yes—yes indeed, Mr Dunn," he agreed, almost hastily, and reached for his glass.

Adam, watching, knew a deep uneasiness. All this had been staged by John Dunn—within him he knew it. He was to be a puppet, to dance when the factor pulled the strings. The fact that the minister was only a puppet also, was small help. Well, he, Adam Metcalfe, would be no man's puppet . . . but he would have to watch how he stepped with this man. For that one revealing ferocious glance had told him much, explained much. Andrew Hardie was afraid of the man; so probably was this Bullough . . . he would have to take hold of himself or he might be, too. John Dunn was no upstart, blustering Jack-in-office, no beggar-on-horseback, but a hard, malignant, dangerous man, possessed of extensive powers. Adam Metcalfe, though born something of a rebel, was no fool. He would have to go carefully!

The meal went on, heedfully.

After the man Colin had cleared away the ruins of a noble cheese, chairs were pushed back and the factor fetched from a cupboard two more decanters, one of claret and the other of the local-distilled fiery malt *uisge beatha* or whisky. Adam had sampled some of the stuff the previous night at Achroy, and found it somewhat drastic in flavour and effect; Ewan MacVarish had suggested that it was a taste that had to be cultivated with some care and diligence—educated into, whatever—for worthy and proper appreciation. He decided now that John Dunn's house was no place to start his education, and contented himself with the claret. The others were nowise constrained by his backwardness.

Bullough produced a bottle of brandy, to ensure that none might go thirsty. "Try some of that, Parson," he cried. "I got that in Dingwall the other day . . . last bottle in the place, thanks to Boney—sink him!"

"Thank you. You had a successful journey I hope, Mr Bullough?"

"Oh, passably, passably. Sheep were a wicked price, like everything else in this blasted war . . . though that cuts both ways, eh! I took all the beasts there were—and two or three buyers were after them!"

"And the other matter . . . did you see the Sheriff?"

"For sure. Two constables are to be sent up in a week or so."

"Eh, but he got more than that out of the Sheriff," John Dunn declared. "He got his papers, all signed and in order. Ye see before ye Henry Bullough, Esquire, Justice o' the Peace and Magistrate of this County."

"Good—my felicitations, sir," Hardie congratulated.

"Strathmoraig will be the better for it. The law must be upheld, or there's an end to all progress. But . . ." he frowned, ". . . only two constables? What are two constables in the face

54

of the task in front of you?"

"'Twas all the Sheriff could spare," Bullough shrugged. "Strike me, there's something of a demand for constables hereabouts these days . . ."

"Two will do well enough," the factor announced, emptying his glass. "I've plenty good men of my own for t'job—the constables will provide the right . . . atmosphere, and two will do that as well as a dozen. All will be done legally and in order on this estate—eh, Metcalfe?" The man did not wait for an answer. "They will not be needed anyway, I think," he went on slowly. "T'folk here know what's good for them—I have made it my job to see that they do, as is only right and proper—eh?" He looked round deliberately at each of them, and his heavy lower lip was thrust out and down in the way it had. "You've done your part too, Hardie." That was thrown out as if he had tossed a bone to his dog. "I don't think we'll have any nonsense at Strathmoraig."

"I hope not," the minister agreed, ". . . but there is a spirit of lawlessness and impatience with authority abroad in the land—even here it is stirring—the spirit that produced the bloody revolution in France and threw up this upstart Bonaparte. At Ardoch we saw the signs of it. My colleague, Mr Henderson, was telling me that Mr Bone was having considerable trouble there in the improvement of the estate. Opposition, resistance, even violence was offered. That idolater O'Brien has been working on them, setting up his false gods, inciting them to defiance, hardening their hearts. He is a danger, a menace to this community, and should be suppressed. We saw the outcome of · his work at Kinlochardoch, did we not, Mr Metcalfe?—brawling and strife and open revolt."

Adam broke his long silence. "I saw misery and wretchedness, unwilling, unhappy people being shipped overseas like cattle, and man-handled if they objected, if that's what you mean," he said evenly.

There was an appreciable pause. Henry Bullough, thrust back in his chair, stared up at the ceiling and hummed beneath his breath. The minister, his bristling brows a bar across his face, moistened his thin lips, glanced across at John Dunn who gazed stonily at the fire and made no move, and cleared his throat. "Young man," he charged, "you are hasty and ill-informed—common failings of youth. The misery you saw was the fruit of seed sown by the man O'Brien, who has taught discontent and the questioning of authority to an ignorant people, bringing forth fears and dejection when they should rather have been filled with hope and inspiration . . ."

"Who is this O'Brien you speak of?" Adam interrupted.

Andrew Hardie almost choked on the name. "Michael O'Brien is the Devil's emissary to this neighbourhood—a popish priest ranging this unhappy country like a ravening wolf seeking whom he may devour, responsible for half the trouble north of Inverness, and spreading sedition and unrest wherever he goes. He is . . ."

". . . merely an interfering busybody who will hang himself in due course," John Dunn said quietly, finally. He turned deliberately to Adam. "Are we to take it, then, that ye disapprove of emigration, amongst other things, *Mister* Metcalfe?"

Adam chose his words. "I am expressing no opinion as to emigration as such," he said. "What I saw at Kinlochardoch was not emigration—it was transportation, forcible and undisguised." Getting no response to that from any of them, he took his courage in his two hands—after all, he was only a youngish man, and one against three . . . and one of them was a devil. "I take it, sir," he said then, "that nothing of the sort is contemplated here . . . ?" He paused. "I . . ." he began, and then halted. Let it stand so—and might the Lord have mercy upon him!

No man spoke then, and a mastiff's loose-mouthed licking and the subdued hiss and crackle of burning logs made only a background for the silence. The factor's great jaws were working strongly, and his head was thrust forward in menace. Then slowly, portentously, he smiled, a smile that was calculating and assured. "Nay, we'll leave emigration to the Government," he said. "We've got plenty to do without that . . . though what Government decides to do is not for me—or you—to question, my young cock. Our job is to clear some tens o' thousands of acres of hill pasture for sheep, and shift t'folk down to . . . alternative holdings on the coast."

"Alternative holdings . . . ?"

"That's right, lad. Right convenient it will be for them, too—near the sea for fishing and easy transport, clustered together in townships instead of scattered everywhere, God knows how, wasting miles of good land. Coast's t'place for likes o' them . . . and if they don't like it and want to emigrate, then we won't stop 'em, lad—we won't stop 'em." He drew a long breath as though after effort taken. It was not often that John Dunn made speeches as long as these.

Henry Bullough suddenly opened his mouth and laughed—and as suddenly stopped, and resumed his contemplation of the ceiling.

"That's our job—that's my lord Alcaster's considered policy," the factor went on. "That's what ye came here to help me with, by God . . . if ye'll be so good!"

"You've no call to question my willingness to do my work," Adam gave back, tight-lipped. "It has been all . . . assumption up to now—you have not tried me yet."

"Aye." Dunn grunted, "Well, ye'll get your chance to show what ye can do tomorrow. We're starting on the preliminary work for the clearing of Glen Luie . . . and a good piece of work for his lordship, too. The estate's been getting a total of little over twenty pounds in rent from that ground: our friend Bullough here's willing to pay considerably more than that for it—eh, Harry?"

"For sure! My offer is sixty pounds for the first year, in compensation for your inconvenience in moving the present tenants, and forty pounds thereafter. That's my offer, squire."

"An offer which the estate accepts," Dunn declared loudly. "So tomorrow, lad, ye start serving notices to quit."

"To move, is it not—to transfer . . . ?"

"Eh . . . ?"

". . . to your alternative holdings on the coast!"

"Ah, of course—transfer, to be sure. Mr Metcalfe, I'm obliged to ye."

57

6

THEREAFTER, with the talk drifting from sheep prices to high prices generally and all the war before them, Adam presently excused himself—and was not detained. With a fulsome wave from Bullough, a frigid bow from Hardie, and a tooth-evident grin from the factor, he got out of that house, and was thankful.

The wind had dropped considerably, and a pale watery sun played its thin smile intermittently over the buffeted land. Not that the land showed any sign of its buffeting; the stalwart pines and the lissome birches betrayed no hint of their ordeal, the reeds and grasses at the waterside that had bowed but would not break had now resumed their nodding gossip, the faded bracken slept too deeply for aught to disturb it yet awhile, and the wiry heather of the hill-sides would not yield to any element save fire alone. Perhaps that land lay too close to the hard rugged bones of the earth to be ruffled by any passing storm.

The man, with the need for action strong upon him, decided to make for Achroy round the far head of the loch. It looked a three or four mile walk, which would just about suit him, for walking-off purposes. He set out with much vigour and decision, and no eye for the scenery. He had serious things to think about, grim, sombre things that would not be blinked, and a course to plot, or at least, some sort of a line to follow. He had learned a lot that afternoon, and had not liked what he had learned. He had known that the factor was an oaf and a bully, but now he recognised that he was far more than that, something much more formidable. Hardie he had thought of as an uncomfortable fanatic, hard but honest; now he was not so sure. And Bullough was a rogue, of that he was certain. As for this sheep scheme, he had been doubtful of it from the first—not of its financial soundness; that seemed to be unquestionable—but of the morals, the ethics of the thing. Now he knew it for what it was, a cynical, blatant piece of avarice at the expense of a helpless people, masquerading under the cloak of estate-improvement and national duty. Cash was all there was behind it—that, and apparently, the Law. There was the sting, the barb of it; Bullough, that gross apostle of the new dispensation, was made a magistrate—as was the factor already, of course—constables were to be provided to see their authority upheld. The State was not disinterested.

He took his dark thoughts and doubts and resentment with him along the high north side of the loch, across the marshland and water-meadows at the green head of it, where the mallards quacked and the rushes whispered and the white bog-cotton danced, and the going was as uncertain as his thinking. It was not that he did not know his own mind—that was seldom a trouble of Adam Metcalfe's—but there were certain salient facts which kept presenting themselves like the unpleasant patches of bog he was now encountering, but which were not so readily got round. Whatever his inclinations, however much he disliked John Dunn, he was under the man's authority, and, within limits, must do as he was ordered. However suspicious he was as to the principle of these 'improvements', they were, as Dunn had said, the considered policy of his employer—indeed, he was here for the express purpose of helping to carry them out. It was not his blame or responsibility . . . so why concern himself? It was no duty of his to set himself up as the champion of these unfortunate people—indeed his duty lay, without much doubt, with the other side, the side that paid him! These were the facts, and he was not going to get over them by wishing they were otherwise—like this headlong river that barred his way.

In his striding the man had reached a broad amber-brown stream that entered the loch out of one of the forking glens. There was no crossing its swift waters thereabouts, so necessarily he headed upstream among the alders and wreckage of its stone-strewn course. It got no narrower, that dark torrent, and presently he was within the open jaws of the glen itself, and still walking. It was a bare, gloomy place of steep screes and tumbled rock from the frowning bald ridges that flanked it, grey and forbidding, but presently, beyond a jutting shoulder of hill, the glen changed its direction and its character, trending away northwards and lifting and widening into a green and shallow valley, open and pleasant. It was not the direction Adam wished to take, but the lusty river gave him no choice but to follow on or to turn back. Being the man he was, he went on.

He found a good track under his feet, and he walked briskly. It was a good time for walking, with the afternoon fading into evening, the scents of bog-myrtle and damp earth rising finely, and a single early star winking palely out of the translucent blue-green that was the western sky. The hill-tops were sharply etched and the higher slopes were bright still, but out of all the deeper corries and hollows and clefts of the valley the shadows were welling and spreading. But all the dark patches that stained the slopes and levels of that green glen were not shadows . . . and the faint acrid smell that came down on the evening air had more than myrtle or earth to it . . . once before he had smelt that smell, after a heath-fire near his native Lakingham, and there too the seared and blighted earth had glowered blackly in a smiling place. But here the sullen stains were all scattered and detached. Towards the nearest he made his way, curious.

It did not require a deal of investigation to reach the heart of the matter. In front of him was a stretch of scorched ground, reeds and rough grass and a few charred skeletons of bushes, and beyond it, on a low mound above the river, a scattered heap of stones. And though the stones were scattered, they were not so much so that they hid the rectangular form of their placing; moreover, a little path led up to the centre of them, and out of their tumbled heart the blackened stumps of beams projected. No, assuredly it did not demand acute insight to perceive what had happened here. Then did all those other burned patches tell the same story? Adam Metcalfe went on up that green glen, with the zest gone out of his walking.

Singly and in little groups he passed them, burnt pasture and broken masonry, each with some tell-tale detail, mute but eloquent—here some fragments of pottery, or a sprawling rose bush, there an accumulation of cattle-dung or a burnlet led through a wooden trough. Not long since, many people had lived in this quiet upland valley. Now they were gone—where? . . . and only the quiet remained.

And it was very quiet. The man had not noticed it before, but he did so now. The river still had its own murmur, certainly, and a solitary wind sighed intermittently over all, occasionally rattling the bare blackened branches of a dead juniper bush. But that was all. And what more had he heard before, then? He did not know, he could not tell . . . but here he felt the quiet, before he had not. The clink of his heel on a stone, the crack of a twig beneath his step, these he heard now . . .

And then, into his preoccupation with the quiet, a sound came that halted him dead in his stride and set the hairs of his neck rising, a horrible sound that made the late hush seem peace itself. It was a wild cackling laugh, essentially mirthless, that rose from a loud gabbling to a high bubbling intensity that was almost a shriek, and sank and died in a choking sob, and left the silence taut and breathless.

The man stood, stiff, tense. The noise came from the direction of another rickle of stones on his left. Slowly he turned, and deliberately, unwillingly, moved towards that spot.

He had gone only a few yards when the grotesque laughter began again, and out of the fallen masonry a figure clambered, a crouching, shambling figure, shapeless in trailing rags and wild-blown hair, that shouted a few words incoherently and shook a bony fist at him, impotently fierce, before turning and making off at a stumbling run up the climbing floor of the glen. And running, the creature laughed again and again, if laughter that sound could be named. He could not tell whether it was man or woman, young or old; only madness was there, and misery and fear and human degradation. Almost sickened, but intensely pitiful, Adam watched till the forlorn thing, bent but swift-moving, was swallowed by the contours of the land. Then he looked at the river to his right, wide still, and at the high rampart of hill to his left and at the long lift of the valley ahead, and found the urge for exploration dead on him. Turning, he went back whence he had come. He drew his collar closer, finding the evening chill.

The light was failing as once again he skirted the loch that had gone steely and colourless, a dulled mirror that reflected neither the definite black of encircling woods nor the uncertain lines of the greying hills. Eastward, the sombre clouds of night were marching, rank upon rank against the ranking mountains, and to the west the blue-green had faded to a toneless emptiness, void and stark, its terrible vacancy only emphasised by that lone star's frigid glitter.

Overhead, the frequent faint whistle and beat of wings indicated the first echelons of the wild duck's evening flighting from the sea.

Having no desire for any further contact with the House of Menardmore that night, Adam had to make a wide circuit of that place, to do so climbing the rising ground north of the loch through its darkening woods and descending into the farther valley beyond, whose inevitable stream must lead him in due course to the Moraig River. A devious road to Achroy, this; he could have rowed so conveniently across that loch, too—if MacVarish's boat was not tied securely to its own stout birch-trunk at the other side of the water. John Dunn would have a boat too, no doubt . . . Let him keep it then, and be damned to him!

He was nearing the strath road, perhaps half-a-mile below Menardmore, and making to cross it, when he noticed a man approaching. There was no mistaking that spare soberly-clad figure. Adam, with no anxiety for converse with Andrew Hardie, could scarcely cross the road directly ahead of him, as his present line must take him, without pause or salute. Nor could he decently change his direction now, in the open and obvious as he was; the man was the minister, and moreover, he had a niece . . . He carried on, therefore, and at the road-side waited.

Hardie approached steadily, a frown on his face. His lean length leant slightly forward and his ash-stick came down heavily at every second pace. His tread was determined, resolu-

62

tion was in every rigid line of him, and he did not relax his frown as he came up with the younger man. To Adam's civil greeting he made no response. Instead, he raised his stick high in front of him. "Son of Belial, consorter with idolaters," he cried impressively, "scoffer, scorner—out of my way!" and he brought down the stick in a grand sweep that missed Adam by inches and all but overbalanced the sweeper. He recovered himself with great dignity and the aid of the same stick, and without pause and more than the single stumble proceeded on his deliberate way. "Woe unto the Unjust Steward, woe unto the Unprofitable Servant . . ." The younger man heard no more than that, for the minister did not look back nor even glance aside from his careful walking. Steadily he continued down that road, desperately steadily, and his stick most evidently was a tower of strength to him. Andrew Hardie was sternly but most indubitably drunk.

His mind working on a new line, Adam Metcalfe went down to cross the haugh of the Moraig River towards Achroy of the birches.

Ewan MacVarish, tacksman of Achroy, in front of his own fireside, was a tight, quietly-humorous man, hospitable and courteous to a degree, but not one to let his tongue run away with him. That evening, after Adam had partaken of his supper, he was invited into his host's room, whence another visitor had but lately gone, a hearty, rather vociferous visitor whose vigorously-voiced brogue all but shook the house. There was no mistaking the country that man came from. But MacVarish had nothing to say about his caller, and it was not for Adam to venture comment.

They sat, then, before a well-doing fire of peats and birch-logs, slippered feet on the iron fire-dogs, leaving the hearth-rug to a black-and-white collie and a slumberous spaniel—Achroy was a widower, with no uncomfortable women nearer than the kitchen to be considered. With his lodger deputy factor, the older man was careful to keep the conversation away from controversial issues, politely but manifestly careful, so that Adam, with information to seek, was restricted to a like circumspection—and yet without emphasis or any constraint. Ewan MacVarish was a companionable man and his reserve did not publish itself. The talk lifted and drifted as easily as the gentle coiling smoke from the Highlandman's tobacco, and the pauses were as easy, and never silences.

But it was a question of MacVarish's that gave Adam the chance to lead the talk the way he wanted it. "And how did you enjoy your first taste of Presbyterian worship, Mr Metcalfe?" he was asked.

"Enjoy . . . ?" He turned the word over on his tongue. "I hardly think enjoyment was intended in that Service. Are we intended to enjoy the worship of our Maker, think you, Mr MacVarish? After this morning I feel there must be some doubt on the matter."

"And you with some justification, maybe," the other nodded, sucking his pipe. "It is a thing that there would seem to be two opinions upon, surely . . . and the Kirk is . . . definite in all its views, you will find. Myself, belonging to the old religion, I take it that man's chief end is to glorify God—and glorifying appears to imply a measure of enjoyment."

"Till today I thought as you do," Adam agreed. "Now I wonder if man's chief end is not damnation!" His eyes lifted to the other's, and both smiled quietly, unhurriedly. Thenceforward their mutual understanding grew steadily. "The pains of hell appear to hold a considerable attraction for some of your countrymen, Mr MacVarish."

"That depends on what you mean by countrymen. In this Scotland, there are two distinct strains that mix but little; my own poor people, the Highland Gaels, and the Lowlanders from the south and east who rule us all. The real Scots they are, these able folk from the Lothians and the Merse and the Borders, strong, hard-working and determined, but damnably sober— and they fear their God with an awful fear. They are the Kirk and the State and all else in Scotland—save only the Army, to be sure. That last is the only thing we poor feckless Highlandmen have been found good for—to fight Boney. Anyone will tell you the same. And the pains of hell sit uncomfortably upon us, despite all the Kirk's good work."

Adam digested that for a space. It fitted in well with all he had observed and inferred so far. "But what about the congregation today?" he objected presently. "Were they not all Highland people, sitting there—good Presbyterians wallowing in fire and brimstone?"

The other shook his head. "That is where you go wrong, Mr Metcalfe. They are not good Presbyterians—hence, to some extent, the fury of the threatenings and slaughters. The Gael at heart is not a good Presbyterian and never will be. As a race he is optimistic and improvident, imaginative and spectacular, sociable and with no inordinate love for hard work—in other words a natural-born Catholic, and the Kirk knows it and hates him for it."

"Then why . . . ?"

". . . why are so many of them Presbyterians? Because the Kirk has a pressing way with it, backed by the State, and more potently still by the estates. The old leaders of the people here were largely Jacobite, and Catholic. When their Cause went down sixty years ago, a whole dispensation in this land came to an end. The clan-system was condemned, and the old faith with it. It is easier to kill a system than a religion, so Catholicism persisted still, but it was suspect and frowned-upon; the new-comers brought their own creed with them, and diligent they were to spread it. The Kirk was very persuasive, and it got its recruits—but it is having its work cut out to make good Kirk-men out of them, I'm thinking."

"So the Reverend Hardie's thunderings are the outward and visible signs of his Church's failure?"

"They could be, then—my own suggestion it is, only. He conforms to pattern, the man, but outdoes most of his colleagues in . . . zeal—a reason for that there could be, too, maybe."

Adam glanced at him. "Yes . . . ?"

The other shrugged. "I wouldn't deny even Andrew Hardie a conscience," he said cryptically. ". . . will you not be trying a drop out of the old bottle, and it distilled not fifty miles from

65

Achroy? I wouldn't say as good whisky was not to be found in the breadth of Scotland, but better would be hard to come by, Mr Metcalfe. The water of these parts is the most suitable in all the West, I am assured, neither too hard nor too soft, by the dispensation of Providence . . ."

Though he tried, Adam did not get his host back to the topic of the minister—not till, with a glow within him and just a faint ringing in his ears, he prepared to seek his own room. And then MacVarish himself returned to the subject in his own way, as though to round-off a discussion that had known no interruption. "Aye," he mentioned, head ashake, "he is a strange man, Andrew Hardie—and weak, weak."

"Weak . . . ?" The young man stared at him.

"Just that, Mr Metcalfe. Mind you the lamp. You will sleep well with that good stuff to warm you. Goodnight to you!"

Like all the rest of his race, Ewan MacVarish was something of an artist in effects.

7

GLENLUIE was wider than the other glens that radiated unevenly from the head of Strathmoraig; indeed it did not approximate to what is generally termed a glen at all. It was merely an indefinite area of land, more or less low-lying, extending between two great sprawling masses of hill, whose buttresses were sometimes two miles apart, sometimes four hundred yards. With its surface as variable as its width, braes, hummocks, bogs, and heath, only the untidy stream that wound and spread its way down the uneven midst of it, substantiated its claim to be a valley. But glen or no, it supported some two hundred people over its five mile course, and the gleam of the walls of its forty or so whitewashed croft-houses was the smile in the eyes of the place.

With the morning bright about them and the oyster-catchers piping shrilly at every stream, the factor's party parted company at the humpbacked Bridge of Luie, to face this glen.

"You'll take the left side of the river, Metcalfe," Dunn directed. "There are fewer crofts that side. Don't miss any, and don't stand any nonsense. Hopkins'll go with you—he'll show you." His eyes narrowed. "Now mind you—if there's the least sign of trouble, strike at once and strike hard. Weakness is fatal. Enforce your authority, and ye'll get results."

"That will be unnecessary, I'm sure," Adam spoke evenly.

"Showing who's master is never unnecessary," the factor rasped. "Happen you'll discover that when ye've been factor a bit longer. There's a lot o' them, and damned few of us. You know your job, Hopkins?"

"Yessir."

"Right. Ye should be finished by the middle of the afternoon. Come on, Harry."

Adam turned across the bridge, followed by the man Hopkins leading a pannier pony, a big stolid fellow with a pronounced accent, one half-closed eye, and the aspect of an ex-pugilist. The younger man was well-content to find him unsociable.

They followed a fair track along the western side of the river, Adam well in front and in a wretched temper. He did not see the soaring larks which sang blithely to the morning sky, he did not heed the tinkle and chuckle and murmur of running water, he did not notice the fragrance which the sun drew from the smiling land, nor any other sound nor scene nor scent of the place—but he did see a single white cot-house set under the shelter of a knoll half-a-mile ahead, whence this path and his duty was leading him, and his frown was black, or grey rather, grey as his heart within him. It was too fine a morning for the work to be done.

Where a little path branched-off up to the house, he halted and turned. "Camusnavoe . . . ?" he asked.

Hopkins nodded. "Name o' Bain or Macbain, Annie Macbain—Missus or Miss, God knows. No husband but a packet o' brats!" and he winked suggestively with the undamaged eye.

"That's enough," Adam ordered sharply. "Wait here, then." And he went up the path alone.

The croft-house was built against the side of the knoll, almost grew out of it, with its humpbacked thatch of reeds shading into the faded grasses and bracken of the bank. Two doors but no windows opened under the low-browed roof, out of the lower of which a lean, small cow eyed the newcomer incuriously. From behind a peat-stack as high as the house came the sound of chopping wood, and thither Adam made his way.

He found a big muscular woman of early middle age, comely and high-coloured, in bursting bodice and high kilted skirt, wielding a purposeful axe on a straggling wood-pile watched warily by a slant-eyed fawn of a child, who, dodging the flying chips, gathered the fruits of her mother's labours. The man was quickly discovered, and the woman straightened up, smoothing her hair and smiling. "*Madainn mhath duibh!*" she said, and half-curtseyed.

Adam coughed. "Good morning, ma'am. I'm sorry to interrupt . . ." and he gestured toward the wood heap. Then the essential hypocrisy of such a conventional expression of regret, considering the scope of his mission, struck him forcibly, and he thrust into his pocket and drew out a paper. "Mistress Anne Bain, Camusnavoe . . . ?" he read out harshly.

Her eyes searched his face, and there was a trace of alarm behind them. "*Mi fein . . . ? Se, tha mi Anna Bàin, Cam's'voe. C'arson . . . ?*"

He looked beyond her, to the hills that may not be moved. "Then it is my duty, my unhappy duty, to inform you that you must vacate this croft by the forthcoming term-day," he said. "Suitable alternative accommodation will be provided down near the coast," and he held out the missive to her.

Hesitantly the woman accepted the paper, opened it, looked at it back and front and turned it this way and that, with a puzzled frown on her face. Then she looked up at him, with a shake of the head and a small anxious smile. "*Cha'n'eil fhios a'am . . . ?*"

Reluctantly Adam took the notice from her and began to read. "Estate Office, Menardmore . . . Take notice, that in accordance with Act of Parliament, the Proprietor of the lands of Camusnavoe in Glenluie, being wishful to resume and occupy the above lands hereby gives notice to Annie Bain or MacBain, sub-tenant and occupier of the said croft and holding of Camusnavoe to leave, vacate and quit the lands mentioned on or before the ensuing term day, May fifteenth, eighteen hundred and nine, leaving the ground clear and unencumbered . . ." His voice trailed away as he looked up at the woman and saw her complete uncomprehension. She was still shaking her head bewilderedly. "*Cha'n'eil fhios a'am . . .*" she repeated, and it required no knowledge of the Gaelic to translate that into "I do not understand . . ." At a loss, he glanced about him for help, casting around for some means of conveying the thing he had to convey. He pointed to himself. "I am the new factor—*factor*," he repeated, and knew by the sudden widening of her eyes that she recognised that word at least. "This is to say," he tapped the paper, "that you must leave—go away from here." And the gesture of his arm included all the croft and its surroundings,

69

and then out, away, vaguely towards the sea, a gesture crude as he found it hateful to make.

Still the woman only shook her head hopelessly, though she reached her hand down to the child and pressed her close to her leg in a motion instinctively protective and born of an undefined fear.

At the movement, Adam turned abruptly. "Hopkins!" he shouted, "Come here." Waiting in uncomfortable silence he tapped the ground with his foot. He might have smiled to the child, made an attempt at pleasantry, but he could not add insult to injury. He was here to work these people's hurt; he would not do it behind the smile of a friend. Hopkins' leisurely approach was expedited by a shout of "Move yourself, man!" and he came, hurrying. "Can you speak any of their language, Hopkins?" he was demanded.

"Not perishing likely," the fellow snorted. "Jabber like a parcel o' monkeys . . ."

"How on earth, then, do you inform the tenants that don't speak English that they are to quit?"

"Jest like Mr Dunn said—hand 'em the notice. If they ain't eddicated enough to read it, that ain't no blame o' yours."

"I'm afraid something more than that is required . . ."

"Not for Mr Dunn, it ain't. That's wot he does. That's the Law, he says."

Adam Metcalfe's jaw jutted. "That may be Mr Dunn's interpretation of the Law but it is not mine. These tenants must be properly warned. Do you know of any of the people who speak English?"

"No, Mister, I don't," the other said, and spat.

"Well, we'll have to find one, and come back," Adam snapped. He turned to the woman, and raised his hat. "I am sorry you have been troubled, ma'am," he said, since he must say something. "I will be back later." And he bowed and swung about, jerking his head to his pitying henchman.

A bewildered woman watched them move down towards the track where the pony waited, watched them till they had passed out of sight beyond the junipers of the knoll. Then she looked at the house, her home, at the little garden and the small scattered patches of tilth that generations had wrested and held from the wilderness, and she looked long, her face expressionless.

They had no great distance to go to the next croft. Set on a little patch of green turf among grey outcrops at the foot of a long heather slope, Knockenra, not whitewashed like so many of its neighbours, seemed little more than a larger grey outcrop amongst the multitude of its fellows, so little did the modest crouching outline of it disturb the contour of the braeside. A few fowls picked about the black pit of the doorway, and away to the flank, across a steep little ravine wherein stunted rowans climbed desperately above a foaming torrent, strips of cultivation, scanty and curiously-shaped, barely scratched the face of the land. At one of these, two or three figures were working casually.

An old man watched their approach from a seat by the byre at the lower end of the house. A tethered munching goat watched too from close by, and ancient and goat had a certain similarity in their expressions and leanness and straggling beards. The old man rose stiffly as they came near, and nodded his head at them, twice, grinning toothlessly. "Ai, ai!" he said.

"Good morning." Adam spoke abruptly. "Is this the croft of Knockenra?"

"Ai, ai . . ."

"You will be Angus Sean MacAngus?" glancing at his paper. "Do you speak English, Mr Angus?"

The other nodded again, cheerfully. "Ai, ai . . ."

Adam drew his hand over his chin doubtfully. "Then, Mr Angus, I'm afraid I have unpleasant news for you. You are required to vacate this croft—leave it . . ."

But the old man had turned away, smiling and bowing, and shuffled into the house from whence he presently emerged carrying a jug of milk and some oatcakes, the staple hospitality of that country. These he offered to the young man, courteously. "Ai, ai . . ."

Adam shook his head heavily. "No—I thank you, but . . . I have come to evict you from your home, to turn you out. Do you understand?"

The urgency in his voice and whole bearing had its effect. The ancient looked up at him, pointed to his ears, and shook his head, and launched into an inarticulate stream of Gaelic.

"Deaf as a post!" Hopkins pronounced. Stepping over, his hand was out to take of the provender when it was knocked aside.

"Leave that alone," he was told. "Have you no sense of decency, fellow?"

The man thrust forward, glared, and thought better of it. "He's offered it, ain't he?" he protested reasonably. "No harm in taking wot you're offered . . ."

Adam turned from him to the crofter, and, touching his shoulder, pointed away, across the ravine towards the strips of cultivated land where the figures were working, and made a gesture as though fetching them back to the croft.

The old man understood at once, and grinning, thrust two bent fingers into his mouth, and hunching further his already hunched shoulders, produced a shrill and penetrating whistle, surprising considering the emptiness of his gums, which pierced the ear-drums and affronted the morning before choking and dying in a plethora of spittle. His beckoning which followed brought a quick wave of the hand in answer from one of the workers, and all three turned from their labour and made for the croft, preceded by a bounding dog. The whistler beamed on his visitors, chuckling satisfaction at his prowess. "Ai, ai . . ." he said.

While they awaited the newcomers, Hopkins moved away by himself till he reached a nearby eminence from which he proceeded methodically to survey the ground around the croft, apparently making some sort of note of what he saw in a small book. Interested, since in all probability the fellow could neither read nor write, Adam observed him, and on his return held out his hand. "What's that you were doing, Hopkins?" he enquired.

"Jest a job for Mister Dunn."

72

"Yes . . . ?"

"Jest having a look over the place."

"You were setting something down on paper . . . ?"

"Jest making a note o' the pasture."

"Pasture? How do you mean—pasture?" Still the hand was outstretched.

Shrugging, the man handed over his book, wherein was crudely drawn a very rough plan of the croft with certain areas in the vicinity shaded-in. Turning back the leaves, other pages were likewise filled with similar plans.

"What's this—what are these for?" Adam wondered.

"Ask Mister Dunn. This 'ere's his book, d'ye see," and he took it back and pocketed it.

Just then the three from the field came round the corner of the cottage, heralded by the bounding, barking collie, a woman, a girl, and a youth in his teens. To them the old man addressed himself volubly, while Adam saluted and waited.

Presently the woman, nodding, turned to the boy and pushed him forward, seemingly with a word or two of encouragement. He gulped twice and spoke, darting-eyed. "Myself hass the English," he jerked. "Angus Sean, she iss saying you the good morning."

"Thank you. Will you tell them I am the new factor—*the new factor!*"

The lad smiled nervously, and rapidly addressed the others. A change came over the company, tension crept into the atmosphere—much more suitable to the occasion, Adam decided wryly. He went on, "I have to inform you . . . tell you . . . that the estate requires all this ground, your croft, for its own use, and you must leave it by the next term-day." He enunciated slowly and clearly, but the boy's anxious frown was eloquent of imperception. He tried again, spacing, his words. "This is a *letter* . . . a *paper* . . . to tell you that you must *leave* . . . leave . . . this croft . . . *go away* from Knockenra. Your laird needs it himself. All the crofters have to go. You will get *new land* . . . down at the *sea*." He realised that his voice was rising; why must he always shout at these people? "You understand . . . ? You

73

must leave by the fifteenth of May?"

The lad's jaw had fallen. "Leave...? Go...from Knockenra? *Cha b' urrainn e bhi!*"

Adam nodded. "Tell them," he said.

He turned away as the boy told, but he could not close his ears to the reception of his news. Into the silence that followed the eventual assimilation of the tidings, he spoke, restrainedly. "I am sorry, desperately sorry . . . It is my duty . . . It is the proprietor's orders . . . your laird's commands . . ."

Still no one spoke. They only stared at him, dumbly, without hostility, stunned and shocked and stricken, like an animal punished for some misdeed it knows not. There were no questions, no remonstrances, only a pitiful passive acceptance of fate. The blow was not entirely a bolt from the blue; other glens had been cleared; the factors were everywhere busy, urgent about their employers' business; the lairds were rediscovering their land, and God's hand was heavy on all the Highlands. So they stood, mute, forlorn, and Adam, looking, could stand no more, thrust the missive of eviction into the woman's hand, and swung away with a muttered word of regret. And Hopkins, winking at the woman and leering at the girl, picked up an oatcake from the platter which the old man still held, pushed it into his mouth, and grinning, followed his master.

A group of half a dozen houses clustered around a wide crescent of haughland pasture constituted the place of Luiebeg. Here, a huddle of foolish sheep, big-horned and shaggy-coated, proclaimed the factor's arrival to all the glen with much fuss and alarm, preceding them up the track in hurrying loud-voiced agitation. The outcry brought people forth from cottage and barn and cow-house, and children and dogs from nowhere in particular, these falling-in behind Hopkins and the pony, so that the progress through Luiebeg took on something of the nature of a procession. Selecting what he judged to be a central position, Adam halted and waited, Hopkins found a dog to kick, and the children withdrew into a knot and talked in whispers.

An elderly man, tall and massively built, whom Adam had

noticed at church the previous day, hastened forward, limping on a stick. "Good day to you, sir," he greeted. "It is surely very fine weather that's in it for the time of the year, yes. Is there anything I can be after doing for you, at all, Mr Metcalfe?"

"You know me, then . . . ?" There was surprise in his voice.

"Yes, then—it was the lad Ian MacErlich that was after giving me the word. You will be the new factor, and staying with Ewan MacVarish of Achroy . . . and him cousin to my own self."

"Indeed!" Adam, who had been congratulating himself on the discovery of an interpreter, now foresaw further embarrassment. "I regret that I should be paying my first visit to Luiebeg under distressing circumstances, Mr . . . ?"

"MacVarish—Donald Bàn, it is."

"I am afraid that I bring you bad news, Mr MacVarish."

"That is hard for you, Mr Metcalfe. A weary road it makes with ill news under your tongue."

"That is so." He nodded, and looking up, met the other's tired grey eyes. "Believe me, I would spare you this, Mr MacVarish, if it were within my power . . ." and he said the thing that had to be said.

After the first quick intake of breath, Donald Bàn MacVarish heard him out unspeaking. Adam would have preferred expostulation, challenge. When he had finished, the other raised his eyes from the ground. "So!" he breathed. "Here, too—must it be here, too!"

It was not a question as he said it, but the younger man answered it as such. "I am afraid it must. It is the proprietor's—the laird's—policy to turn all this land over to sheep . . . in the national interests." His mouth twisted on the phrase. "I am afraid that there is no hope that he will reconsider his decision."

"The laird, is it!" The Highlandman's voice betrayed its first hint of bitterness. "Aye, it is a laird we have got, now—though never one of us has seen the great English lord that does be calling himself that same. In the old days it was a Chief that we had—now it is a laird, whatever. A difference there is, Mr Metcalfe, for sure."

"I believe you . . . though I have heard tell of some chiefs, too, who have discovered the need for 'Improvements' on their estates!"

"Aye, God pity them. They have broken their trust, and with it they are breaking their people . . ."

". . . but not the Law, Mr MacVarish, not the Law—which is the important thing, is it not?" That man, hurting and hurt, must twist the knife in his own wound; he could not do anything to make things easier for himself.

"'Tis yourself that is saying it, sir. I do not know—I am no lawyer. But can you tell me this, Mr Metcalfe . . . can your lord be showing any papers—deeds is it, or titles?—to this land that he is emptying?"

Adam eyed the man strangely. "I couldn't tell you, but no doubt he can. Why shouldn't he . . . ?"

"Because it is not his land, at all. It is the clan's land. The chiefs never owned the land. MacVarish of Strathmoraig never owned Glenluie, or any more than the place of Menardmore."

"Then who did?"

"Clann Varish its own self. The Chief had the placing of it out to tacksmen, like this Luiebeg to myself and my father before me and my father's father, and his share of the produce of it, but that was all. He did not own it, whatever."

"But this is important," Adam cried. "I had no idea—I doubt even if Alcaster has. Such a system is unknown in England." He turned to the other on a sudden thought. "Tell me, does Mr Dunn know about this, d'you think?"

Donald Bàn nodded his head slowly. "Yes, then—he knows. Ewan was after telling him long since, when first the word of clearing came out."

"Yes . . . ?"

"He asked Ewan to produce the *clan's* titles," the other said simply.

"Ah—I see." He could not fail to see. "John Dunn would say that. And there are none, of course?"

"Never the one, at all." With a deep breath, the older man lifted his gaze to the line of the enduring hills, and his look held a direct and terrible clarity of vision. "So we must go," he went on, then, and once more that was a statement and no question. "Down to the sea, I think you said, Mr Metcalfe? Somewhere down at the shore?"

"Yes, somewhere round about Invermoraig, I believe. Mr Dunn says the alternative accommodation is adequate. I have not seen the place myself—I only arrived on Friday . . ."

"That could not be expected, whatever," Donald Bàn acceded politely. "An unpleasant duty it will be for you altogether, and you new come to the place. If there is any way I can be helping you . . . ?"

They were so polite, so damnably civil, these people. Adam almost hated them for it. If only they would show some fight . . . ! "Yes, Mr MacVarish. I have to deliver these notices to each of the tenants. If you would be so good as to come with me, and explain . . . I cannot make myself understood . . . Not a very pleasant task for you, either, I'm afraid, but it would be a help both to them and to myself, perhaps . . . ? Thank you, Mr MacVarish, I am much obliged. You will tell them that any suggestions or—er—complaints they may have to make, I will take note of and pass on for consideration by the factor, but . . ." his eye met the older man's, and he shook his head, ". . . I would tell them, too, that they would be . . . unwise to hope for much . . . for anything . . . at all."

The Highlandman inclined his head. "I understand," he said evenly.

"Come on, then." Adam turned wearily. "This first croft is . . . ? Farquhar? Ah, yes—Nial Farquhar. We will start there, then."

And that thing they did.

And so it went on, the sorry progress—the six crofts of Luiebeg, and Balnacoul and Tomglas, and Badandubh and Ruaig. "I am sorry. . . I deeply regret . . . No, I am afraid not . . . Down to the sea . . . Yes, the coast . . . You must go . . . must go . . . I am sorry . . . No, you must go . . . I will tell Mr Dunn, but . . . I am sorry . . ."

With seven crofts still to do and Camusnavoe to re-visit,

Adam called a halt. It was late afternoon, with all the bright promise of the morning lost and forgotten in a grey dreariness that a searching wind brought to the hills; Donald Bàn had his beasts to get in and his wife sickly and tied to the house, Hopkins was impatient and surly, and Adam himself was weary in body and mind. Enough woe had been wrought for one day, anyway.

He thanked MacVarish at the door of his own house, and declined refreshment from that inborn gentleman. "My debt to you is heavy enough," he proclaimed. "I have destroyed your peace and undone the work of generations; I have made use of you shamelessly and involved you in a task that you must have loathed; I will not eat your bread as well. Leave me a little of my pride, Mr MacVarish."

The other nodded his understanding, and they parted.

Leaving that place, men—elderly men—looked after them dully, silently, a woman withdrew inside her doorway as they passed, and from their path a party of children ran, fearful. Adam, set-faced, saw all of that, and more, and seeing, walked on steadily. He saw the green glen that he had been in last night, deserted and desolate. He saw the mad, shambling, mouthing figure that had pointed at him and gesticulated, forlorn and desolate as the glen. He saw an endless succession of deserted glens and staring unhappy figures that pointed at him, desolation in their eyes. And why—why was he, Adam Metcalfe, implicated? What was he doing on that road that led down those desolated glens? He was about his master's business, that's what he was doing, earning his living. That was it—he was making his daily bread! He was tasting his own hell that day, the man.

Nor was he finished, yet. Dunn and Bullough had arrived back at Menardmore nearly two hours previously, and having refreshed themselves, were awaiting Adam's return with grim anticipation. The factor greeted him with his usual directness. "Ye've taken your time, Mister," he growled.

"There was no particular hurry, was there?" the other gave back, and his voice was tired.

Dunn's smile proclaimed his notice of the fact. "Oh, none at all, none at all," he allowed. "Maybe ye'll have discovered that this factoring is not just the simple job ye thought it was, eh? Where's Hopkins?"

"Outside, I suppose." That was shortly said, and brought forth a meaning stare before Dunn swung about and marched from the room.

Henry Bullough spoke from the hearth-rug. "We were getting quite anxious about you, lad," he announced—though neither of them had looked it. "No trouble with the crofters, eh?"

"Not what *you* would call trouble." If there was little attempt to hide the accent on that 'you', the big man gave no sign of noticing it.

"Good," he said. "Not that there should be any cause for trouble, of course, but with these illiterate, uncivilised folk you never can tell, eh?"

Adam's glance was wordless but eloquent—eloquent enough to bring the big man's observations to a sudden close, and to set him swinging on toes and heels before the fire, eyes on the ceiling. "Aye—ah—um!" he concluded.

John Dunn's heavy-footed entry brought to a close a silence that the younger man considered to be suitable rather than uncomfortable. He strode straight up to his assistant, halting barely a yard from him, head thrust forward, legs wide, in the aggressive way he had. "Ye haven't finished—ye've not done much more'n half, sink me!" he rasped. "What in hell's name have ye been doing, man?"

Adam gave back stare for stare—he must, now, or be for ever lost—and he took his time to answer. "I was doing an unpleasant task as . . . decently as I could," he said quietly.

"Decently. . .!" the factor almost roared, and his great hands clutched and strained in their own grasp. He enunciated with difficulty. "Damme, your job is to do *what* you're told, *when* you're told, and *how* you're told. I'll decide how it's to be done, Mister—you'll *do* it. I'm master here, and things will be done my way—see?"

"And is it your way to issue eviction notices in English to Gaelic-speaking tenants, by the hands of people who speak no

79

Gaelic?"

"Eh . . . what? Curse me, what d'ye think? D'ye think I could put that heathenish jabber down in writing, even if I wanted to? The King's English is good enough for John Dunn—and for the tenants. The King's English—that's all that's required."

"I think the tenants are legally entitled to a little more than that. The position must be made clear to them . . ."

"God—I made it clear enough for them today . . . and it'll be clearer still on term-day, I promise ye. And *I'll* decide what the Law requires here, Mister. I'm magistrate, and don't you forget it. Hopkins says . . ."

"Yes—what does Hopkins say?"

The sudden grate in Adam Metcalfe's tone warned the factor, who, whatever else he was, was no fool. For only an instant the beady eyes that had held Adam's wavered, and then clamped back again. "He says ye've still six or seven crofts to do, damme." The words started uncertainly and ended almost in a shout that was the measure of his disconcertment.

Adam knew that was not what the man had been going to say, and knew too that he had gained a point. He was in a mood to follow it up. "I came here as Lord Alcaster's Deputy-Commissioner, not as your lackey," he told him. "If you must discuss me with estate servants, I would imagine that you would keep the fact to yourself."

John Dunn did not move, did not speak, but his neck seemed to grow thicker and redder above his soiled cravat, and his breathing became a noticeable thing. Adam, sitting with the man's clenched hands level with his throat, knew a choking sensation born of a thrill of physical fear, but he swallowed it and held his eyes steady.

As had happened once before, it was Henry Bullough who spoke; either he did not relish the tension, or he sought to help his friend. If his friend needed that help, then Adam was not dissatisfied. "No need to take it that bad, Mr Metcalfe. John Dunn's the last man to be over-familiar with servants—eh, John? It's just that he likes to see his instructions carried out by his own—er—thorough and efficient methods. It will not take you long to get into his ways—good ways that produce results. You'll be working hand-in-glove in no time, I'll warrant." Adam produced the suspicion of a smile. "It's not to be wondered at, lad, that you didn't get along too well the first day—these Highland critturs would rile anyone—but firm handling is all they need, and they're meeker than a flock o' my own sheep—you'll see."

"That certainly seems to be the accepted practice hereabouts," the younger man agreed sardonically.

"It's that or nothing, lad. One man, or a small group of men, can only impose their will on large numbers of folk by knowing their own minds and letting the others see that they are prepared to carry out their plans to the limit—and beyond, if need be. You've got to show that you hold the whip-hand and the only way to do that is to crack the whip!"

"A little reminiscent of Bonaparte's theories, perhaps, Mr Bullough—what we're supposed to be fighting against?"

The other guffawed. "Maybe it is. Old Boney's a clever man; he knows what he wants and he knows how to set about getting it . . ."

John Dunn, who had taken a pace or two back and forward, broke in ruthlessly. "Enough o' this!" he snapped, very definitely himself again. "Metcalfe, I'm going to be very patient this once—but I would not advise you to rely on it in future! You want a Gaelic-speaker to explain the position to the crofters? Very well, you shall have one. You can go right down to the Manse tonight, and tell Hardie to go with ye tomorrow. He knows enough of the wretched lingo to make himself understood—though, sink me, I can do that myself without knowing a word—eh, Harry? Aye, damme, Hardie's just the man for ye, lad."

"Mr Hardie may not be agreeable . . . he may have other plans for tomorrow . . . ?" Adam viewed the suggestion without enthusiasm.

"Mr Hardie will be agreeable," Dunn stated definitely. "You tell him from me . . . or, ahem . . . you might request him to do so with my compliments. He'll go. Right . . . !" The factor wheeled about and made for the mantelpiece and his pipe. "If ye want to eat here, the man Colin'll get ye something," he jerked over his shoulder.

Adam rose. "I will make my own arrangements, thank you," he said stiffly.

"As you will, Mister . . ." John Dunn grinned.

8

A DAM METCALFE trudged down the road to the Kirkton of Menardbeg in the creeping dusk, with his pride intact—like his hunger. He might have rowed back across the loch to his dinner at Achroy and delivered his message in the evening, but he preferred to get this sad day's work done and over . . . and who knows if a soft-eyed young woman, hospitably inclined, might not take pity on a man still wanting his dinner! He was young enough to have the notion help two weary feet along a benighted Highland road.

A cheerful gleam of lamp-light from one of the Manse windows seemed to beckon and welcome warmly—and that might even be the warmest of his welcome—and the night drew the closer in its jealousy. As he crunched up the river-bed gravel of the rough drive a dog barked shrilly, hostilely, in tune with the night, and the man knew a quick surge of wary enmity, reflex of some primitive instinct deep-buried. Then from the byre behind the house a cow lowed slumberously, a homely, soothing sound that banished the uncertain threat of the dark and the dog, and cast its comfortable benison on all the night.

Light steps followed the hollow thud of his knocking, and the door opened to silhouette Alison Hardie's admirable figure against the soft glow of a candle. "Is that . . . oh, it's you, Mr Metcalfe!" she said, and waited quietly.

He could not see her face, with the light behind her, but he could hear her voice, and she was not hastening to hale him within. So he spoke formally. "My respects, ma'am. I have a message for Mr Hardie from the factor . . ."

She stood for a moment, and the candle-light made a subdued halo around her plenteous hair. Then she quickly turned about, and with a cast back, "Come this way, please," she led the way down the lobby. The man closed the door behind him, and followed, frowning.

Opening the door on the right into the same small apartment that he had been in before, the girl preceded the visitor. "A message from the factor—by Mr Metcalfe," she announced, and her voice, which could be lively, was expressionless.

In that pleasant room, cosy in the warm light of log-fire and lamp, Andrew Hardie lifted himself out of an armchair to bow stiffly to his guest. "Good evening, sir," he said, and so stood. Adam was aware of little welcome in that house.

He was brief himself. "I regret to trouble you at this time of day, Mr Hardie, but I come on Mr Dunn's business, not my own," and he gave half a glance sideways as he said it. "He presents his compliments and asks if you will be good enough to accompany me tomorrow up Glenluie, serving eviction notices?"

"But I was under the impression that you were doing Glenluie today, Mr Metcalfe . . . ?"

"I was—but not speedily enough for Mr Dunn. I do not understand the language, and, apparently, am possessed of quite unnecessary scruples about explaining the exact position to the crofters, with the result that barely half my side of the glen has so far been informed of its fate."

"And you wish me to assist you in bringing these people to a proper understanding of the position?" The minister's eyes were not on the other man but on his niece's back. She had turned to leave the room after announcing the caller, but on Adam's first words had moved over to a side-table near the door, to tidy odds and ends thereon with some display. There she still stood, her back turned to the men, her head bowed.

"It is Mr Dunn who wishes it," Adam corrected carefully. "He evidently considers that your presence would be . . . helpful."

"To whom?" It was Alison Hardie who asked that, tensely, chokingly, as though it had been forced out of her. She faced them now, flushed, her fingers gripping the edge of the table behind her.

Surprised, Adam looked at her. "To the estate, of course," he answered her crookedly, "—to the factor, to lawful and settled authority generally, to the national cause, even—wool for uniforms, mutton for food, profits for some, and glory for all! Who else is to be considered, I ask you?"

"Only the crofters," she said bleakly. She made no attempt to respond to the man's irony.

"The crofters!" he cried. "Who considers the crofters . . . ?"

Harshly Andrew Hardie intervened. "Child, you would do well to mind your own affairs and not concern yourself with matters you do not understand," and he lifted his stern stare to throw a meaning glance toward the door.

"I am no child," Alison Hardie denied, and indeed it was no child's voice that said it. "I am only a woman, but I know right from wrong, I think." She spoke jerkily, as if by an effort, and Adam Metcalfe, watching her, perceived that the girl was taxing herself to speak thus, forcing herself to an assertion, a defiance, that her whole nature shrank from. She was not a brazen woman, this, but soft-eyed—though firmly-chinned below— warm and of an amicable nature, and she had been brought up in a stern tradition of strict respect for her elders. "You may talk of the ultimate benefit to the country, but you cannot deny that these people, the crofters, are being harshly, cruelly, dealt with, and they have done nothing to deserve it. And if it is harsh for the factor and his, his associates"—here she threw a disdainful glance at the visitor—"to treat them so, who represent nothing more than a distant landlord's interests, then surely it is wrong, a sin, for you, their minister, to assist at their hurt. They are your parishioners, your flock . . ."

"They are no flock of mine in Glenluie," her uncle grated. "Papists, nine-tenths of them, idolaters, false-swearers, followers of that evil man O'Brien! If they were my people, Kirk-members, Mr Metcalfe would need no interpreter."

"Donald Bàn MacVarish is no Papist! And, anyway, have you not a duty to them all—they are all your parishioners?"

"It is my duty, yes—it is my privilege—to advise them, for their own good and for the greater good of many." His eyes lifted to the ceiling, and an upraised hand evinced the professional preacher. "These things are above and beyond you,

Alison. Leave them to men, whose province they are. Leave us now, girl."

For a moment or two she hesitated, and the very evident rise and fall of her bosom proclaimed her emotion. She was well-made, that girl, and womanly, and Adam Metcalfe, not unimpressionable himself, had to find some outlet for his admiration—beyond that written eloquently, if unconsciously, on his face. "Miss Hardie—if there were more like you, this country would not be the same place, at all!" he said. He paused and glanced towards her uncle, and his voice, which, for that one sentence, had been his own and natural, took on a different inflexion. "Who knows if these Highlands of yours would be able to play the—er—useful part for which a far-sighted Providence has so apparently cast them—eh, Mr Hardie?"

But he was not looking at the minister now, and for a brief spell the girl's eyes held his, as though seeking the man behind the words. Then, with a strange perplexed shake of the head, she turned abruptly towards the door. Adam, with a swift stride, reached the handle first and held the door open for her. "Bravo, Alison Hardie!" he murmured as she passed him.

If she heard his words, she gave no sign, and slowly, reluctantly, he closed the door behind her.

"You will forgive the clatter of a foolish child, Mr Metcalfe. My niece is hardly herself tonight," he was told. "Women's havers and the uninformed charity of a quean . . . She will learn in time, the girl."

"I am just afraid that she will," the other answered.

Andrew Hardie's fierce eyebrows rose, for that was significantly said, but he made no comment. "About tomorrow," he inquired, "would it be suitable if I met you at, say, the Bridge of Luie . . . ?"

Adam Metcalfe walked back to Achroy through sighing, creaking woods and by whispering waters, and noticed none of it. Indeed, he was more than half-way there before he recollected that he was ravenously hungry.

9

IT was while listening for the second time, constrainedly, to Andrew Hardie's somewhat impassioned interpretation of his statement to the crofter of Altbran, that Adam Metcalfe noticed the smoke. It appeared to come from the direction of Camusnavoe, which they had left despondent barely the hour before, not from the house and steading itself but from the open ground beyond. He watched the drifting brown curtain of it absently for a space, before turning back to attend to the work on hand. And Andrew Hardie not only demanded attention, he compelled it. His Gaelic may not have been fluent but it was eloquent—even to the younger man who knew no word of it—and if he appeared to have considerably enlarged the scope of Adam's original statement, there was no doubt that he was impressing his hearers. Colin Dubh mac Ian, tenant of Altbran, positively wilted before a sonorous barrage of words that quite evidently comprised declamations and censures and retributions. The frequent upflung hands and upraised glances told their own story; Heaven was involved, and God, the great and terrible God of Scotland's Kirk, demanded that the landlord's will be done. The minister's methods had been noticeably efficacious at Camusnavoe where they had left Anna Bain in tears and fully understanding the position. Here, it appeared as though he would be equally successful. Today, obviously, was going to see much more progress than yesterday. Adam Metcalfe looked on, tight-lipped.

Hardie seemed to be working up to a climax in his dissertation when Adam noticed that a change had come over the expression of Colin Dubh. Where previously his eyes had held distress and despair, now a sudden alarm was manifest. Adam turned to follow the direction of his gaze, and saw what he saw. Across the Luie, at the other side of the glen, smoke was rising from two places—not the blue plumes of peat-reek from cottage chimneys, but the yellow-brown fumes of burning vegetation. He glanced back to what he had seen at Camusnavoe. The smoke there was spreading and rising, fanned by a morning breeze.

It was a moment or two before Andrew Hardie noticed the preoccupation of his listener; when he did, his voice, far from falling, rose higher in righteous wrath, till, that having no visible effect, he also followed the other's stare. What he beheld, however, appeared to occasion him no concern, for he turned back to the unfortunate Colin Dubh, and with a wave of his hand, seemed even to make use of the conflagration to give added point to his remarks. No doubt flames and burning fitted in very aptly with a theme of judgment and hell-fire.

"What is all that smoke, Mr Hardie?" Adam Metcalfe interrupted sharply.

"Merely the old pasture being burned, I expect," the other answered briefly.

"Why burned?"

"To improve the pasture for next season. It has to be done regularly, if the herbage is to have any heart or worth to it."

"Our friend here,"—indicating the crofter—"seems to be somewhat upset by it, nevertheless?"

The minister shrugged. "I think I have already indicated, Mr Metcalfe, that these people are generally incapable of seeing more than a yard in front of their noses!"

The man Colin Dubh, encouraged perhaps by some inflexion in the factor's voice, gripped Adam's arm and broke into a stream of emphatic Gaelic. The younger man listened, schooling his expression to immobility that no false hopes be raised. "What does he say?" he asked.

"Oh, just the usual thing—protests and complaints."

"I can see that—what is his special trouble? Something to do with this burning?"

The other drew himself up. "It is the usual contempt for authority. He demands that *his* pasture is not burned. He claims that it is his own, that he grew it. He takes to himself the exclusive credit for clothing the hills with heath and the meadows with grass. The laird, the owner of the ground . . ."

". . . did not grow it, either," Adam interrupted tersely.

Affronted, Andrew Hardie turned on him. "Would you deny the elementary, the sacred right of a man to do what he considers best with his own property, sir?" he demanded sternly. His voice rose stridently. "The Lord Himself, the Keeper of the Vineyard, saith 'Is it not lawful for me to do what I will with mine own?' It is the very root and foundation of all order and authority. A man in your position, sir—his master's steward . . . !"

"A man in my position is an unhappy man indeed." Adam took him up quickly, bitterly. "I appear to be both a fool and a knave; I am neither a profitable steward nor an effective—er—shepherd . . . only a wretch with a conscience. I will give you a quotation, Mr Hardie. 'Ye cannot serve God and Mammon.' Who, think you, are we serving here?"

The other's eyes steeled. "Young man, beware how you mock your Maker," he warned, and his voice quivered. "Mind you, your every word will have its due recompense. Will you set yourself up to judge those whom God has set in places of authority? Will you . . . ?"

"All right, all right!" Adam said wearily. "Will you tell this unfortunate man that he has my sympathy . . . for what it is worth. I will put his point of view before the factor, of course . . ."

In silence the two men left the croft of Altbran, and took the heather northwards.

Mid-day was well past, and only one more croft was left to do, when Adam Metcalfe and his companion and the boy with the pony, nearing the brown wastes of high moorland now, out of which the glen was born, were halted by a hail. About a quarter of a mile back a figure was hastening after them, limping on a stick. That man would be Donald MacVarish. Without a word, Adam turned and walked back to meet him. Minister and pony-gillie stayed where they were.

As he drew near, it was to be seen that the older man had not been sparing himself; they were a good three broken heather miles from Luiebeg, and his breathing was deep, as was his colour, and his face ran with sweat; also his washen-grey eyes were brighter than they had seemed yesterday. But his greeting was quiet and decent, for all that. "Good day to you, Mr Metcalfe—your pardon, and me shouting on you."

"Surely, Mr MacVarish. What can I do for you?"

"I do not rightly know if there is anything you can be doing, at all," the other panted, ". . . but I had to be trying, whatever." He turned about and waved with his stick, toward where an ominous dark film was rising, even above the line of an intervening spur of hill, to stain the afternoon sky. "Yonder is an ill thing, Mr Metcalfe, the work of an ill mind. That smoke may mean starvation, and the death of beasts . . . and men. If you could be stopping it, yourself, it's many that would bless you, sir."

Adam looked away. "I am afraid . . . I do not like it myself, but . . . What do you mean—starvation . . . death?"

Donald Bàn looked at the man who was assistant factor intently. "Maybe you do not understand, Mr Metcalfe—small blame to you indeed, and you but new here. Here's the way of it. The crofter grows his corn on his small bit tilth for winter feed for himself and his beasts—and always it is little enough, by God; the winter is long, long, and meal scarce at the end of it. But last harvest was bad—rain, rain, and the corn black and sprouting or washed away in the spates. Already the beasts are poorly and half-starved—there is no feed for cattle here in the winter . . . and the winter is not done yet, at all. Each year it is the new spring growth of the hill pasture that is saving them, the green shoots that's in it under the old dead grass and heather. And that same is now burning, Mr Metcalfe—to be making better pasture for the laird's sheep next season! The beasts will starve, the calves will die, and nothing will be fit for the journey down to the new ground that's to be in it near the sea. And if the beasts starve, the people starve—and them all they have. God— does the man be wanting us all finished and done with alto- gether?"

"Surely not," Adam asserted, but without conviction. "I had

no idea . . ."

"And where is the man's right to be doing it, then?" the other went on tensely. "It's still tenants we are, till the term, and all our rents paid. We have paid for that pasture till May . . . Mr Metcalfe, is there anything that you can be doing, at all?"

"I do not know—but I can try, by God Almighty!" Adam swore. "Wait here a moment, will you?" and he swung about and ran back whence he had come. To Andrew Hardie he spoke briefly but firmly, handing over the last eviction notice. "Will you kindly deliver this notice yourself to Corrievreck—I have to go with Mr MacVarish just now? It may be irregular—but there are many irregularities being committed this day! You have done most of the business so far, anyway . . . I will meet you on your way down." And leaving no time for questioning or protests, he left them there and came back to Donald Bàn. "Come on, Mr MacVarish—show me the way," he directed. And within him, behind the fire of hot anger that the other flames had kindled, a cold quiet voice murmured, "Fool, fool . . ."

The two men did not speak much on that journey, and the younger man had no occasion to shorten his step on account of Donald MacVarish. They were still something over a mile away when, half-an-hour later, they emerged from an open wood of gnarled and stunted birch into sight of Luiebeg. Donald Bàn paused and pointed, but did not speak. A thin wisp of smoke was rising from the braes beyond the farthest croft of the little township.

Adam nodded. "They waste no time," he commented shortly, and pressed on.

Luiebeg itself seemed deserted as they hastened through. Up on the surrounding slopes men and dogs could be seen hurriedly rounding-up and driving down the scattered live-stock. But most of the people were congregated at Nial Farquhar's croft, the men standing in a sullen despairing knot, the women, in the Gael ever more practical than their men-folk, helping Nial's wife with her beasts, the children everywhere, hushed or vociferous.

And Nial Farquhar needed help. What a mile back had been but a wisp of smoke, had now grown into a great billowing cloud obscuring in its murky folds the thin afternoon sun. It rose from a long snaking line of flame, short-tongued but vicious, that, fanned by the freshening breeze, crept forward steadily or leapt in sudden rushes over the faded bent-grasses and bracken, deer-hair and bare heather. Already the menacing belt of fire had come alarmingly close to the rough steading of the croft, and the watchers were beginning to cough and rub their eyes with the acrid sting of it. A few of the small rough-coated black cattle had been hurriedly driven in and penned temporarily within the steading, where they charged to and fro, bellowing lustily; two or three stirks which either had escaped or had never been caught were dashing about outside, stiff-legged, tails high, pursued by the distracted Nial and a couple of yelping excited dogs. Before the house a pair of goats, tethered, rushed wildly, now across, now around, their protracted circle, bleating incessantly, and near the midden a milch-cow, obviously far-gone in calf, had fallen, seemingly with a broken fore-leg bent under her, and was lowing piteously, Mrs Farquhar attending. And all around, the squawking scuttering poultry ran, eluding women and children and being moodily kicked at by the men. Against a background of the crackle and hiss of the fire, the noise at that place achieved pandemonium.

Even as the newcomers arrived, a stretching arm of the fire reached out to a clump of junipers adjacent to the steading, which went up with a roar, tossing a shower of sparks and flaming fragments high into the air. Inevitably some of the embers landed on the roof of the poor buildings, a roof of dry reed thatch that in a few moments was smoking in half-a-dozen places. Shouting, Nial Farquhar left his foolish stirks to their own devices, ran for the byre and clambered up on the hump-backed roof, beating about him with his snatched-off jacket. Donald Bàn waved his staff and gesticulated at the other crofters, and at last the men threw off their fatalistic stupor and went to help.

But it was too late. The dry weather of the last few days

assured that. That roof was made to burn. The dead withered reeds of its thatch caught like tinder, and in a minute all the little fires had joined up into one great blaze, despite the fire-fighters' efforts. Farquhar escaped down just in time, with hair and beard singed and clothes smouldering. He did not pause, but, wild-eyed, stumbled round the building to tug and throw open the timber barrier which penned in his beasts within the compound formed by the steading.

He was not too soon. Frenzied with the flames and smoke from the blazing roof, the cattle were milling wildly, and already two of the younger stirks had been knocked over in the rush and were in danger of being trampled to death. The open gate saved them. With starting red-rimmed eyes and wide-open nostrils, the beasts swung and dashed for the gap, struggled and plunged within it, and were out, scattering all before them. Away they charged, downhill towards the river, and after them ran the shouting men. There were rocks and bogs and other traps for maddened cattle down there. And as they thundered off, the burning roof collapsed in red and reeking ruin. Out of the conflagration a blazing hen flew screeching . . .

Adam Metcalfe had seen enough. Looking about him for the men who had wrought thus notably, he felt his arm taken and he was turned round, to find Donald Bàn pointing to where, beyond a jumble of stony hillocks, a group of men and two ponies could be seen, moving slowly. He nodded briefly, and started forward in the same movement. MacVarish followed him.

There were four men in that group, big lusty fellows, specially-chosen factor's men, and, sad the word, two of them were Highlandmen. They carried with them a small portable brazier which glowed redly, progenitor of many fires that day, and on one of the ponies bundles of bog-fir torches dipped in resin. As Adam came up with them from over the hillocks, Hopkins was consulting his little book detailing the pasturage areas, and his companions were re-fuelling their brazier with knots of bog-fir from a pony's pannier-basket.

Metcalfe went straight up to Hopkins. "Are you doing this—

burning this land—on the factor's instructions?" he demanded without preamble.

"That's right," the other agreed cheerfully. "Mister Dunn's orders."

"Perhaps Mr Dunn doesn't fully understand the law. These tenants have their rights, and this pasture you are destroying is theirs till term-day."

"That ain't no concern o' mine," Hopkins shrugged.

"Is it not! Perhaps the judge—the sheriff—will think differently. You are accessories to a serious offence."

"I'll risk that," the man grinned insolently. "I reckon we can leave Mister Dunn to deal with the sheriff—eh, lads?" They all laughed.

Adam's features were set. "I see you are a fool as well as a rogue, Hopkins," he said slowly. "D'you think the factor could explain away what you've done back there? You've burned down half the man Farquhar's croft, destroyed his buildings, and injured his stock—and Lord knows what you may have done elsewhere!"

The other spat. "That ain't no great loss, Mister—their bloody crofts is jest stones and mud and turfs, and their bloody cattle's jest mangy skeletons, not worth a toss, the lot o' them. And ain't we saving time, after all—kick me if we ain't! They'll all be cleared out o' here in a couple o' months, the whole bloody lot o' them, and good riddance to 'em, says I." Something in Metcalfe's expression must have struck him, for he hesitated and went back to his original defence. "Anyway, it ain't no concern o' mine—we're jest carryin' out Mister Dunn's orders."

"Then you can carry out *my* orders, now!" Adam snapped, and his voice gave no hint of the doubts within him; the trouble with Adam Metcalfe was that his judgment was apt to keep pace with his temper, a discomfort to any man. "I am in charge of this side of the glen, and your action in damaging tenant's property has created an entirely new situation. You will do no more burning till I have consulted Mr Dunn . . . and you will keep a civil tongue in front of this gentleman!"

"Oho—a gentleman, is he!" the man jeered. "He's jest a dirty

94

crofter like the rest. And see here, my young cock, we take our orders from the factor, and no-one else—see?"

"You will do as I tell you—and you will say 'sir' when speaking to me . . ."

"Oh, we will, will we! Hear wot's talking. 'Sir', says 'e—'think again', says I . . ."

Smack! Like the report of a musket, Adam's open hand struck the man's face and ear, a ringing stinging buffet—that was, however, only a slap, the warning corrective blow that is the reward of insolence. What followed thereafter happened as quickly as it was unpremeditated. Hopkins, an ex-pugilist, instantly with the blow threw up his hands in a boxing posture, and one of his fists, coming up, knocked the younger man's chest. Whether he intended to strike back is not to be known, but in the heat of the moment Adam assumed that he did. Quick as thought he hit again with his left, not an open-handed skelp this time but a fierce swinging hook to the curve of the jaw, that sent the big man staggering, his head up and back. Adam Metcalfe had done some boxing himself, and that upraised uncovered jaw shouted aloud for punishment. Lunging forward, his right fist whipped up in a beautiful clean uppercut that took the point of a stubbly chin just where it could do most damage. There was a crack and a crunch combined, and with a grunt the fellow sagged and toppled backwards, backwards against one of the waiting ponies. The beast quivered in fright, reared, and bolted, and one of its hind hooves just grazed the falling man's head. Hopkins lay still.

It all happened in a few brief seconds. Metcalfe was as surprised as anyone. He stood over the prostrate body for a moment, brows wrinkled, then stooping down, ran a hand over the man's scalp and neck, raising the head a little, to be rewarded with a groan and a mutter. From the fellow came a strong smell of spirits; it is doubtful if the former prize-fighter would have been so easily disposed of if he had not been indulging fairly freely in the *uisge beatha*, the whisky, of the despised Highlanders. Satisfied, Adam straightened up, and turned to the three other factor's men, who eyed him with considerably increased respect.

"You understand?" he proclaimed. "There will be no more burning till I come back."

They glanced from each other to their fallen comrade, and nodded.

"Now where is Mr Dunn—do any of you know?"

One of them pointed across the wide valley to where, beyond the river, hung the pall of other fires. "Like as not he'll be over there . . . sir . . . or he may have gone back to the House for his dinner," he volunteered. "He likes his dinner at the right time, the factor."

Adam nodded shortly. "Right," he said. He turned to the remaining pony, the one with panniers. "Take those baskets off," he directed, and while one of the men did his bidding he walked back to Donald Bàn MacVarish, who had stood watching the proceedings from a little way behind. "I apologise for that man's remarks . . . and for my own exhibition," he said. "I'm afraid it has all been rather a vulgar display of bad manners. If you will excuse me now, I will go and see if I can find John Dunn."

The other's lined face betrayed the faintest of smiles. "Your manners were very adequate to the occasion, I'm thinking," he told him gravely. "I thank you . . . but," he laid a hand on the younger man's arm, "you will not be doing yourself a hurt, at all, Mr Metcalfe?"

"Don't worry about me," Adam returned. "I'm doing this for my own sake as much as yours—and little enough I am likely to do, God knows! I will go now—but I will be back."

He strode back to the garron and, taking its head, turned it round, and with a jump heaved himself on to its broad bare back. The creature side-stepped in astonishment, backed a pace or two, and then stood docilely, with the habitual placidity of its kind, till a couple of heel-jabs in its ribs caused it to toss a shaggy head, cast an enquiring glance backward, and set off at a long, slow trot. Adam, bobbing about uncomfortably on a back as flat as a table, his feet trailing in the high heather, took a good grip of the beast's plentiful mane, and swallowed his pride in his horsemanship. With only an improvised stall-collar to steer with and a seat that was uncertain, to say the least of it, it was a case of blind instinct and Providence rather than equestrian skill. He clapped down his hat, and hoped for the best.

Donald Bàn looked from the rider to the fallen Hopkins, now rising unsteadily to his feet, to the rolling smoke-cloud that was shrouding the glen, and back to the rider again, and he shook his head.

Swaying and heaving his way down through the heather, Adam Metcalfe had scant opportunity for deliberation, but he was aware of feeling rather more satisfied with himself than he had done for some time. He was at least doing something, however doubtful the outcome, and he had enjoyed delivering that left-and-right—even if his knuckles had not come unscathed out of the encounter. He had been wanting to do something like that for quite a while. For too long he had had to be passive, an onlooker; here was action at last, precipitate and scarcely judicious maybe, but at any rate he felt more of his own man again.

But down on the track that followed the river towards Bridge of Luie the going was easier, the pony modified somewhat its unique bone-jangling gait, and the man had a chance to consider—consider what he was going to say to John Dunn.

Adam Metcalfe considered the question for some way down that glen, and got little good from his considering. His worthy judgement gave him small comfort, and less confidence, in his ability to convince Dunn of the error of his ways. Error—that could be ruled out; expediency only would carry any weight with that scrupleless man. And could he anyway convince him that this latest piece of thuggery was inexpedient? It was doubtful, to put it mildly . . . and the methods he had employed with Hopkins were scarcely suitable for use on the factor.

Perhaps if he had had to jog quietly along that track, with his meditations, for much longer, the man might have been in poor fettle to deal with the factor when at length he should come up with him. But, as it happened, he was just passing the croft of

Camusnavoe, where a soot-begrimed woman was attempting to salvage the charred remains of her only small stack of bog-hay that had survived the winter, when something across the river attracted his attention. Two loping dogs had come into sight over there out of a fold of the long slope that lifted and rolled up from the water-side, and though they were most of half a mile off, he knew those dogs. Sure enough, a few moments later, Dunn himself emerged into view, striding homewards, parallel with Adam, and alone. The young man nodded grimly to himself and tugged the pony's head round, downhill towards the river's edge.

The Luie, though swift, was shallow hereabouts, fringed with a wide belt of bleached and rounded small stones. The garron took to its amber waters without hesitation, and plodded its way across with the minimum of fuss and splatter, placidly picking the easiest route without guidance from its rider. The farther bank, beyond the stones, was steep and unsound, but Adam wisely gave his beast its head, and it found its way up with undemonstrative efficiency. At the crest he pulled it round, and slanted off at the trot in the wake of the factor.

He came up with his man on the fringe of a small wood. John Dunn turned at the thud of hooves, and stared; his mastiffs came bounding back, baying furiously.

"Sink me, what's to do now?" the man cried.

"Quite a lot, I'm afraid," Adam jerked, a little breathless with the jolting. He was about to slip off the pony when one of the hounds leapt up, heavy lips back, ponderously malevolent. It did not touch him—it was probably only a characteristic demonstration—but the shelt shivered and sidled, and at the second bound, shied nervously. Adam liked that pony, and he did not like the dogs. As the brute came up the third time, the toe of his boot caught it just below the great slobbering jaws, and it fell back with something between a yelp and a snarl. The factor snapped a brief word at his dog, and took a stride forward, his brows black. Adam decided to stay where he was for the present, and sat still.

"Well . . . ?" John Dunn demanded.

"I understand that you authorised this burning, Mr Dunn?" and he waved his hand at all the blackened, smoking brae-sides.

"Authorised . . . ? I ordered it."

"Is that so! You have already informed me that it is no part of my duty to teach you the law, Mr Dunn, so no doubt you are fully aware that your action is absolutely illegal?"

"*I'll* judge the legality of my actions."

"Right—and knowing your attitude, I suppose there is no use in my expecting you to have regard for the elementary interests and common rights of the tenants? That spring pasture is essential to the crofters, and it is theirs till term-day."

John Dunn took a pace further forward, and gripped the pony's neck with a hand that trembled ever so slightly, and his bare bullet-head, thrust forward and up, was menacing at Adam's flank. "It is not theirs—nothing is theirs," he said, enunciating slowly and clearly. "Everything in Strathmoraig belongs entirely to the estate and Lord Alcaster—whose interests alone, as factor, I serve. And Mister," he tapped the other's knee with a thick, short forefinger, "the sooner you get it into your fool head that you serve the same interests *only*, the better for you, I say."

"I'm afraid I can't agree with your conception of the duties of factor," Adam gave back evenly. "As I understand it, he should act as a link between landlord and tenant, and he has his responsibilities toward both. I . . ."

"You will understand just what I want ye to understand, curse ye," the man hissed, "or . . ."

". . . or what?"

"Or, by God, I will break every bloody bone in your body!" John Dunn roared.

Adam Metcalfe looked down at the coarse red face that strained up towards his own, and though it would be incorrect to say that he felt no fear, sheer distaste for the man was the stronger emotion—though he was glad that he had not dismounted. And, in a way, he was relieved, too; it had had to come to this, eventually, and, a sensitive man, a softer weaker part of him had dreaded the event, might have sought to avoid it. Now they were down to stark reality, and he need no longer fear that he might not come up to his own standard. Now they had touched bottom, and he need only be natural. Adam Metcalfe knew worse fears than that of physical hurt.

"So now we have you!" he commented, grimly but steadily. "I guessed it would not be long before you descended to threats of violence, Dunn—your kind usually does. Violence is your substitute for wits—and a damned poor substitute at that!"

"You young whelp, you'd better get out of this before I start on ye." The factor spoke thickly. "I've stood all I'm standing from you—Lord God, I've stood too much!"

"All right—but before I go, I'll tell you what I came for." He drew a deep breath, and somewhere within him he knew a sudden emptiness and a quick constriction. "I have taken it upon myself to countermand your orders; I have told your men to burn no more pasture meantime . . ."

"You've *what* . . . ?" That was a bellow, and with the words the man's whole body tensed and crouched, one arm flung back and the other hand came down with a crash on Adam's thigh.

The younger man acted rapidly. He threw up his knee with all his strength, drove the other one into the pony's belly, at the same time wrenching its head round towards the factor. The beast, nervous already, jumped, danced, and swung round, head tossing, its rider only retaining his seat with difficulty, while Dunn stumbled forward and nearly over-balanced. Adam jerked the brute's head back so that it reared and let fly a kick at one of the mastiffs that started its leaping again, all almost in the same movement.

"John Dunn," he shouted, "use your brain. You should thank me for what I've done! D'you want a riot here, among these people? You can drive people too far. You'll have serious trouble over there."

Dunn said nothing, but came on slowly.

"You fool!" Adam cried. "Do you not know when you've gone too far?" Searching the other's baleful eyes, an idea struck him. He thought quickly. "There's trouble brewing over there,

I tell you. The last I saw of your man Hopkins, he was unconscious—struck down. Things looked ugly. There's buildings burned and stock injured and men angry . . . and there's a lot of them and few of us—if you get them really roused."

The factor had paused. "I'll teach them . . ." he snarled. But the direct glare of his beady eyes had wavered.

Adam went on swiftly. "Violence breeds violence. Will it do your sheep schemes any good, or the estate, or Lord Alcaster's interests, if you raise the country? Do you think his lordship wants the sheriff up making enquiries as to how his estates are run?"

"Blind me, what in hell's name's the sheriff to do with it?"

"Quite a lot, I should think. Your men have committed serious offences—punishable offences. If the tenants appealed to the sheriff . . ."

"They wouldn't dare, the scum," the other snorted. "And even if they did, d'ye think the sheriff would take their side against mine, against the estate and the Commissioner?"

"He might . . ." A longish pause, ". . . if they were supported by the Deputy-Commissioner . . ." Even as Dunn lunged at him, Adam, backing his beast, threw down his last card, that weak, unsubstantial card that he had played once before doubtfully, ". . . and Alcaster's friend!" he cried.

And again that spurious card took the trick. The factor, hands groping, checked himself with a violent effort, turned on the mastiff still leaping near the garron's head, and grasping it by the neck, swung the great brute in the air and threw it far from him, in a gesture wherein baffled rage was as eloquent as almost incredible strength. And so he stood for a full minute, staring, his squat massive frame heaving with the depth of his breathing, silent in a venom and fury that was beyond all words.

The other, as he sought to control the agitated pony, strove to control his own voice. "Plain speaking today, John Dunn—perhaps we understand each other better!"

The older man gave no sign that he had heard. Only his looks were eloquent—and they spoke volumes. Thus he remained, swaying a little, as though he waited for something—something

101

that did not come, however, for suddenly, without another word, John Dunn turned on his heel and left that place, and his dogs, heads down, slunk after him. And he went back, not the way he had come, towards his men and the trouble, but back down the glen towards Menardmore, with a fixed and heavy tread, and he did not look round.

Adam Metcalfe, patting and stroking his garron's neck, watched him go, a stocky, resolute figure, potent even in eclipse and dangerous always, till the folds of the land swallowed him up. Then, turning his beast, he too went back whence he had come.

10

BACK through the smoke, Adam came to Luiebeg, and found that the situation had not remained static during his absence. Something of the picture of strife that he had painted for John Dunn's benefit had actually materialised, though in rather different colours. Trouble reigned in the clachan of Luiebeg, clamour and the clash of tongues, and from the heart and storm-centre of it all, rose a rich Irish brogue, lusty and emphatic.

Threading his way through the press of crofters, their women, their children and their dogs, Adam reached the core of the disturbance, where, within a rough circle of far-from-disinterested onlookers, men disputed violently. Hopkins was there, with his three colleagues, and two newcomers, obviously estate-servants, one of whom, supported by his companion, looked decidedly the worse for wear; Donald Bàn was there, and his cousin Ewan MacVarish of Achroy, and with them another man, who, undoubtedly, was responsible for most of the noise. A little red-faced, bright-eyed man, this, hot-tongued and fluent, dressed in patched and stained and faded homespuns, and crowned by a bashed and dusty black hat of vaguely clerical aspect. He was talking now rapidly and vehemently, and supporting his points with passes and thrusts of a business-like ash-plant. ". . . and if ye so much as make another remark like that last, you great bull of Bashan you," he was crying, apparently addressing Hopkins, "I'll break your thick ugly skull for ye, same as I've broke the creature here's, so I will, sure as there's a living God!"

"Take that stick from him," Hopkins shouted.

"Don't you dare lay a hand on me, ye spawn of Satan!"

"Father," Ewan MacVarish intervened mildly, "here is Mr Metcalfe, the new deputy-factor. Mr Metcalfe—Father Michael O'Brien."

The other faced about, and glared fiercely. "So you're Metcalfe!" he said, and looked Adam up and down critically.

"That is so. I think I have heard of you, sir."

"Why wouldn't you? Sure and I've heard of you, too, and not all of it bad, either—and that same's more than you'd say for me, I'll be bound. But you're on the wrong side in this devil's business, Mr Metcalfe."

"I am Lord Alcaster's representative, Mr O'Brien."

"And is that you proud of the fact?" That was fired at him like a shot.

Adam took his time to answer; he was entitled to. "I think my feelings in the matter are my own affair," he replied formally.

"That they are, and it's myself that had no right to be asking you," the other agreed handsomely. And then, with a lightning change of face that left his hearer gasping, "And now will ye call off your ruffians, that would be molesting a servant of Holy Church about his Christian duties!" he demanded, almost ferociously.

Blinking, Adam turned. "Well, Hopkins—been distinguishing yourself again? You're making quite a day of it, aren't you?"

The man, still looking a little shaken from his recent experiences, was glaring truculently at Metcalfe, and for a moment or two no words would come. Then, "The factor . . . Mr Dunn . . ." he got out, chokingly.

"I have just seen Mr Dunn, and he concurs with my handling of this situation," Adam inserted crisply.

The other looked his disbelief. "But this man," he pointed at the priest, ". . . he's wanted. Mr Dunn wants him, the constables is after him."

"You seem to be much in demand, Mr O'Brien?"

"Aye so, my popularity overwhelms me. But I think the people here need me more than Mr Dunn does." His blue eyes, strangely blue for a man well past his youth, flashed fiercely. "Mr Metcalfe, I demand in the name of justice and humanity that this criminal outrage against the crofters cease, and that due restitution is made by the estate!"

Donald Bàn laid a hand on the Irishman's arm and began to

speak, but Adam cut him short. "I have spoken to John Dunn, and the burning is to cease forthwith. But I am afraid I am not in a position to make any promises about restitution."

"They are entitled to . . ."

"Yes—but you will appreciate my position. I am only deputy here. I can only . . ."

"Deputy to a blackguard and a scoundrel!" Michael O'Brien cried. "Deputy to a bully and a tyrant! It's a grand position that ye hold, Mr Metcalfe."

Adam coughed. "I must ask you to moderate your language, sir. Mr Dunn is my superior . . ."

"Would ye muzzle the truth in the voice of God's Church!" That was like a trumpet blast.

And, from a little way off, like the echo of the trumpet, he got answer. "That is not the voice of God's Church. That is the lying voice of the idolatrous harlot of Rome, seducer of the ignorant, deceiver of fools!" Through the ranks of the crofters Andrew Hardie clove his way, and they stood aside politely to give him passage. "That man is the emissary of the Devil, the apostle of disorder, who would lead you head-long into the pit of anarchy and confusion." In the centre of the circle he halted, head up, brow fierce, a commanding figure, and his searching glance swept the gathering. "Why is he allowed to stand here, free, spreading his poison at will? Why is he not taken in charge?"

Hopkins, to whom this demand appeared to be addressed, shrugged, and pointed at Metcalfe. "Ask 'im," he said viciously.

Hardie looked enquiringly at Adam, who bowed. "I trust you were not incommoded by my leaving you so abruptly back there, sir?" he mentioned. "My presence was required down here rather urgently."

The minister made a motion of his hand as though he would brush aside all such verbal dalliance. "Mr Metcalfe, you may not fully appreciate the position, but the authorities are very anxious to lay hands on this man. He is a dangerous agitator, who, under the guise of religion, is spreading sedition and discontent amongst these ignorant people. He must be apprehended."

"I am afraid that I have had no authoritative instructions on this subject," the younger man returned smoothly, "—and you will appreciate that interfering with the liberties of a minister of religion is a matter not to be embarked on lightly! Anyway," in a different tone, this, "—I am no constable, sir!"

"But—it is your duty to have him arrested. The well-being of this community demands it."

"Well-being, is it!" Michael O'Brien could no longer contain himself. "By the God above ye, do ye call this well-being?" and his stick described a circle to include all the smoking glen-sides, swishing alarmingly close to his fellow-clergyman's nose in the by-going.

Hardie stiffened, but disdained an answer. "Mr Dunn will be most disappointed assuredly—incensed, I might say—if this, this, ranter is not held, Mr Metcalfe."

"Mother of God—ranter!" the priest exploded. "I'll rant ye, ye long-shanked stick of Pharisaical misery, ye whited sepulchre you! You it is, and such as you, that . . ."

"Enough!" Hardie cried. "I wonder you dare to show your face in this place, without lifting up your malicious voice in abuse against those in authority."

The Irishman answered more soberly, but no less earnestly. "I dared because it was evident that these unhappy people needed help, and that against your very authorities that should be their stay and protection. I saw the smoke of their sorrow from afar, and came. Many of these people are my children in God. Ye would not have me elsewhere than with them in their need, would you?" That was spoken with obvious sincerity and a quiet dignity that was impressive. Adam perceived that he was not really a small man, at all.

But Andrew Hardie, a master of oratory, was not impressed—or if he was, he gave no sign of it. "Their need is not for such as you," he said. "Their need is for a proper recognition of their position and their true friends."

"Friends!" the other cried. "Would you be naming yourself that?"

"Naturally."

"Then God save them from their friends, I say. For your own ends, for worldly ease and reward, ye support an utterly selfish landlord and an unscrupulous management in the oppression of the people under your spiritual charge. It's thirty pieces of silver ye should get for . . ."

"Silence!" the minister thundered. "I will not stand here to be insulted—here, in the centre of my own parish—by this renegade, this outcast. Mr Metcalfe," he rounded on Adam, "you will not stand by while I am insulted, while your master, Lord Alcaster, is traduced . . . ?"

Adam answered him gravely. "I would not presume to interfere in a difference of opinion between churchmen. This appears to be a question of the duties of the clergy, a matter I am not competent to judge upon."

"Scoffer!" Andrew Hardie's voice rose almost to a scream as he turned to Hopkins. "Take that man! In the factor's name, I command you—all of you. Arrest him, in John Dunn's name."

"You cannot do that—you have no authority . . ." Adam was saying, when Hopkins' bull-like roar drowned his words.

"To hell with 'im, the bloody cockerel—the parson's our man! Come on, boys!"

Adam raised his voice, O'Brien shouted, Hopkins' men themselves were not silent at Hardie's strident urging, yet, as they pressed forward, a single voice, quiet but sibilantly intense, pierced and vanquished the uproar. "Stand where you are! Touch Father O'Brien and I fire!" it said.

In the sudden uncanny silence, all eyes turned to where, at the priest's side, Ewan MacVarish stood, still and determined, in his hand a small pistol, richly-mounted, cocked, and unwavering. With the menace of that figure before them, no man spoke.

In his own time, Achroy went on. "We are going now, and no man is following us. You understand? I would not hesitate to shoot any who would interfere with this man, and that is God's truth." He looked at Adam. "I am a man of peace, Mr Metcalfe, but there are times when a man will do what he must—you know that your own self, I think. There are many in this unhappy, betrayed country depending on Father O'Brien's

107

ministering, and they will not lose the last comfort they have, if I can be helping it."

Silent, Adam Metcalfe nodded.

Hardie was beginning to speak, when the pistol jerked round viciously. "Keep you quiet, Andrew Hardie," he was told. "You have said enough this day." MacVarish stepped back a pace or two. "Right, Father?"

The priest shook his head sorrowfully. "Ewan, man," he sighed, "more faith it is that we need here and now, not fire-arms ... or ash-sticks. Still and all," the beginnings of a smile flickered in his blue eyes, "we will not reject the means Providence in His wisdom has provided." Turning his back on Hardie and Hopkins and the rest, he ran his eye over the silent, watchful crofters, and shook his head again. Then he raised his hands above his head, palms out, face upturned. "God the Mighty and Merciful keep and guide you," he cried. "God the son of Mary strengthen and sustain you. God the Quickening Spirit comfort and bless you, and let no evil or the malice of men touch the living tender souls of you. Amen." With the briefest pause, arms still upraised, he broke into sonorous Gaelic, most evidently repeating the benediction. And as he finished, no sound broke the silence, save only a clear trilling, from high above, where a lark made fervent praise as at the very gates of heaven.

Adam Metcalfe watched the scene with wonder and astonishment, and just a trace of grim amusement—the serene, shabby figure of the priest, the ranked, head-bowed crofters, most of whom had sunk down on their knees, the hostile group about the frowning minister, and, in the centre of it all, the motionless, purposeful man with the pistol that glinted evilly, menacing. As a parson's son, he had seen many benedictions, but never one such as this.

It was Andrew Hardie who broke the hush. Looking away from the pistol, its holder, and the priest, he found something that he could vent his fury upon. Kneeling amongst the crofters was a man who did not belong to Luiebeg, or Glen Luie at all, a strapping fellow dressed in a length of tartan cloth and a torn shirt and little else. "Ian MacErlich, will you get up off your knees—back-slider, heretic!" he commanded, "Will you damn your immortal soul, bowing down before the idolater?"

Ian More sprang to his feet. "My soul is my own, and my knees are my own, and Michael O'Brien is no idolater," he cried. "A good man he is, and a good minister, for all he has not a double house with a slate roof, and the factor's silver in his pouch!"

"Hold your tongue, you fool . . ."

"I will not, then. My tongue is my own, too . . ."

"Quiet boy, quiet." O'Brien intervened. "Your tongue is your own, for sure, and long it is, at that. Come on with ye, now—'tis time we were away out of here. Mr Metcalfe—sorry I am that this had to be the way we meet and part. Another time, maybe, you will see a servant of Holy Church in a better light."

Adam, his position delicate, nodded in silence.

"Come on, then, Ian, Ewan . . ." With a sigh, the priest turned away, taking MacErlich's arm, and the people made way for them on either side. Stepping backwards, Achroy moved after them a few paces, till, well clear of the throng, he paused and bowed.

"Good-day to you, gentlemen," he said. "You will forgive what has been necessary, I hope?"

Hardie gave him his answer. "You will suffer for this day's work, MacVarish," he declared, and his voice trembled.

"I may, indeed—but not in my conscience," Achroy returned levelly, and turning around followed the others. He kept his pistol still in his hand. They had not gone far when Ian MacErlich looked back. "Never again will I darken the door of your church, by God I will not!" he called. Michael O'Brien took his arm and jerked him round.

The press of the crofters murmured amongst themselves, shifted uneasily, and melted away, leaving the group of Southerners, watching. Donald Bàn raised his eyes to meet those of Adam Metcalfe, grey eyes, tired and full of trouble.

11

WITH the boy and his pony disappearing downhill towards his cottage near the loch-side, Adam frowned down at the cloak over his arm. This was not his cloak—it was Andrew Hardie's. The man must have taken his when he left him, frigidly, ten minutes ago. They were both black. . . Hardie had gone on to the House of Menardmore; no doubt he had much to discuss with John Dunn. For himself, he had seen quite sufficient of both of them for one day, and he had no desire to go back to Menardmore simply to exchange cloaks with the minister. He glanced again after the pony-gillie, but he was just passing out of sight and hail—anyway, the lad would be tired. He could have the thing delivered to the Manse, of course . . . he could deliver it himself. He tapped the ground for a moment with his toe and then nodded to himself. He could, indeed; wasn't it the obvious thing to do? He might be in time to lend a hand with Clara.

He was not that, but, getting no answer to his knocking at the Manse front door, when he went round to the little farmery behind the house it was to find the milking still in progress. Leaning within the doorway of the thatch-roofed byre, he sniffed, and not for the first time, drew a quiet pleasure from the homely warm smell of the place. From the line of cows came the rattle of a chain, the gusty sigh of a full-uddered beast, and the hiss and froth of milking. A black-and-white cat came and rubbed against his leg, mewing, wide-mouthed but almost soundless.

Alison Hardie, her head pressed against the broad flank of a brown cow, her fingers busy, glanced up and round when she perceived the man's shadow across the floor, and for just an instant her brown eyes held a smile of welcome. But quick as thought her eyes clouded and the smile was gone, and she looked at him levelly. "Yes, Mr Metcalfe?" she said. She did not interrupt the rhythmic motion of her hands.

The man had seen that first gleam, as well as what followed, and knowing her attitude as he did, he was not dissatisfied. She had expressive eyes, that girl. "You are busy, Miss Hardie. Had you any trouble with Clara today? I hurried—just in case I could help."

"You should not have done that—you have been busy yourself today, very busy, I understand. Have you finished your . . . business now?" Her face was down-turned again, and her voice was even and cold—and hers was a voice that was not meant to be cold.

"Yes," he said abruptly—so abruptly that she looked up again, quickly. He was silent for a time, while the cat weaved and purred about his legs and the subdued sounds of the byre went on—and failed to soothe him. She was looking at him still, and something questioning and uncertain in her look led him on. He stepped out of the doorway over to the tail of her cow, and stood above her. "You are not very generous to me, are you, Alison Hardie?" he demanded of her.

Her brow was down on the beast's side once more. "Generous? I don't know . . . why should I be generous to you, Mr Metcalfe?"

"Because I think that you are usually generous. You look as though you should be. Your eyes are soft—it is the first thing I noticed about you—but you are hard on me, unfair . . ." He spoke jerkily, earnestly, without the veneer of flippancy that he had used towards her, and more than her, in the past. It may have been the experiences of the day that had done it. It may have been the air of simplicity and permanence about the byre and its affairs that was responsible; ever since Christ the Lord was born in a cattle-shed, men have recognised the peaceable worth of such. Perhaps it was the very essentiality of the girl herself, as she sat there beside her beast, working at a task that was simple and frank and older than history, with her skirt kilted above the knees that gripped between them the wooden pail into which the thin milk jets played.

"You should never trust a woman's eyes, Mr Metcalfe," she

111

asserted, with an attempt at archness. It was only a poor endeavour.

He looked down at her. She was warm and flushed with the heat of the cow, but he noticed how the pink faded and died before the pure pallor of her breast, that was broken, but never sullied, by the shadow of its dividing. She wore a coloured kerchief over her hair, but that hair was not such as could easily be disciplined, and tendrils and curls of it found their way out from all constraint. Her sleeves were up-rolled, and the play of muscles in a well-rounded arm was not without fascination. Alison Hardie may have felt at a disadvantage with all this frankness, for, under his scrutiny, she presently stopped her milking—though her pail was barely half-full—and, getting up from her wooden stool, emptied the milk into a larger vessel, at the same time splashing some into a wide flat dish on the floor to which three cats came running, tails up. And so, passing a hand over her throat and neck, she sat herself down again, more carefully arranging her skirts—and having some little difficulty with the pail therefore. Then, looking up at him, herself again, she spoke. "I would not like to be ungenerous to you—or anyone else—Mr Metcalfe."

That was sufficient for the man. Of a sudden he was aware of a need for confession and sympathy—to be natural, himself, no longer playing a part, as he had had to play it since ever he had come to this place. All at once he knew his loneliness, his perturbation, and a little fear, and he wanted a confidant; and here was this girl, with a problem of divided loyalties of her own, and who did not want to be ungenerous.

"Don't you see what a difficult position I'm in, what a false and hopeless position?" he demanded, pleaded. "All my sympathies are with the people here, the crofters, but I am employed by the proprietor and have to work for his interests. It is his policy that I must carry out—not my own—and if I do not do so, then I am failing the man who pays me."

The young woman said nothing, and he went on, seeking his own conviction as much as hers. "I know that their interests are so much more vital than his, their homes, their livelihood, their

112

very lives are affected, against merely a small fraction of one man's income—and some other's profit—but does that entitle me to support their interests against his?"

"Might not—should not—their interests and his be the same?" she asked.

"The same . . . ?"

"Yes. Is not a well-doing contented tenantry good for any estate?"

He shook his head. "I am afraid Lord Alcaster looks for more from his property than contentment."

"He gets his rents, doesn't he?"

"Yes—but not enough in a year to pay for a single night's gaming."

"But that is wicked—shameful!" she cried. "Would he ruin a whole people for *that*? For they *are* his people, not just his tenants—isn't he of the blood of their chiefs?"

"I am afraid that is a fact he would prefer to have forgotten, Miss Hardie."

"I dare say." She had paused in her milking, and her eyes were no longer soft. "But blood—and responsibilities—are not things that can just be forgotten, Mr Metcalfe. Could you not . . . Oh!"

Her cow, with all this unusual interruption of its milking, had become restive, and more than once the girl had had to speak soothingly to it. Now it was swinging its tail about like a pendulum, and one violent flick had caught its milker quite a buffet on the side of her head. "Belinda, you wretched beast!" she protested, and caught the straggle-haired tip of that long tail and tucked it firmly between her leg and the milk pail that she held between her knees. "Could you not influence him, make him see what he is doing, Mr Metcalfe?" she went on, then. "You are a friend of his, my uncle tells me."

The man smiled wryly. "I am afraid that I am not quite such a friend of Lord Alcaster's as I have led certain persons to believe," he confessed. The cow's tail jerked out of the girl's grip, and started its swinging again. Adam caught it, and held on. "We used to be friends—we were brought up together but, nowadays, I fear, no advice of mine would much affect him,

113

especially where his pocket is concerned."

"Oh."

"Yes." He felt rather ridiculous standing there holding that beast's tail up like an animated pump-handle, so he crouched down beside her; it seemed more natural that way. "I suggested that I was closer to him than is the case just in order to influence Dunn, in favour of the crofters," he resumed. He was anxious, eager, that she should understand. "I have done what I can, you know. I have argued by the hour, threatened—though I had really nothing to threaten with. I have done my best for them, and when there was nothing I could do, I have tried to soften the blow a little. Today, I even knocked Hopkins down, I all but came to blows with John Dunn and, er, somebody else, and became a sort of accessory to an astonishing Irish priest. I tell you . . ."

He stopped. A young woman, plump and comely, had appeared from behind another of the cows to empty her milk into the larger pail, and she was eyeing him with undisguised interest. Adam got to his feet in some confusion, and dropped the tail; he had not realised that there was anyone else in the byre. A perfect fool he must have looked, squatting there . . . The young woman grinned broadly, bobbed her head, and went back to her task. He cleared his throat and stood, frowning.

From her stool Alison Hardie looked up and smiled to him, quite gently. "You can tell me all about it—presently," she said. "I am nearly finished Belinda, and Seana can do the rest today. We'll climb up the knowie at the back, and I'll get the whole story. Will that do?"

She was not so ungenerous, after all, was Alison Hardie.

And, presently, tell her he did, as they climbed unhurriedly the birch knoll behind the Manse, and came in time to a fallen pine—fallen, but not dead—providing shelter with its branches from most of the winds that blew. On its levelled trunk they sat themselves down, without discussion, with all the wide strath of the Moraig River before them, while Adam unburdened himself, and felt himself the better therefor. And the girl sat, intent

114

and commentless, and the man had no fault to find with her listening.

He did not stress the part Andrew Hardie had played in that day's work, but for all that her uncle's role must have been fairly apparent, though she gave no sign. It was when Adam reached his encounter with John Dunn, relating how words had all but given place to action, that the quality of her listening changed. From being attentive she all at once became tense.

"You should not have done it, have risked it," she cried. "That man—he is evil, dangerous!"

"He may be, but I must counter him, and go on countering him, if anything at all is to be done for these poor people. He is the sword that strikes them. I can only try to blunt that sword."

"Don't—you must not risk violence." She leaned forward and grasped his arm in her sudden agitation. "You *must* not. Don't let him touch you. It is too dangerous."

Surprised, and not ungratified, by her evident concern for himself, he shook his head and smiled. "Don't worry," he said, man-like, "I can look after myself." He took the opportunity to stroke that hand on his arm, and that was man-like, too. "John Dunn is just a loud-tongued bully," he lied. "He is . . ."

"No," Alison Hardie whispered, and there was a wealth of conviction behind the word. "He is vile, horrible. Those hands . . . !" She took a deep breath and spoke slowly, as though keeping her voice under control by an effort. "They say John Dunn killed a man with those hands. I . . . I found it—the body," and with a choke, her face was down within her own hands, as though she would shut out the picture before her mind's eye.

"Good God!" The man stared in front of him. He remembered vividly those great groping hands, gripping, straining within each other, as he had seen them many times. As in a flash he realised the significance of many things—Bullough's constant shadowing of the man, his loud-voiced eagerness to smooth over difficulties when a clash seemed imminent, his heavy bonhomie when tempers rose. Bullough was anxious—and with reason. And himself—how near to that clash he had come, many times, how very near . . .

115

Then he turned to the girl at his side, and his expression changed. "My dear—how terrible for you!" An arm went round her, hesitated, and sank back to his side. "I am sorry," he said inadequately. "Tell me."

She looked up, dry-eyed. "Not just now, please—some other time, perhaps. But you *will* be careful, Mr Metcalfe?" she urged, forcedly calm. "Do not provoke him. It would be . . . awful, and it would help no one, if, if . . ."

"Quite," he agreed soberly. "I will be careful. Thank you for being concerned for me."

She shook her head, unspeaking.

Adam went on, "The trouble is, there's not much that I can do for the people here without making trouble with Dunn." He shrugged dispiritedly. "Not that I have done much—anything at all, really. A few acres saved from the burning—to be lost at term-day, anyway; the lives of a few poor half-starved beasts prolonged for a week or two more; a little barren sympathy, that cannot avert any part of their hard fate, but may have the effect of raising false hopes. That is the sum of my efforts."

The girl spoke kindly. "I don't know, but I think perhaps that you have done more than just that, Mr Metcalfe. You have done more, a lot more, than . . . others, who have more call."

There was silence then, for a little.

Adam followed the train of his thoughts. "Does Mr Hardie know—about Dunn, I mean?" he asked suddenly.

Alison Hardie looked straight ahead of her, and nodded slowly.

The man, belatedly, perceived his lack of tact. "Not that it is any business of mine," he added hurriedly, and made matters no better.

"You are quite entitled to ask," she allowed—and declared, "My uncle cannot expect to avoid criticism. I cannot defend his attitude, I can only understand it . . . and hate it!" It was the girl's turn to confide, and the words came with a rush as though in release and relief. "He is determined in his course—nothing will move him, nothing. I have tried, how often I have tried, but it is no use. I am either a child, uninformed, with no judgment, or a

116

woman, sentimental and hysterical. He cannot see—he will not see—what he is doing, that he is helping to ruin the lives of the very people it is his duty to cherish. He, who worships justice, cannot see that he is trampling justice underfoot . . . or perhaps he can see it!" she added more slowly, and there was horror behind her words. Then she shook her head. "I should not be talking to you like this. It is wrong, undutiful . . . You will think that I have no respect, no modesty . . ."

"No, I do not think so," he said gently.

She went on: "He—my uncle—would be furious if he knew. And yet . . ." With a sudden change of tone she turned to him. "No need for me to ask where he is now? He will be at Menardmore . . . ?"

Adam nodded. "He took my cloak by mistake. I have brought his with me—this is it. That was the reason, or rather,"—he risked boldness—"the excuse for my visit." This passing without remark, he continued. "But why does he do it? I can't understand why a man in his position, representative of the supposedly all-powerful Scottish Kirk, should ally himself so completely with the estate against the people in his care."

The girl looked at him curiously. "I would have thought that you would have jumped to the obvious conclusion, Mr Metcalfe . . . though it is not quite so simple as that, I think."

"You mean, he prefers the powerful, the winning side—the easy course?"

"I mean that he works for the side that pays him, that's all," she said wearily. "So many of the other parish ministers do the same. You do not understand the financial system of the Church of Scotland, Mr Metcalfe?"

"I'm afraid not—something like patronage, I suppose?"

"Maybe. The minister's stipend is paid by the heritors of his parish, not by the Church . . . and there is only one heritor in this parish!"

Slowly Adam inclined his head. "I see—patronage at its worst. We have the same sort of thing in England—don't I know, who was brought up on it. But I had always imagined that your Scots Kirk was different, made of sterner stuff. But even so,

I can't imagine an Episcopalian clergyman acting quite as your uncle is doing—and we've got some classic examples of our own. Even under pressure, I don't see why he need be so whole-hearted, so fervent, in the cause of the proprietor."

"There is a second reason, I think, beyond self-interest. I should not say it, I know, but I am afraid that he has come almost to hate the people, the crofters. He says that they are all Papists, Catholics, at heart. And knowing that he is failing them, siding with their oppressors, he is the more bitter against them. He is not a happy man, Mr Metcalfe. All the time, I know, there is a warfare in his own mind. He knows—he must know—what he is doing, and the knowledge is bitter and sour in him. And it is getting worse. His sermons have become more and more terrible. I am perfectly certain that his railing and denunciations are the product of his own unhappy conscience, and in damning them all he is damning himself. Sometimes I fear for his mind . . ."

"I see what you mean . . . but why, in Heaven's name, does he continue to violate his conscience, then? Surely, for the sake of his peace of mind, his own self-respect—if not for his congregation's sake—he would be wiser to risk trouble with the estate and at least not actively help in the wretched business?"

"I think that I can answer that, too," the girl went on, and her voice was tired and curiously flat. "We come of humble stock; my grandfather was a poor fisherman in Crail of the Kingdom of Fife. Always my uncle had to struggle against poverty. He worked himself to the bone to pay for his studies at the College of St. Andrews. Between studies he had to work in the boats, in the fields, at the salt-pans, to keep himself, and later his mother, when my grandfather died. Many and many's the time that he went without food in order to buy the books he needed. And his first charge was in a poor fishing village in Angus, where he had to work his own boat and plough his own glebe to make his stipend keep him. Then he came here . . . you see how it is? He will not give it all up, what he has built up here, his security, his comfort, his books, his authority, to risk poverty again—he will not."

The man nodded, unspeaking, and for a little only the tree-tops murmured, and the sigh of the river came up to them softly, and from somewhere, near or far, a wood-pigeon breathed its soothing benison on the evening.

But Alison Hardie was not soothed. With almost a sob she broke the silence. "But what right have I to speak, to judge him—I, who live on his bounty, who share his comfort? Ever since my father, a ship-master, was drowned at sea ten years ago, he has kept me, and, in his own way, been kind to me. A poor return for his charity, judging and condemning the man whose bread I eat! I am just as responsible . . ."

"Hush, child—never say that," he urged her. "You are his housekeeper, aren't you? You manage his farmery for him. He does not keep you for nothing; if you did not do it, he would have to hire someone else. Your soul is your own, Alison Hardie. You should not speak that way."

"No, I should not speak that way," she took him up swiftly. "I should not be talking like this at all—and to you, practically a stranger. What will you think of me . . . ?"

Adam glanced at her face, but there was only sincerity there. All along, there had been only sincerity, her voice reflecting the travail of her mind. She was a laughing, soft-natured girl, this, warm and impulsive, and young, ill-cast to carry this woeful burden of grief and shame. The man's heart went out to her, sitting there, crouched a little forward, forlorn, but facing the thing she was not equipped to face. A small shiver, occasioned by distress or apprehension or just the chilling evening air, shook her, and he picked up Andrew Hardie's cloak from his knee and slipped it over her shoulders and tucked it about her, and his arm remained around her. She did not move, she gave no sign.

Presently he spoke. "I think more than well of you, my dear. Believe me, I would be happy to be as satisfied about my own position. You know," he suggested carefully, "you and I ought to hold together. Our problems are not dissimilar, and we could help each other quite a lot, I am sure, possibly to the advantage of these Highlanders whose need is great. I would be grateful for

119

your help, and proud to lend you mine."

Still she did not speak—but was it only in his imagination that she inclined just the merest degree nearer to him, that he could feel the slightest pressure against his side? It could be, too—but what was wrong with an imagination like that?

"It is a good thing to know that you have a friend," he said then, and that was all he said, and sufficient for that time. He had a kind of wisdom of his own, that man—sometimes.

And so they sat, amidst the still dark pines and the whispering gentle birches, and the cushat and the river and the questing restless mountain air had the silence to themselves. Below them light and colour was draining from the haughs and slopes and woodlands, from all the strath save only the pools and rapids of the Moraig River, which still held in its gleaming links a pale memory of the sun that the hills to north and west had swallowed. Above them the tranquil companies of the gulls glided seawards, constant as time, deliberate as time, and there was no end to their gliding. And at their feet the teeming legions of the ants wrought ceaselessly and silently along chosen age-old paths, and by the very order and tempo of their business contributed their quota to the evening's living hush.

And sometime therein the man's arm tautened and drew closer, gradually, and the girl stirred, but gently, and did not lean away. And presently the cloak slipped from her knee, and as her hand moved down to retrieve it, so did his, and two hands replaced that cloak, one within the other, and so stayed.

Thus they remained, still but aware, till Adam began analytically to question the wisdom of wisdom, and to wonder if always the instincts of a gentleman were necessarily more commendable than the instincts of a man. There were, after all, a number of sound proverbs anent the grasping of opportunity . . .

Consideration on these lines was veering towards action, when the man felt the girl's whole body shake within his arm, twice, thrice, a shake that was a convulsion and no shiver or tremble. Alarmed, he looked at her face. Alison Hardie was torn

120

with great sobs, and her eyes were brimming with glistening tears.

"Alison! Good Lord!" he cried. "What is wrong? Are you ill . . . unhappy?"

Gallantly she choked back the emotion that was racking her, and those brown eyes held a strange gleam that was born of more than tears. "I am all right . . . please forgive me," she gasped. "I will be . . . quite myself . . . in a minute. It is so foolish . . . just the way I feel . . . and it is not unhappiness."

"No?" he wondered doubtfully.

"No." She was quite definite. "You will not understand . . . it is just a sort of—of relief. I have not felt so sure, so safe . . . for so long. It is not unhappiness, I assure you." Gently she drew the cloak closer about her and rose to her feet. "I must be getting back to the house now. I have things to do—and my uncle may be coming back. I hope he is not back already . . . ."

"Would he disapprove—of you being up here with me, I mean?"

"No." She shook her head, and her voice went flat again. "Not so long as he thinks that you are a friend of the Earl of Alcaster, Mr Metcalfe!"

"I see," he said, and, after a moment, "I wish you would call me Adam—it is my name, you know, and more suitable between friends."

She was already moving down-hill and she did not turn round, but she nodded her head.

At the Manse gate they paused. "You will forgive me if I do not ask you in?" the girl hoped. "When he has been at Menandmore, my uncle is sometimes . . . ."

"I understand," Adam assured her. He held out his hand. "Keep a stout heart, Alison Hardie. As Ewan MacVarish would say, I think, 'You have got yourself a tail, now'. Mixed anatomy, but sound sense."

She smiled, and took his hand. "A tail—yes, that was what I needed."

"It is a thing we all need."

"Yes. You have one yourself—now. Good night."

He raised his eyebrows censoriously. "Good night what?"

"Good night . . . Adam."

"That's better," he said.

The man walked back to Achroy, and his step was light. Even the chill wind that came to him out of the mouth of Glen Luie, loud with the evil smell of burning, weighted his tread only for a matter of minutes.

12

IN the weeks that followed, a strange unnatural calm settled upon Strathmoraig, settled and lay, and almost oppressed the place, covering but never dispersing the current and cross-currents of emotion and strain and passion that held that wide upheaved land in their uneasy grip. John Dunn, no doubt for reasons of his own, had no comment to make to his assistant, either by speech or action, on the events of the day of the burning. Apart from being a little grimmer, a little more silent, he was his usual compelling self, curt, cunning and decisive. The minister, too, allowed himself no alteration in his attitude of austere correctitude.

Affable he never was; more definitely hostile he did not appear, to Adam or to the mass of his parishioners. His services and sermons were fiercely condemnatory, but then, always they were that; his denunciations of the Church of Rome and all its works and adherents were frequent and furious, but that too was normal. And Ewan MacVarish, from the moment of his casual and unspectacular appearance at supper that night onwards, was most apparently the quietly courteous unassuming Highland gentleman, and nothing else. That this was the man who had most violently held up the lawful authorities of that place at the muzzle of a pistol, seemed entirely improbable. As for the crofters, like any other non-corporate entity, they were inarticulate, as always, waiting in silent apprehension, unreasoning and uneasy hope, or full resignation, for what was to be. In this atmosphere of wary precarious calm, no man found, or looked for, peace.

And throughout it all a chill and gusty wind blew and eddied, rain-laden and dismal, shrouding the tops of the hills for three unbroken weeks in a grey mantle of streaming ragged cloud, and soaking the slopes and valleys and blackened pastures—pastures that, had that wind come two days earlier, would not have been blackened.

Men saw, and waited.

For Adam Metcalfe it was a time of watching and abiding, of stress and mounting anxiety, and of a growing appreciation of the falseness of his own position. He was not long in discovering that he was now invested by the tenantry as the champion of their cause; not an unnatural development, perhaps, but none the less at variance with the facts. From his role of more or less passive sympathiser he found himself erected to that of active protagonist, and he was not very happy about it. Instead of being the proprietor's representative, he was fast being accepted as the representative of the other side, and much was being expected of him. It would not do, it would not do at all.

And there was so little that could be done for them, anyway. The longer he remained in Strathmoraig the more obvious that became. These people were fated to exploitation; their whole history made sure of that. A patriarchal community, deprived of or deserted by the chiefs and leaders on whom the whole structure of their society was founded, and in whom the nominal ownership of their land was vested, they were an obvious prey for the hard-headed developer from the South. A simple, easy-going people, entitled to claim cousinship with their chief, and accustomed to the intimate and personal jurisdiction this entailed, they were lost and bewildered before the cold and remote intricacies of the Southern law, sharpest weapon in all the armoury of the progressive incomers, a law set forth in a language that they could neither read nor write and few could understand, a law potent in the punishment of transgressors. A race of martial tradition, hunters and herdsmen, forbidden their weapons by decree since '45 and, until recently, their national dress, and neither industrialised nor particularly industrious, they were marked out as recruiting material in a state needing more and ever more soldiers. And the cream, and far deeper than the cream, gone, what was left was apt to be the more easily handled. Even their culture now militated against them, a culture deep-seated and widely-held—if seldom understood, or

124

even perceived, by the Southerners—that drew all its inspiration from the more distant past, and gloried in exquisite lament in the fabulous deeds of legendary figures, not to be presumed to be emulated in the lesser stature of modern men, a culture as unproductive of present action as it was laudatory of the past. Their very religion weighed down the loaded scales, for, whereas the dour Calvinism of the rest of Scotland could have urged resistance and a fight for their rights, the mild fatalistic form of Catholicism that was their heritage, an expression of their character, whatever the present nominal creed, enjoined acceptance of the inevitable—God's will be done. Indeed, they had no choice; their cause was lost before ever the battle joined. Something of all this Adam Metcalfe learned gradually, with growing distress.

It was a chance remark of Henry Bullough's, some ten days before the Term, later substantiated by John Dunn with terse amusement, that sent Adam forthwith to the Manse at Menardbeg with the brimming cup of his disgust. It was not the first time, by any means, that he had been back, but this time he went in desperation. He had discovered that the estate was making absolutely no provision for housing the crofters who were to be evicted down to the coastal areas. Apparently the cot-houses that they lived in now were their own property, built by themselves or their forefathers, so, it was claimed cynically, their re-housing was no responsibility of the estate's. Let them build themselves new houses when they got there, was the cry— if their miserable heaps of stones and turfs and sticks could be so called. And as though that was not enough, they had made a new decree that no timber was to be cut for roof-trees. It seemed that these black houses were largely built around a central spine of timber, carefully selected and shaped. So this new prohibition meant that these dispossessed tenants must carry their present roof-trees with them when they moved, and so were prevented from erecting any new houses prior to the demolition of the old. In other words, all these people, old men, women and children, were going to be left down at the coast, after a journey of up to twenty miles, without house or roof or any shelter at all.

125

If the weather should remain like this . . . ! It was outrageous, the last straw, and he, Adam Metcalfe, was not going to be identified with it, he was not!

Alison Hardie looked at him anxiously. "But what can you do, Adam?" she asked. "It is beastly, vile—but what can you do?"

He hesitated before he answered her. "I could do what I should have done long ago," he said slowly. "I could resign . . . get out."

Her eyes widened. "You mean . . . give it all up, everything?"

"Why not!" His voice was rough, almost aggressive. "Why should I stay here? I am doing no good . . . and I do not enjoy it, I assure you." His eyes flickered away from hers. "If I had known the situation I would never have come at all. Why should I fight and struggle—ineffectually—and put up with that brute Dunn and his oaf of a friend? I am sorry for these people, desperately sorry, but they are no responsibility of mine—they are not my people. If they would only show some spirit, some fight . . . I wanted to fight Napoleon. Alcaster said I would be better up here. He was wrong. I can still go and fight Napoleon." He was not looking at his companion; hardly was he speaking to her. It was to himself that he was speaking, arguing, and it was inward that he was looking . . . and seeing only her widened eyes. "Can you say, honestly, that it is my duty to stay?"

Dumbly she shook her head.

Her silence seemed almost to enrage him. "But you think I must stay, for all that—I know you do! You think that to go now would be the act of a coward. But why should it, my God! I did not come here to be a hero, to lead a revolt against my employer. I have a duty to him, haven't I, and if I cannot discharge that duty, then surely I ought to go, and at least not remain here under false pretences? And my staying is useless, anyway; nothing that I can do will alter these people's fate, or even ease their burden the merest fraction."

The girl looked at the ground, and her tone was troubled. "I thought . . . I think that just your presence helps—gives them the last gleam of hope they've got. Your being there is maybe a sort of sign that all the world is not against them. If you go . . ." her voice trailed away.

"If I go they will know the truth, the plain truth—and that might be the best thing for them . . . better than relying on a broken reed." He was the more dogmatic for her contention. "If they would rely on themselves—do something, get together and have a real revolt, a riot even, they might at least get their state known, cause a stir, and make Dunn more careful in his methods. But it is not for me to lead them that way."

"No," she swallowed. "No, indeed."

Sharply he glanced at her, but when he spoke again the brief storm had passed, and his voice was his own again, but a little weary. "Why should I stay, then?" he reiterated. "For three weeks I have lived in an atmosphere of strain and suspicion and ill-will, with violence behind and the threat of it all about and the certainty of more of it to come. That house—Menardmore—is like a prison—worse, like a mad-house. Dunn scarcely speaks, just looks and looks, and Bullough laughs and laughs. It is not . . . pleasant. And they are not dissatisfied with themselves, that I am sure. And Achroy, too. The place is not the same. MacVarish is polite, kind, but somehow he is distant, preoccupied, and on edge. He is away a lot, too. There is no peace in that house, either. It is the same everywhere I go—even here. And I can see no betterment to come. There are dozens of glens to be cleared, and no limit to the size and number of the sheep-runs they plan to make, no limit to their ambitions. Then why must I stay, with it all no concern of mine? Why must I stay?"

The other answered him quietly, evenly. "No need to stay then, Adam," she said.

"But I must, you see," he said then, as quietly, but his voice had grown firm, vibrant. "I must . . . because I cannot do anything else. It is your fault, Alison Hardie. I cannot go . . . and leave my heart at Menardbeg."

She stirred under the directness of his regard, but did not look away. Nor did she speak. Only a hand lifted and hovered—they were on the birch-knoll behind the byre, she a foot or two above the man—hovered, to run lightly, gently, through his hair. And she shook her head again, and, being a woman, meant this or that or the next thing thereby, and so stood. She was not ineloquent in her silences, that girl.

The man found in her quiet gesture all that he needed at that moment, and knew peace for the first time in Strathmoraig. And presently he caught that hand as it left his head, and kissed it, not fiercely but never lightly, and turning away, he left her there.

Adam Metcalfe required all the peace he could find in these days. The very next evening he arrived at Achroy to find a keening woman and no one else in that grey house amongst the burgeoning birch-woods, no one else—save only the corpse of Ewan MacVarish, lying on his own bed and covered with the tartan of his own plaid. From the weeping housekeeper, dubious in her English, it was only to be learned that the body had been found at the foot of some cliffs near the far end of the loch that morning, with the neck broken. The path above the cliffs was bad, bad, and the place clear where he had fallen, so it was said. Woe, woe, and he the fine gentleman . . . !

Ewan MacVarish had not been home the previous night, but that was not so unusual an event. And now he had come home for the last time. Long Adam stood by the bed of a man whom he would like to have called his friend, stood staring, till the woman had left the room, and after that. Then stooping, he turned back the cover from over that face. And looking, he stiffened, froze, and somewhere beneath his scalp, nerves stirred and tingled. He had never seen a man with a broken neck before, admittedly . . . But those weals and great bruises all about the throat, blue and black and evil! Almost he could imagine great fingermarks about that discoloured and twisted throat . . . He saw great hands groping, groping . . . With a shiver he replaced the tartan plaid, and waited for a moment, head bowed, eyes unseeing. Then hurriedly he left that room and went downstairs, and his face was set, hopeless. What could he do . . . ?

128

13

THEREAFTER, since he must, the man sought to swallow his horror as best he could and went about his work as usual, and kept his own counsel.

They were very busy on the hill these days, Dunn and Bullough and himself, prospecting the farther northern glens, for sheep ground, selecting hirsels for winter sheltering, surveying the rotative availability of the pasture, deer-hair, cotton-grass, mosses, and bents—and finding it all distressingly suitable. They ranged far and wide, by paths and no paths, through vast forests of birch and pine, by great lochs and remote valleys under the stark glare of frozen snows, east beyond the deepest penetration of the thrusting sea-lochs, west to the very rim of the western ocean, Dunn acrimonious and tireless, Bullough heavier-footed but determinedly hearty, Metcalfe silent, watchful. Twice they stayed away all night, sleeping in lonely croft-houses, where they were welcomed without question and treated generously out of a humble store, hospitality that stuck in Adam's throat, knowing the future that they were planning for the givers. And the nights he did not relish either, in dark smoke-blackened rooms, sleeping but fitfully, and waking and listening to his companions' breathing, listening, with the dread image of Ewan MacVarish's dead face before his eyes. Only on the few occasions when he was sent off on his own to examine the possibilities of some side glen or out-of-the-way tract, did Adam achieve any real appreciation of the beauty and grandeur of the country he was exploring, the long brown flanks of the hills, scarred with red and shot with green, the far austerity of the high tops, preoccupied only with the dizzy immensity of the pale heaven, the sparkling, rushing rivers, ale-brown and frothing white, the blue jewels of the lochans set securely within the emerald and gold of quaking bog, and the wide, lifting folds of the heather moors, rolling, rolling, the playground for the cloud-shadows at their racing. All this he saw, then, and only sometimes appreciated and seldom indeed enjoyed. It was as well for Adam Metcalfe at that time that deep within him a small fire was burning, glowing, outwith and beyond the reach of the chill flood of hatred and despair in which he was caught. Quietly and steadily it burned, now and again flaring up in a blaze, more often gently glowing, for the warming of his soul.

It was after one of these two-day trips that Adam, taking his usual brief leave of the others outside the House of Menardmore, was hailed back when half-way to the loch-shore, by a bull-like roar from the factor. He was nowhere in sight when Metcalfe, having toiled once more up the hill, reached the rough terrace before the house. Choking back his usual hot indignation at the man's manners, he paused, shrugged, and frowning his reluctance, entered the doorway, past the crouching, glowering dogs, and the nervous, shifty-eyed Colin.

In the only room he ever used, John Dunn stood in his usual position, wide-legged before the fire, and facing the door. "Friends of yours, Metcalfe," was all he said.

It was Lieutenant Seton of the 91st, and his impressive uncle, the Colonel. They had arrived the previous evening from Kinlochardoch, and failing to find anyone at Menardmore had put up at the Manse for the night. Old Jehovah Hardie had not been riotously welcoming, but his niece with the hair and the eyes would have made up for half a dozen of the worst that the Kirk could produce. Astonishing thing to be related to that stern collection of dry bones—ripest thing he'd seen since Greenock, b'Gad! Thus Alexander Seton.

Indeed Mr Seton was extremely affable, even if his uncle, as ever, was more noticeably military and non-committal. He hoped that Mr Metcalfe had not forgotten him, nor his promise to visit Strathmoraig, nor even the fine clutch of recruits he was to have for him. They could do with them, too, it seemed. So far their drive had been disappointing, most disappointing. No spirit about the men, no sense of their obligations to their country. And worse still, the whole place was getting practically empty; a serious matter, as the country would find out to its cost.

Where would they be—dammit, it was a question of where would old Boney be—if the Highland regiments were not kept up to strength? It was these damned improvements that was the trouble. Oh, the devil . . . ! Profuse apologies all round. But it was the very deuce, if they saw what he meant . . . after all, they could hardly go over to the Americas or whatever deuced place it was the fellows were shipped to, for their recruits, could they now? Skye was bad enough—scarcely enough to raise a single Platoon out of the whole island—but that last place, Ardoch or Kinardoch or whatever it was called, was the worst yet—not a man there; they would hardly credit it, but not a single man. Nobody about the place at all, nothing but a lot of baa-ing sheep. So here they were, a bit earlier than they had expected, but relying on Strathmoraig to make up for the rest and provide them with a Company at least.

Adam Metcalfe was hardly encouraging. "I'm afraid that you have chosen rather a bad time, Mr Seton."

"Bad . . . why?"

"Today is the 23rd of May. In five days it will be the Term, and the people hereabouts are going to be somewhat . . . preoccupied this Term."

"Stab me—not more improvements?"

"More improvements." It was John Dunn that spoke, crisply. "And I say ye've chosen an excellent time, Mister."

"Ah . . . er—thank you." Seton stared from one to the other. "Glad to hear it, I'm sure." He looked at his uncle, but got no help from that quarter. "I say," he went on, "I take it that you've no objection to our recruiting amongst your people here . . . ?"

"On the contrary!" Dunn went so far as to attempt a bow. "I'll do my best to assist ye, lad—the more ye enlist, the better I'll be pleased. Anything to help a friend o' Mr Metcalfe's," and he grinned broadly, but not at the soldier.

"'Pon my soul, that's uncommon handsome of you, sir."

"Don't mention it. Here, gentlemen, we'll drink to this—happen Mr Metcalfe'll join us, for once. Harry, fetch over those glasses. Here's to the success o' your recruiting—may ye enlist every bloody Highlander in the place! Don't mind Metcalfe—he has no head for liquor . . ."

Later, inevitably, the question of accommodation arose, Strathmoraig being unprovided with an inn. The newcomers would have stayed at Menardmore, of course, but the factor produced no urgent suggestion that they do so. Indeed, he appeared to assume that they would put up at Achroy with Metcalfe—so conveniently vacant, and so convenient, too, to be beside their friend for the planning of the recruiting drive! The blade of John Dunn's wit was cutlass rather than rapier. Mr Seton had no fault to find with the amenities of the Manse, and, winking, was for leaving well alone. But the Colonel, bestirring himself, had to admit that he found the parson-fellow trying, deuced trying. And Adam, with a sudden access of hospitality, was much put about on the Colonel's behalf, claiming his comfort to be absolutely essential. It was not often that he found himself in agreement with the factor. So Achroy it was, the Lieutenant retiring in good order before superior pressure, but keeping his powder dry. Thitherward Adam led them, with no undue delay. Dunn appeared to find the situation diverting.

At Achroy life retained at least a semblance of normality. The sudden death of Ewan MacVarish had created surprisingly little stir, outwardly at least. Comment thereon was extremely guarded, and the one or two leading questions Metcalfe advanced were unproductive of information. The funeral, however, had been a strange affair. Two nights after the tragedy Adam was awakened by stealthy footsteps outside his room, and, feeling for a heavy stick that he had taken to carrying about with him, he opened the door and peered out. Three or four men were engaged in carrying the body of Ewan MacVarish downstairs. Even as he had stared, his shoulder was roughly gripped and he was jerked round.

"It's your bed is the place for you this night," he was told, at Ian MacErlich's tersest. "Get you back in, now."

Donald Bàn's voice came quietly from the stair. "Is that yourself, Mr Metcalfe? It's sorry I am you've been disturbed. It is just the last small thing we can do for Ewanie."

"I see," and on impulse, "Could I come along, too? I had a great regard for Ewan MacVarish."

Only for a moment had the other hesitated. "Surely, sir. It is kindly thought," he said.

So Adam, throwing on a few clothes and his travelling cloak, had followed the strange cortège through the sleeping woods till they came to the mouth of a little glen striking up into the hills to the south, where quite a concourse of silent folk were awaiting them. Following on, without a word spoken, the whole party had moved up the glen. They were perhaps half-a-mile up, when from the darkness ahead of them a sound had risen, a strange sobbing bubbling wail, that, sending shivers down Adam Metcalfe's back, rose to a scream, intense and prolonged, before moderating to what presently became recognisable as notes, music—if not melody. The man had never before heard the bagpipes, but recognised that this could be nothing else. To the high sorrow of a wild lament, then, fast and slow by turns, stern and melting, and inexpressible in its sadness, that mute indefinite throng had followed on, climbing as the little valley rose sharply, till in time the piping seemed to become louder, to come closer, and they were in a level open place wherein the remains of tumbled walls loomed darkly. And there, amid the moss-grown ruins, a grave had been dug, and as the pibroch sank to a close, a voice lifted in its place, an Irish voice rich and strong and sorrowful. So Ewan MacVarish, tacksman of Achroy, had been buried, darkly but never unseemly, with the last rites of his Church. And in due course the gathering had turned and melted away, silently as it had come, leaving the dead to the night and the ruins and the unknown piper. Long the woeful dirge had followed them down, rising and falling but ever fading, till, in the open strath, the hills had swallowed it up. At the door of Achroy, Metcalfe had had his hand taken, and pressed, by Donald Bàn MacVarish, and that was all. He had gone back to his bed, but he had not slept.

So Adam remained at Achroy, for the time being. There was no new tenant, for the estate was not going to renew the tack or lease. Donald Bàn was the nearest relative, and he was not anxious to burden himself with extra plenishings just then, with a removal of his own looming ahead of him. The old housekeeper made no move to leave; this evidently was all the home she had. And the factor apparently had no immediate plans for the use of the house. He did, however, impound most of the stock of the little farm attached, by way of casualties and escheat . . . which was as good as any excuse to use, and convincingly legal. He also gave six weeks' notice to quit to each of the half-dozen crofter sub-tenants on the tack, and immediate dismissal to Mairi MacErlich on the grounds of her husband's wilful neglect of his holding, to follow bad company. Word of this last reached Adam Metcalfe by the person of Mairi herself, child on one arm and a poor bundle of her things in the other, with a letter from Alison Hardie. Alison felt a responsibility in the matter since she could not persuade herself that her uncle was unconnected with the business; he had spoken violently against backsliders, and renegades from the company of the elect, in his last sermon, prophesying with significant conviction immediate Divine vengeance. So she pleaded Adam's aid. Mairi MacErlich was expecting another baby. What were John Dunn's reactions when he heard that his assistant had taken in the MacErlich woman and her children is not to be known; but he said nothing—meantime. Ian More himself paid another clandestine visit late the following night, to express with some magnanimity his appreciation of the arrangement, leaving thereafter for whatever quiet place he had come from, in highly dramatic fashion. That was Ian More MacErlich.

Thus passed the days, and the nights, of the end of the month of May, and all men waited. From the outer world came two reports. That Napoleon was pressing hard in Spain, Sir John Moore had been killed, and Austria had come into the war again. And that the emigrant ship that had sailed from Kinlochardoch had been sunk by a French privateer in mid-Atlantic, with less than a dozen survivors.

14

THE twenty-eighth of May dawned still and fine, a day such as the hills dreamed over, with white diaphanous tendrils of mist clinging to the higher corries, the mountain tops clear against the sky's palest blue, and the myriad of spiders' webs, heavily bedewed, sparkling and gleaming on every bush and shrub and tussock. The touch of frost had disappeared, and only a mild air out of no airt in particular ruffled the polished surface of the water, as Adam Metcalfe rowed across the loch to Menardmore. It was early—Dunn had told him to be over early that morning—and the two officers were not risen when he left Achroy, though he had one of their soldier-servants in the boat with him, to row it back for them to use for fishing later in the day. Seton had approached him the previous evening, asking whether it would not be a good idea if they were to come with the factor's party next day—see what was to be seen, and maybe pick up a recruit or two on the rebound, you know—and had been quite painfully surprised by the vehemence of Metcalfe's reply. So they were going fishing. It was going to be a good day to be fishing. Adam might have used his oars more zestfully if he had been going fishing himself.

At Menardmore he found the ponies out and harnessed and Dunn striding back and forward before the house in obvious impatience. With hardly a nod to his colleague he turned, shouting, "He's here, Harry. Come on, blast you," and set off at a great pace. Hopkins followed with a pony, and three other men with beasts behind, while Adam glumly brought up the rear, to be presently joined by a panting but persistently jocose Bullough. "A grand morning, lad," he puffed. "Grand. Just listen to them larks. Only one sound I like better than larks—or maybe two. And that's sheep bleating—and good liquor coming out of a bottle! Ha! Strike me, John's in a devilish hurry this morning, eh? Great one to go, John. Lot to do today, though.

God, ye'll see me up on one o' them ponies soon, I'm telling you. Why walk when ye can ride, eh—even on one o' them?"

Indeed John Dunn was in a hurry . . . as to devilish, that might be right too. And there would be a lot to do, undoubtedly. Adam's answers were monosyllabic.

Down the sandy road that led west they went, the ponies' hooves clopping and crunching in the quartz-grit, the pannier-baskets creaking as they swayed. Past the great folds and the in-fields, where the ranks of Bullough's stolid tups, breeding rams, chewed steadily, morosely, the pasture that had once been the arable of the crofting township of Menard, and over the wooden bridges that spanned the streams that came each out of one of the radial glens that fanned out from the head of the strath. It was when they passed the last of the bridges, a stone one, high-arched, that Adam turned to look curiously at his companions. They had passed both the roads that led up Glen Luie, and they had passed all the other glens likewise, and they were still going westwards. He would have asked where they were going, but for his foolish pride.

By the time that they had passed the Manse at Menardbeg, and a mile more, and crossed the Moraig River by the same ford he had used the first day that he had come to the place, and the little cavalcade was lifting to the gradual steady rise of the wide southern flank of the strath, he knew that there was going to be no eviction that day—and the knowledge wrought in him such an unreasoning tide of relief that he was almost overwhelmed, bewildered. For weeks he had dreaded this day, the twenty-eighth of May, the last day that the crofters had been given to remain in their homes; the thought of what he must witness, and help to achieve—God pity him—that day, had never left him, preyed on his mind. And here was sudden relief, temporary only, without a doubt, for one day merely perhaps, but relief never-theless. He began to appreciate that it was a very fine day, and presently he was emulating the larks and whistling a stave or two in its favour. John Dunn threw a sardonic glance or two backwards.

Climbing steadily southwards it was soon apparent that they

were making in the direction of the mountains of Ardoch. What they were going to do there, Adam had no idea—unless it was concerned with the dispute about boundaries that had been going on between the two properties for months. Not that he greatly cared—it could have nothing to do with evictions; all that southern ground had been cleared already.

That day was spent amongst the tumbled wastes of the high watershed that sent down streams, south to Ardoch, north to Moraig, with Bone the Ardoch factor and some of his people, settling the question of the march between the two estates, a problem that had become acute with the great numbers of sheep that both sides were driving up to these high pastures for the summer grazing. It was not just the simple matter of fixing a line where no line had been fixed before, for there was a long tract of debatable ground, and the incidence of water, access, and more particularly, shelter, relevant to both parties, had to be considered. It was not an acrimonious business; the factors seemed to get on very well with each other—indeed, it almost appeared to Metcalfe that there was some sort of arrangement between them, in which the furtherance of their employers' interests may or may not have been the primary motive. But it was a tedious business, with every glen-let and corrie and col of the wide no-man's-land to be surveyed and considered, and every stream and patch of good pasture to be inspected and bargained over, and little cairns of stones to be built every few hundred yards to make a boundary that would be completed by a dry-stone dyke as soon as time and labour permitted. After due instructions, Adam with one man and a pony, and one of the Ardoch people, was sent westwards to extend this line towards the sea, while the main party turned eastwards.

So all the day he worked contentedly enough, under the warm regard of the sun, tempered by the thin wind of the high places, measuring, assessing, discussing. The Ardoch representative, an elderly disillusioned man, was easy enough to get along with. With no small talk and little information either to give or to seek, there was one query he did put with some interest. Why had John Dunn chosen *this* day to start this work? At Ardoch they had thought it rather strange—though they had been trying to get the job done for a long time. Not that the day mattered to them; with only three large sheep-farmers as tenants on the whole place, term-day was no longer a busy time with them. Those days were past. But, from what they had heard, they had imagined that this might have been quite a busy day on Strathmoraig . . .? Adam, wondering himself, was unable to provide much enlightenment.

With progress made, but only a small fraction of the task done, they parted company in the early evening, to go their separate ways and meet again the next day. It was late when he reached the hushed haughlands of the Moraig River, too late, he restrainedly decided, to call in at Menardbeg as he passed. He was almost regretting his manners when, back at Achroy, he discovered a bored colonel in sole possession, with the information that his nephew had been over at the Manse all evening, curse him . . . could Mr Metcalfe rattle a dice at backgammon, by any chance?

Mr Metcalfe could not, Heaven be praised!

The day following, Saturday, conformed to an identical pattern, the early start, the long day on the hill prospecting, debating, and the lengthened journey back in the creeping grey of the evening. This time he did not hesitate as, returning, he passed the Manse. He was still later than yesterday; having stumbled most of his length in a black peat-hag, he was in no condition for visiting—and anyway, Seton would never be there again tonight.

Which was where he was wrong.

Tomorrow, then, it would be no less than a duty to attend at Menardbeg.

The military gentlemen had been invited to take their dinner with the factor on Sunday, and Adam, elaborately, had been included in the invitation. His acceptance had been governed only by the claims of expediency.

It was during the forenoon, that—being insufficiently a

hypocrite to attend, for purely personal reasons, a church service in which he was unable to achieve any trace of the feeling of worship—Mairi MacErlich, wood-gathering, came on him, on his back, in a glade among the birches near the loch-shore, contemplating the green tracery of the leaves and the slow procession of the clouds, and considering various things. She looked down at him thoughtfully before she spoke. "There is no turning out of the crofters yet at all, then, Mr Metcalfe," she said, ". . . excepting just my own self?"

"No," he agreed. "Apparently not."

"It is a good thing, that."

"It is—as long as it lasts."

She nodded, "Yes." And looking behind her, "Watch you, Ian Beg, and see you don't be falling into the water, now. He is a right *borach*, that one, and him just the same as his own father. There are some that do be thinking that Mr Dunn has his mind changed."

"I would like to think so, but . . ." The man shook his head. "Why should he?"

"They are saying that God, and your own self maybe, have changed his mind for him."

"Fools!" With sudden anger Adam sat up straight. "Blind, self-deceiving fools! I have done nothing, *can* do nothing— nothing, I tell you! Why can't they recognise that, stand on their own feet, and stop looking for help from me? Dunn will do as he wills, without reference to me."

Mairi MacErlich was unmoved by his outburst. "Yes, then," she said evenly. "Ian More said that same." Her tones, quiet and equable, held a quality of calm and tranquillity, wherein seemed to speak the voice of patient, enduring, accepting womanhood of all ages. "Ian Beg, will you take your foot out of the water, now. *Tha mi cumail suil ort, Ian 'ic Ian*. He says John Dunn will do anything. He says John Dunn killed Ewan MacVarish."

Adam looked up sharply, and then, almost involuntarily, glanced about him. "Ian More says that? Why?"

She shook her head. "I cannot say—Ian More says it." She turned, unhurriedly, in answer to her son's cries, and moved down to the beach, where she rescued Ian Beg from six inches of water and the fear of imminent death, and led him back, dripping and clamorous. The man watching, saw for the first time, from the carriage of her shoulders and her slightly deliberate movement, that she was indeed carrying a third child. "Wheesht you, wheesht you," she charged the boy. "The factor and Achroy were unfriends from the day Dunn came, and him wanting this place of Achroy and Ewan not for giving up his tack. Ian More was after saying always that the man would be doing Ewan a hurt . . . that was the way of the pistol. Come on with you, *oganach*, and you with half the loch in your pocket— come on, or it's sneezing you'll be by bed-time, little trout." Moving away, with the sticks she had gathered in the loop of her apron, she turned, "If you should be seeing Miss Alison, Mr Metcalfe, will you be telling her my thanks for her kindness?"

Of the dinner at Menardmore, the less said the better. No one appeared to enjoy the occasion—except, perhaps, John Dunn himself, whose appreciation of his victuals was a thing constant and unaffected by circumstances, Andrew Hardie appeared to be in a profound ill-humour, and was not noticeably concerned with hiding it; Lieutenant Seton's initial ebullience sank and died away fairly early on, and even Henry Bullough seemed to find the Colonel's heavy silences and glassy stare too much for him, and for the nonce gave up his self-appointed role; as for Adam Metcalfe, he had on him that wary, watchful silence that he had come to wear like a garment in that place, cramping and unnatural as it was to an otherwise reasonably cheerful temperament. Even Dunn may have found the atmosphere irksome, for, after the meal, when they got down to pipes and wine, he went so far as to announce that he had hoped Miss Hardie would have been there to entertain them, but unfortunately she appeared not to have felt well enough to come. Which brought forth solicitous enquiries from Bullough, and an urgent demand for particulars from Alexander Seton, followed by the announcement that, since it was no doubt just the vapours or the megrims or whatever deuced name it was the dear things gave to their little troubles, he would go with Mr Hardie later when the latter went back for his evening service, and endeavour to cheer her up. To Hardie's objection that this was quite unnecessary, he turned a deaf ear. Thereafter, the Lieutenant, at least, was slightly more lively.

Discussion of the recruiting campaign was unproductive of elation. Despite the factor's blessing it had been practically barren so far. Two or three open-air meetings had been held amongst the crofts, and individuals had been approached, but without effect. The men were uninterested, spineless, and without pride—and of course there were not many of them of military age, anyway. Conscription should be applied—it was most undignified for officers and gentlemen to have to stump the country pleading with Tom, Dick and Harry to do their duty. Though, of course, one volunteer was worth half a dozen conscripts . . . Dunn was sympathetic. He thought a little pressure might yield results. He would see what he could do . . .

The question of eviction was not discussed.

When, earlier than usual, then—but by no means too soon for some of his fellow guests—Andrew Hardie rose to go, he was accompanied by both the younger men, since Adam was certainly not going to remain behind in that company. They left the three of their elders reaching for fresh bottles, as though getting down to business. Relief seemed mutual. Which of the trio was likely to be the better man at the end of their entertainment might have provided an interesting subject for speculation.

The three men on the road to Menardbeg, after a first brief duel between the minister and Seton on the needlessness of their errand, found little to say to each other. Harmony, noticeably, was lacking. Hardie strode half a pace in front, Seton and Metcalfe level, but scarcely side by side, and each found the other's presence redundant.

It would be about half-way to the Manse that Adam, out of the corner of his eye, caught a glimpse of white moving amid the trees at the far side of the river. He watched carefully, but not obviously, and presently saw it again, and more, and smiled to himself, for the first time that day. He would know that kerchief anywhere. Holding his tongue, he walked on for about a quarter of a mile to where a slender footbridge crossed the Moraig.

"I will leave you here," he informed them, then. "My road to Achroy lies over the bridge, there."

Hardie did no more than nod shortly, but Seton looked at him in some surprise. Metcalfe had not actually said that he was coming with them to the Manse, but the thing had been assumed. "You are just going back to the house, then?" He did not sound in any way disappointed. "Shall I convey your respects to Miss Hardie?"

"Yes—yes indeed," Adam agreed solemnly. "Please do—if the opportunity presents," and with that he left them, and slanted down the bank, to cross unsteadily the swaying sagging erection of wire and rope and laths, precarious-seeming but veteran of a hundred storms, and so to reach the little woodland path on the other side, and follow it back in the direction he had come.

He came up with her in a grove of sombre pines, after some twenty minutes brisk walking. The deep pile of the pine needles deadened his footsteps, and he was quite close to her before she heard him. She walked well, he noted, carrying herself with a lissome ease and a careless lift of the shoulders that was a pleasure to watch. He watched. Then a cracking twig gave away his presence, and she turned about swiftly, with an urgency that gave the lie to the seeming ease of her going.

"Oh," she said, on the intake of a quick breath, "it's you! It's just you, Adam."

"Yes—that's all. Just me. Who did you expect—young Seton?" He had not meant to say that. He had not been thinking about Seton. It just came out, from the sharp edge of his tongue.

"No," she said, and she made no attempt to use the woman's weapon that he had put in her hands, as she might have done. "I wasn't expecting anybody. You gave me a start, that's all. I was just on my way to Achroy."

Her ingenuousness made his remark seem foolish, petty, and so, a man's pride being what it is, it was necessary to be still more childish, all in self-defence. "What a pity!" he proclaimed. "Mr

Seton is just on his way to Menardbeg to see you, and here you have missed him!"

She was patient. "But I was not going to Achroy to see Mr Seton—it was you I wanted to see."

"How kind." He bowed, confirmed in his folly, and aware of it. "And what can I do for you?"

Alison looked at him, puzzled. "Is there anything wrong, Adam?" she wondered.

"Wrong—of course not. Everything is fine, splendid. I have just been enjoying Mr Dunn's hospitality, pressure is to be brought to bear to ensure that Strathmoraig does its duty by a country with a strange preference for Highland soldiers, and the crofters are already thanking God and myself for changing the factor's mind on the question of evictions."

Troubled, she fingered the tassel of her scarlet girdle. She was not wearing her Sabbath clothes this Sunday afternoon. "It was that I was coming to see you about," she said. "It is strange—good, of course, but ... I did not know what to think. And I had no news ..."

"News!" the man interjected. "Surely Mr Seton has been keeping you abreast of the news?"

She looked away. "Mr Seton had other things to talk about." He was working, pleading, for this, and she was by no means without spirit, the girl.

"I dare say," Adam agreed, with heavy significance.

They were walking on together, slowly, between the brown aisles of the trees, but now his companion checked, and halted. "There is no need for me to go on to Achroy now that I have met you," she declared. "And ..." a pause, "... it would be a pity, as you say, to disappoint Mr Seton," and turning around, she started to retrace her steps, at a noticeable increase of pace.

The other hesitated for a moment, and then hastened after her, and fell into step beside her, frowning. This was damned ridiculous—and precisely what he had asked for.

So they walked, unspeaking, along a little path that was only a slight flattening of the thick carpet of the pine needles, convenient roadway for the endless columns of the ants, whose wood this was. But their silence was not the wood's silence, but a brittle, uneasy thing that clashed and had no part in the grave hush that was about them. Soon it was a struggle between their poor silence and the wood's, and since the place was vast and potent, presently the one enveloped and swallowed the other, and they walked in the wood's quiet and not theirs and Adam ceased his frowning.

It was a capercailzie, hobgoblin of the northern forests, that released them, bursting deafeningly from a juniper bush beside the path, and beating its way blindly deep into the farthest fastnesses of the trees. They both started, the girl gave a small choking cry, and the man's hand was at her elbow. "Just an earthquake or something of the sort," he reassured.

"Oh!" she gasped. "Those brutes—aren't they just wicked! I'm afraid I am all nerves just now."

Adam nodded. "We all are, I think—hence..." he faltered, "... my recent display of ill-manners. I apologise, Alison."

She laughed a little. "I am glad that is all it was," she said. If there was reproof in that, he could not claim that it was unmerited.

Soon she spoke again, and now her voice was serious only. "What does it mean, this leaving the crofters in their homes? They were all expecting to be moved out on Friday. Do you think that something has made him pause, some doubt—or is he just not ready?"

"I am afraid that I have no idea—he has given me no inkling. But it is only two days, you know."

"I know—but he is a man who always makes a point of carrying out his threats. He said that they must move by the twenty-eighth of May, and he has not done anything about it. It is not like John Dunn..."

"That is true. It is strange." He rubbed his chin. "There is only one faint possibility that I can think of. I wrote a letter to Alcaster some time ago—just after the affair in Glen Luie—and sent it south with a packman, who was to see it on to the mail coach at Dingwall. But—no, that is out of the question. Even with the greatest possible speed, going and coming, he could not have sent word back yet. Anyway the chances of it having any effect are remote—I sent it for my own conscience's sake, rather than for any good it might do."

They had come to a green alleyway between the pines, where a sizeable burn chuckled its shallow way over scoured, grooved stone and polished gravel. At its fern-dotted edge, the girl paused. "The Allt Ruadh," she mentioned, "—the Red Burn. I have always liked this burn. It makes such a green path for itself through all the brownness. I wonder why it was called red?"

"Not very suitable, certainly, unless it has changed its character. Something to do with blood, probably—that is the usual explanation for the numerous red rivers of this world."

"Yes..." She accepted his hand to cross the stepping-stones. "Yes, I dare say ..." And then, "It was terrible about Ewan MacVarish, wasn't it!"

He stood beside her on the farther bank, and nodded, unspeaking.

"I have been afraid for Ewan ... for a long time." Her voice was unsteady. "Adam—will you not do what you were speaking about that day, last time I saw you? Will you not go south?"

The man turned to regard her, the appeal and earnestness of her, and he was strangely moved. "Why, Alison ...!" he began, but did not finish. Instead, he gave a short laugh. "Didn't we decide, that same day, that it was out of the question?"

She shook her head, as though in sorrow. "But this is serious, Adam—desperately serious. I wish you would go."

"Do you, Alison?"

"Yes," she said, firmly.

He considered that, for a moment or two, not the statement but its implications, but not as rationally as he could have wished. There were things astir within him that were not rational, at all. He answered at a tangent. "We cannot make things as easy for him as that, I think. Anyway, he would not dare ..."

Their eyes met, and hers were wide. "Then you, too, think that Ewan was ... murdered?"

He did not admit it in so many words. "He may not have been

145

. . . I have no proof. It was only an idea of mine . . ."

"Not only your idea," she corrected. And then, with a return to her former urgency. "Don't you see, then—you must not stay here. For my sake, Adam . . ."

The man took a deep breath. "For your sake!" he cried. "It is for your sake that I will not go." He stopped. "No, perhaps that is not quite true. Say . . . that there is much that I would do for your sake, Alison Hardie, but not this. I will not go south yet awhile. I told you why, the other day."

Abruptly she turned away, and moved over to the water's edge. As abruptly she sat down on a flat-topped stone amongst the nodding ferns. Adam eyed her dubiously. He was uncertain of his road, now; he did not know his road at all. And quite suddenly he knew that it was intensely important that he should take the right road here and now. He had been going with the tide, so far. He was accepting this easy effortless progress thankfully, in conditions that were far from easy and where all else was effort. Now it was time to stop drifting.

He moved over to stand beside her, and there was no certainty in him, save only that he knew that his goal was precious. "Alison," he began, "I want to apologise for the way I talked the other night. I want you to forgive me, for a, a special reason. I was strung-up, weak, and foolish—worse, I acted like a spoiled child laying my burdens on your shoulders. I am sorry."

When the girl did not speak, nor look up, Adam stooped anxiously. "You do understand . . . ?"

Her voice seemed to come from far away. "I think so . . . now. You did not mean the things you said that night."

"That's right. I've been thinking about it, and I would not like you to have a wrong impression."

"Then why are you here—why are you not going back to the south?" she asked wearily.

"What . . . ? Good God, I don't mean *that*! I don't mean that I didn't mean that last bit, if you understand me—I meant that I didn't mean . . ." Hopelessly he shook his head. "Sink me, don't think that, anyway." Then he was plumped down beside her on her stone. "Alison," he cried, "I have nothing to offer you—

146

nothing. No position, no security, no promise for the future, nothing. Lord, how can I ask you for the thing I want?"

Still she looked away, and he could hardly hear the words that came, eventually. "What is it that you want, Adam?"

"I want you to give me your heart to keep, my dear," he said deeply, steady-voiced now it had come to the bit.

His companion threw a quick glance at him, and away. "But—I need it myself . . ." That came in a rush.

"You do not. Mine you have got—I told you before, meaning it—have had, irrevocably, since first I saw you herding cattle. And I need a heart, your heart, Alison Hardie. It is cold, cold, without any heart at all . . ."

After a moment, she spoke. "So that is why . . . !" she said, quietly, almost pensively.

"What is why?"

She looked at him now, right at him, smiling, and her eyes were soft indeed. "That is why my breast has been so, so warm of late, and full, nearly bursting, despite all the trouble in it . . . Your great warm heart has nearly choked me sometimes, I think. Take mine, then, Adam—I am only a weak, silly girl, and I have no need for two . . ."

She said no more, nor did she have opportunity just then. Their love, that had germinated and budded and grown modestly under dark clouds and evil winds, was all the fiercer in its sudden blossoming.

15

THERE are not many, perhaps, who will blame Adam Metcalfe that, in the next week or two, local conditions and problems receded a little in their urgency, if not in their gravity. They were not disregarded or forgotten, nor could they be, but neither were they the ever-foremost challenge to thought and whetstone of the mind. Something else, essentially more personal, had assumed that position. Besides, Strathmoraig appeared to have reached a pause in its progress towards economic soundness. Day succeeded day without event; the factor's establishment was all busily engaged in the formidable task of delineating the southern march with Ardoch, the crofters found increasing cause for an optimism that is at once the blessing and curse of the Gael, and the military mission continued, in between fishing and social occasions, to speak with the voice of one crying in the wilderness—with appropriate results.

John Dunn was a man of his word. As the days passed, he suggested that Mr Seton should take a trip north and west, to the remote regions of Altbea and Druim and Loy where there were one or two quite populous townships, untapped so far in the matter of recruiting. There was no need for the Colonel to fatigue himself with the tiresome journey, but Metcalfe would go along with him, and at the same time collect the rents of one or two of the tacksmen thereabouts—which, in their usual fashion, they were holding on to till somebody came to fetch them—and one or two other jobs as well. There would be a year's accumulation of petty disputes to settle—good practice for a young factor. He, John Dunn, usually went himself, but he wanted to get this Ardoch march business finished with. With a day and a half both going and coming, and a couple there, they would be away five days—not longer, with plenty of work waiting to be done. A fine trip for a pair of young men.

And so it was. With Alison Hardie no longer a cause of

contention—now that Adam knew just where he stood, and could afford to be generous—and certain divergencies in their outlook accepted, Alexander Seton made quite a good companion. And good weather, an invigorating, challenging country, freedom from restrictions and especially from the grim atmosphere of Menardmore, all helped. They went out into the wilderness, expectantly, and knew no disappointment therein; with extreme good fortune they managed to shoot a roe-buck among the shadows of evening, and fried its liver for breakfast the next morning; they even went so far as to climb a great hill, for no other reason than the vista of the unknown that it would give them, and the dare of its soaring buttresses to their young manhood. They also did what they went to do, Adam, with the interpreting help of one of their two Highland pony-gillies, donning the mantle of Solomon with some little success, and Seton convincing no fewer than eighteen of the younger men of Altbea and Druim wherein their duty lay. He was rather proud of this; it was all his own doing. He got no assistance from his fellow-traveller.

On the fifth day, then, they returned across the wide moors and through all the long glens that led towards the great basin of the hills where gathered the multitude of streams that went to make up the Moraig River. It was late afternoon, with the yellow sunlight slanting at their backs, when the little party topped the last ridge and looked down upon the parallel valleys of Glen Evoch and Glen Luie. Long they looked. Each of the glens was dotted with small patches of black, new patches, out of some of which white walls stood starkly. And, barring the fowls of the air, no living thing was seen to move in all the spread of them. The stale smell of burning came wafting up to them on the warm air.

John Dunn was a man of his word, indeed.

Adam Metcalfe moved silently amongst what was left of the croft-houses of Luiebeg, and the rage that was in him was near to bringing tears to his eyes—and not rage only, perhaps. He had left Seton and the gillies back on the heights, there, almost without a word, afraid to speak, and had come striding down into the ravished valley of the Luie, his face set, his eyes busy.

There was much to see, mute, but shouting to highest heaven in its eloquence. The work had been done with obvious thoroughness. Not a single roof had been left intact in all the glen—old thatch burns readily. Walls had been thrown down, fences levelled, and gardens trampled. At one croft a dead dog lay across the doorless threshold, its body contorted, and from it a swarm of flies rose, humming. At another, the splintered sticks of poor furniture scattered before a gaping homestead told their own violent story. At another, a heap of wings and the like in a corner, and poultry feathers blowing about everywhere, spoke as clearly. There was nothing left, nothing pertaining to the people of Glen Luie, that had not been removed or methodically destroyed. Even the little dams that had widened burns into duck-ponds or washing pools had been breached, and dry sand and gravel was all that remained. And everywhere, charred beams, burnt thatching, and the blackened remains of plenishings, affronted the eye and tainted the air.

Adam's grievous wanderings brought him to what had been Donald MacVarish's house. A number of crows flapped heavily up from the carcases of two goats which lay before the destroyed steading, still tied to the ropes that had tethered them. There was another, lying within the scorched shell of the house—at least he thought it was a goat. Within the doorway, a bed was jammed. The half projecting had escaped the flames, even to the hastily-thrown-back bed-clothes, revealing a hollow where a body had lain. Donald Bàn's wife, of course, had been an invalid . . . And all about the doorway and the bed, a whitish substance lay, scattered and piled in little heaps. At first he took it for sawdust, till, tracing it to its source, he knew differently. It had come from a large brass-bound chest that now lay up-ended, smashed, and riven, obviously by axe-blows, amongst the trodden vegetables and broken fruit-bushes of the garden. Adam knew that box. It was MacVarish's meal-chest, that a prudent saving man had not emptied throughout the long winter, knowing that there would be no more meal to be had for man or beast till next harvest.

That chest was symbolic. There were other things to see, but Metcalfe had seen enough. He left that place, and set off down the glen, hurrying.

He had not gone far when he noticed a man, two men, sitting up on the top of a bare-topped hillock near the road. Changing direction, he clambered up to them. One of the pair he knew, Dickson, one of Dunn's men. He touched his cap quite respectfully as Adam came up.

"What are you doing . . . here?" he was demanded.

The fellow jerked back his head. "Watching that none o' them come sneaking back," he said, and he patted a heavy pistol at his belt. "Factor's orders. This 'ere's a orficer o' the Law."

Without a word, Adam turned on his heel and left them there.

John Dunn was not at Menardmore—only the man Colin, who informed that they were clearing the Braes of Arletter district that day, and would not likely be back till late. Adam wasted no time. He got out a fresh pony—ponies were plentiful at Menardmore—saddled it, and made off at the stolid beast's best pace down the strath road.

In the yard behind the Manse, Alison Hardie came running, at his clattering arrival. "Adam!" she cried, clinging to him. "Oh, I am thankful to see you. It has been terrible, terrible. You seem to have been away for so long . . . Oh, my dear . . ." and she dissolved into incoherences.

One arm about her, he smoothed her hair, and held her close, whispering a word or two, till she looked up, blinking her eyes but smiling wanly.

"I was afraid, desperate . . . I was terrified in case he might have attacked you, laid a trap for you out in the hills . . . some lonely place . . . But now you are back, it is all right."

He pressed his lips to her brow. "Dear kind heart . . ."

"Your own heart . . . isn't it?" she reminded, a little unsteadily. "Adam, it has been a dreadful time."

"Tell me," he said.

She told him, brokenly, disjointedly, but the picture that her words painted would have been clear enough to a man with

151

much less imagination than Adam Metcalfe. The day after he had left for the north, been got out of the way, John Dunn had struck. Glen Luie it had been first, with all his own men, and Sheriff's men from Dingwall, and some of Mr Bone's people from Ardoch. And her uncle, God pity him! Dunn had been like a savage, absolutely ruthless, knowing neither decency nor mercy. He said that they had been told to be out by the term, they had not gone, and so they had forfeited all legal rights. His waiting had just been a trap. He had given each crofter only a few minutes to get some things out of his house, before setting fire to the thatch. Those who protested were beaten, assaulted. Old people, children, the sick, were dragged out, their belongings tossed out after them or smashed deliberately. The beasts and cattle had been rounded up, some of them impounded. Dunn had given his men drink . . . they were mad, beasts. Such things were done, unspeakable things . . . Morag Macleod that was due to have a baby in a month or two had had a seizure . . . she was dead now. Old Ellen Campbell was dead too. She was eighty-six, and had died outside her own house as the roof blazed. Angus Og, her grandson, had carried away her body over his shoulder . . . Seana Maclean, in the byre there, had told her all about it. She had been up at Luiebeg visiting her mother, and saw it all. It was vile, sheer ferocity. They had all been driven down the long road to the coast—she had seen them passing the Manse—laden down with what they had been able to save, driving their poor cattle and sheep and goats. She had seen furniture tied on the backs of cows, women with a child on their backs and three or four pinioned and squawking poultry over their arms, dragging sleds heaped with their belongings. And it was eighteen miles to the sea. That was Glen Luie. The next day it was Glen Evoch. Then Corrievar. Today it was Arletter . . . the same hideous nightmare!

Adam listened white faced, his eyes burning, and the grip he had of her arm left it bruised for days. But she did not notice it then. She had done the little that she could, she told him, almost protested—the desperately little, giving food and refreshment as they passed the Manse, lending her pony, going a little way with

152

them, trying to cheer the children. But it was so pitifully small a help that she could give, and their need so great. She had had one woman and her child in the byre for two nights—the child was sick—till her uncle discovered them and turned them out. Dunn had issued a decree that anyone in the strath giving shelter to the evicted would be evicted themselves. Her uncle! Oh, she was ashamed, mortified. Never again could she show him any respect, any affection . . . He was telling them that it was all God's will, a punishment for their sins, but a blessing for the future, assuring them that earthly trials were the food of the soul, and threatening with damnation all who objected. He was saying that they should be grateful to the estate for providing them with alternative holdings at the coast. Grateful . . . ! According to Seana, conditions down at the shore were awful, beyond description. There was nothing there, nothing—just rocks and seaweed. The people were sleeping amongst the rocks . . .

The man straightened his shoulders. "That's where I should be," he said, nodding his head. "That's where I am going, now." ·

"Now—tonight?" she wondered. "But it is a long way, Adam—eighteen miles. You have come far today, already. You must be tired."

He laughed shortly. "I am not tired. This pony will have me there before dark. If you will give me something that I can eat on the way . . . ?"

"Of course. But . . . what are you going to do there, Adam?" There was fear behind her question, the quick weak fear that is born of a woman's love.

"God knows!" he told her, grimly. "All I know is that I must go—at once. It is necessary. My, my soul is involved in this, somehow." He took her hand in his. "Anyway, it is probably better that I do not see John Dunn tonight . . . as I feel at present . . ."

"Yes," she took him up quickly. "Yes, indeed." Then she raised her head, as in decision taken. "I will come with you, then."

For a moment or two he looked at her, and the flame went out of his eyes, to be replaced by something softer, but even warmer than flame. "You would do that, Alison Hardie . . . ?" he wondered, deep-voiced. But his head was shaken. "No," he said. "Not tonight, my dear. Thank you—but it is not necessary, I think, or advisable. Tomorrow, if you will . . ." He smiled a little. "My soul it is, remember. You keep my heart safe here."

The girl looked up at him. "I will do what you think best, Adam," she said quietly. "I will get what you need, now."

"Yes," he nodded, "and you will remember that I love you."

Solemnly she answered him. "I will remember," she agreed, and there was pain behind that as well as pleasure.

16

DUSK held the land, a spreading shadowless dusk, by the time Adam reached the mouth of the Moraig River, a colourless half-light in which the weary trudging figures that dotted his road became impersonal and unreal—and in which the heavy pall of smoke that hung over the strath lost its ominous identity, and merged into the gloom of the night. But, turning the last shoulder of hill, with the estuary and all the level sea before him, he was suddenly in a different light, a different land, where shadows there were, bold and black, and colour, sombre but definite. Seeming to come from the sea rather than from the sky, a dull gold, murky, metallic, that became polished, gleaming, as it reached the very rim of the western ocean, casting on the banked clouds of grey above it the pale reflection of its own glowing. It was the sea retaining the memory of a day that the land had lost. And small, foreshortened, and starkly black, the scattered islands of the Minch lay etched upon the golden plate, their long shadows staining darkly the heaving waters, the streaming sands, and the flat machair that fringed the shore.

The man turned his beast's head northwards, his heels dug impatiently at the flanks of the quiet deliberate animal he rode. He was not alone, now; before him, between his arms, a girl sat, a child of ten or eleven, that for the last hour or so had slept against his breast, exhausted, soothed by the even rhythm of their going. He had picked her up, footsore and weeping, to relieve a woman well-nigh distracted, with a baby in her arms, an old doddering man to lead, half a dozen assorted beasts to drive, and the remains of her worldly goods in tow. That woman had cursed, in mixed Gaelic and English; she had cursed the man Dunn that was the staff to their backs, she had cursed the laird, their Chief—she had spat—that had sold them, blood of his blood, for baaing sheep; she had cursed her husband that had let himself be taken for a soldier to fight the battles of them that oppressed them; and she had cursed her own mother that had borne her to see this day. Adam, intensely pitiful, had found himself only silent before her affliction. But she had given him the child.

So he jogged up that darkling sea-board, with the hills rising sheer on his right, their crests and ridges grey and indistinct, merging with the night, and the jagged rocks of an iron coast just below him on his other hand, at their eternal warfare with the snarling frothing waves. Here were no level sands, no spreading flats; that had been only about the wide estuary of the river. This was a shore of stone and foam, of black headlands and blacker coves, of frowning cliffs and striding reefs, and of occasional small bays backed by crescents of grey-green machair, on which shingle the long Atlantic swell beat endlessly, a rugged battle-ground whereon the mountains cast their challenge to the sea. There was no breadth of land between the water and the soaring screes and heather. The rough track rose and fell, now at a cliff-summit, now at the tide's edge, a sore road for man or beast. The pony took it, staid but staunch. They passed many that night, making less satisfactory progress. The camps of those who could go no farther lined the route.

The man reached the end of his road suddenly, without previous intimation, rounding a steep headland and slanting down into the dark pit of a deep bay. Then he was amongst the evicted. At first, he thought it was only a prolongation of the weary procession behind him; there was the gleam of a few fires, certainly, but then, so was there at his back. But soon it was apparent, from the numbers and from the character of their encampments, that this was no temporary halting-place, but journey's end. Yet even here, as far as he could see, there was no breadth of land between the beach and the towering hills. This could never be the place ... Stooping, he asked at one group for Donald Bàn MacVarish.

A lad detached himself, and led the way through and past numberless shadowy clusters of people, that stood or sat or lay about the heaped piles of their belongings, groups small and large, couples and households and families. Only one or two amongst the many had fires lit. There seemed to be some attempts at tent-making, though the great majority had only the canopy of heaven for roof. Children were very evident, children who shouted and played, running from throng to throng, and in and out amongst the hobbled beasts that strayed everywhere. Dogs barked and fought, voices were lifted suddenly, out of the night, and sank again, and from somewhere indefinite a low and mournful singing rose and fell in weary monotony.

It was all so different from anything that Adam had imagined. He had expected to find the people all scattered and dispersed amongst their new holdings, each household endeavouring to set up some sort of a shelter till they could get houses built—not huddled together like this around the shore, like survivors from a shipwreck. And where were their holdings . . . ?

He found Donald MacVarish in what was practically a cave among the rocks, quite near the surf-drenched beach. Adam, dismounting, and so awakening his young passenger, waited while his guide slipped within. He was trying to comfort the child's sudden sobbing when Donald Bàn came out. The two men eyed each other for a moment or so, and then the Highlandman held out his hand. "You are back then, Mr Metcalfe!"

"I am back," Adam allowed heavily.

The other looked at the weeping child. "Come, girleen," he soothed, "'*De tha cur doilgheas oirbh?*" He stroked her head. "Peig!" he called, and handed her over to the woman who came. "It is hard on the little ones," he said.

The two men sat on a slab of stone and watched the tossing waters, black now but edged and flecked with deadly white, heaving and reaching and sinking in their ineffectual fury—like the seething thoughts of many who sat thus on that coast that night. Adam shook his head. "I cannot even begin to tell you what I feel about this," he said. "No words of mine . . ."

"Yes, it is bad," MacVarish agreed.

"It is worse than I could have expected. Behind you the glens are a smoking wilderness, and here . . ." He gestured around

157

them. "This is terrible. Have you all been packed together like this since Tuesday night?"

The older man half-shrugged. "What else can they be doing? There is nowhere else for them to go, at all."

"But the new holdings . . . ?"

His companion turned around on his seat, and pointed behind him at the dim bulk of the hill, and his voice, for Donald MacVarish, quiet man, was very grim. "There are our new holdings," he jerked. "Strips, narrow strips, up the side of Meall Garbh—rock, screes, and a sprig of heather, ten acres to each household, and it steeper than the side of a roof!"

Adam stared at him. "But . . . Good God, you don't mean . . . That's not all the land he's given you?"

"Just that, Mr Metcalfe."

"But . . ." The younger man's jaws shut with a click, and in silence he contemplated just what this all meant.

The other, after a moment or two, went on, in that reasonable and impartial tone of his, that could on occasion be soothing, impressive, or infuriating. "There is not enough pasture on the face of Meall Garbh to keep two families, let alone sixty, and there is no arable in it, at all. And there is no place that you could be building a single house, by reason of the slope of it." He picked up a piece of dry seaweed and turned it over and over in his hands, hands that were apt to be noticeably still. "So that is why we are packed together like this, Mr Metcalfe. A township, the factor says we will have to make here on the machair, a township."

The younger man waited.

"John Dunn is not wanting us here at all, I'm thinking," MacVarish went on. "He's for having us out of the place altogether, the man. How are we to live, whatever? There is nothing for our beasts on the side of that hill—Anna Bain's brown cow has her leg broken on her already with the place. There's only the goats could be making anything of it. The little soil that we could be scratching amongst the rocks would give no more than a handful of grain. He says that we can eat the fish of the sea, but we have no boats, no nets, and little of the skill

158

of it. And how can we build houses, with no wood for the roof-trees? There are no trees here, and none to be cut if there were. He will sell us wood, he says, at a price, but we have no money. There is no peat, no wood for fires, except the driftwood from the beach . . . John Dunn is not wanting us here at all, I say. "

"I am afraid that you are right," Adam acknowledged. "He . . ."

"Sure and he's right!" a voice broke in from behind them, a strong voice, forceful and angry, sounding strangely vital after MacVarish's dispassionate calm. Adam turned, to find Father O'Brien at their back. "Dunn wants this land empty, for his own ill ends, and devil the care has he how many human souls he crushes getting it. The man is a monster, Mr Metcalfe, a fiend in the shape of a man."

"I know it, sir."

"And your Earl is little better, a heartless grasping idler, worthless descendant of a great line—and a fool, into the bargain."

Adam shook his head. "The rest he may be—but Alcaster is no fool."

"Is he not. Lord pity him! Selling his salvation for another man's profit."

"What do you mean?"

"I mean that it is only a fool would imagine that a hireling, and a blackguard into the bargain, would be so urgent about his master's interests as this John Dunn—use such violence, take such risks, do as he has done. He is playing his own game, with his employer's property, and the lives of a whole people."

"I see that he will stand to gain through Alcaster's increased rent-roll. A grateful master . . ."

"Pshaw!" the priest snorted. He was not conspicuously priest-like, then or any time. "Think you that is all Dunn is going such lengths for—the problematical gratitude of a grasping master? Mark my words, whoever else is a fool, your factor is not . . . only a knave. I have good reason to believe that he is deeply involved in Bullough's sheep-rearing schemes, finan-cially involved—his all is in it. Ewan MacVarish found that out—rest his soul! It is most convenient, to be sure! Bullough decides on whatever slice of land he wants, and the factor, his partner, decides how much they will be pleased to pay in rent for it. Even if they double and treble the little bits of rent the crofters could afford to pay for their holdings, they are getting the land at bargain price. For, mind you, they don't get just the crofters' holdings, but *all* the land, all the hills and moorland for leagues and leagues. And that is not all, look you. You will see, the estate will soon begin to do quite a lot for these magnificent new tenants. New houses will be built for the shepherds; fences and walls will be put up to keep the sheep from straying—haven't they started already over Ardoch way? There will be roads made, bridges built, and water controlled—improvements indeed. And at whose expense? Alcaster's. And for whose benefit? Bullough's . . . and John Dunn's. So your earl gets his rents doubled and trebled for nothing, and thinks he is an astute man of business, while the sheep-farmers get vast tracts of land, a whole province—since their ambitions are boundless—at a tithe and less of its value, with privileges galore . . . and the people whose land it is, clan's land, occupied and worked for untold centuries by their forefathers, get . . . this!"

Adam Metcalfe had stood up, to face him. "It is inhuman, devilish," he conceded. "Nothing that you could say would be stronger than my own condemnation, but . . . why, in Heaven's name, do your people lie down under it, allow themselves to be treated as of no more consequence than beasts—less, indeed? Surely, if only they had united and shown some fight, some violence even, since that is the language John Dunn would best understand, they might have bettered their position, for he cannot wish to have to bring in outside aid—more especially if what you have just told me is the case. He will not want enquiries and investigations. By their meekness the crofters have just played Dunn's game. Even now, here, a demonstration of some spirit might gain them some concessions at least!"

"How are we to fight, and our young men all away at the war?" Donald Bàn put in. "Is it the women, and old men and children, you'd have fighting, Mr Metcalfe?"

"And why not, to be sure!" O'Brien interrupted. "It's grand fighters the women can be—leastways they can in Ireland, bless them." He grinned, and for the moment his features were boyish only. "I mind the time . . ." He stopped, and shook his head. "I do not, then. My sorrow, that was a long time ago, and all forgotten. *Omnia mutantur, nos et mutamur in illis.*" Then suddenly, he turned to Adam and thrust out his hand. "Man, Metcalfe, it's you I agree with entirely," he cried. "'Tis the fighting spirit they need, and often I have said it, too—have I not, Donald MacVarish?" He coughed a little. "Privately, of course, since I am a man of peace . . ."

The Highlandman looked up, and there was just a hint of a glint in his washen eyes and a twitch at his lips. "I have heard you, man of peace," he said mildly.

The other coughed again. "Aye—very well so," he said. "Anyway," returning to the younger man, "it is my opinion—like your own—that your advice given to these poor folk might yet do some good." His glance became keen, direct. "It would have to come from one outside themselves . . . and it would come better from one such as yourself, a man of the world, than from a servant of Holy Church!"

Adam met that glance, and presently nodded slowly. "Yes, I see what you mean," he said, almost reluctantly.

The other lifted a hand, palm open, in an expressive gesture. "'Tis a saying, that the road hardest on the foot is easiest on the soul, my son," he said. And with a touch to MacVarish's shoulder, "Time it is that we were at our prayers and our sleeping, Donald Bàn," he suggested.

They moved back from the water's edge together.

The Highlandman, rather ridiculously, seemed anxious for his guest's comfort. "I doubt I'll not can offer you much hospitality this night, Mr Metcalfe," he apologised. "A plaid or two you can have, but for sleeping . . . you'll maybe not be caring to sleep in the cave with the body . . . ?"

"The body . . . ?"

It was the priest who answered. "Bridget MacVarish died this morning."

161

Adam shook a hopeless head. "That, too!" he cried. "I am sorry . . ."

"I am not." Donald Bàn stopped him, quietly. "Better so. I could wish my own self with her."

"Not yet awhile, old friend," O'Brien told him. "Work there is for you, first."

The other looked up. "Maybe. A poor vessel I am, but willing."

Adam Metcalfe lay that night under the pale stars of a dark that was never black. Weary as he was, he was long in sleeping.

Cramped, chilled, in the stark light of a grey morning threatening rain, Adam surveyed the crowded strip of links at Bay of Tarve, and found it an even grimmer sight than he had realised behind the screen of the twilight. The grey-green sickle of the machair, between the beach and the sharply-rising hillside, was littered with people and beasts and poultry and plenishings, in apparently hopeless confusion and general uncleanliness—how, indeed, could it be otherwise? Stone was everywhere, gleaming quartz-shot stone, outcropping from the machair, bared on the harsh flank of Meall Garbh. Nowhere were there any trees or bushes, nor much vegetation at all save the bent-grass and the wiry heather. Along the rocks a number of figures crouched, fishing listlessly for rock-cod, with improvised lines and without much success. Over all an atmosphere of dejection and despair hung like a cloud. These people were down, stricken, most evidently. Perhaps it was his hunger that depressed him—he had refused Donald MacVarish's generous offer of a little thin porridge and milk for breakfast, saying that he still had some food with him. That was a lie, well intended; he had given the last of the provision Alison had made for him, to the youngster he had carried at his saddle last night, whose need had been great. And if *he* was hungry, what hunger there must be about him here . . . ! And he was condemning their dejection!

Adam was to be involved in another funeral that morning, his second during his short stay in Strathmoraig. Donald Bàn's wife was to be buried today, and another with her. It had been a problem finding anywhere with sufficient depth of soil decently to cover the bodies—that is the sort of place it was. But by making use of crevices between the rocks and of loose stones from the beach, something in the nature of a sepulchre was contrived. Father O'Brien had blessed and hallowed the ground yesterday. Donald Bàn was a Presbyterian of sorts, but he would not have his wife laid to rest by Andrew Hardie.

The business was not done perfunctorily or in haste; indeed, practically the entire evicted community, men, women and children, followed the bodies, that were wrapped in plaids and borne on rough biers on the shoulders of men. Ahead paced two pipers, whose lament, if less eerie than that other Adam had heard, was no less dolorous. Father O'Brien, in a crumpled vestment, followed the bearers, with Donald Bàn behind and the silent throng at his back. It was not far to the burial-place, so the pipers, by no means finished their voluntary, trod up and down a patch of turf nearby, and played their sorrow to its choking end, their eyes fixed and their cheeks scarlet. In the throbbing silence that succeeded, a great sigh went up from the company. Then, into the thin screaming of the wheeling sea-birds, and the shudder and sigh of the waves, that place's own lament, Michael O'Brien's voice rose clear and strong.

The burial-service was perhaps half-over when Adam felt a touch at his elbow, and turned to find Alison Hardie at his side. His smile of welcome may not have been entirely suitable to the occasion, but the young woman remembered her manners. Nodding towards the grave, she whispered, "Bridget MacVarish?"

"Yes—and somebody else, too. You've had an early start today, surely!"

"Ssh!" she said. Thus early does a woman commence to take a man in hand.

With the service over and the pipers returning to their refrain, the priest made his way towards them. "Good morning to you, Mistress Alison," he bowed. "You are a long way from home."

She flushed ever so slightly. "Not farther than I could wish to be, Mr O'Brien," she answered quietly.

He considered that for a moment, and nodded. "You will have your reasons," he allowed. Then he turned to the man. "'Twould be as good a time as any, this, to be giving your good advice to the crofters," he urged. "Donald MacVarish will be saying a word or two of thanks when we get back—the custom it is, though there'll be no hospitality to go with it, this time. Then will be the time for you."

The girl looked from one to the other quickly. "What is this, Adam . . . ?"

It was the priest who answered her. "Mr Metcalfe thinks that the folk should show some spirit, some fight, against their oppressors, if they are to survive at all. I say he is right, and should tell them so."

Alison's glance was anxious. "Right, maybe—but it is a big thing you are asking him to do."

"I know it, child," the other agreed. "I do not forget that Mr Metcalfe has his responsibilities towards his employer, however unworthy, when I suggest that he has still higher responsibilities as a Christian gentleman."

The girl began to speak, but Adam interrupted her. "I will speak to them," he announced briefly.

"Good, then."

Alison said nothing then, but she squeezed his hand.

Back at the encampment, with the crowd lingering, Donald Bàn, climbing on to a heap of stones, said what he had to say quietly and without heat. Adam understood nothing of it, though he did hear the name of Ewan MacVarish mentioned. Then another older man got up, quavering but more loquacious; no doubt he spoke on behalf of that other anonymous deceased. Frequently his voice broke, and once or twice he raised a gnarled fist above his head, in a gesture pathetic rather than defiant. When he finished, brokenly, something like a groan went up from the people.

The priest raised an eyebrow at Metcalfe, who moved over to him. "If I speak to them in English, how many will understand me?" he demanded.

164

"Enough to tell those that don't," came the answer. O'Brien stepped up, and spoke a few words in Gaelic. Then he motioned to Adam. A murmur of curiosity and expectancy ran through the assembly.

"I am not going to tell you all how sorry I am for you, or how much I regret what has been done to you," he began, speaking strongly, perhaps rather too strongly—that old illusion that by shouting he could make his English understood. "I *am* sorry, but my sorrow will not assist you at all, any more than your own. Some of you, no doubt, are disappointed in me. You hoped that I would be able to help you, and I have been no use to you at all. But I could have told you from the first that I could do little for you—I said as much, more than once—and if, by showing that I sympathised, I have led you to rely in any way on my efforts instead of on your own, then I have only done you a disservice by my sympathy. For I say to you that the only efforts that will really help you must come from yourself—all of you. You must fight, you must not lie down under the factor's whip, you must show that you are not dumb beasts, to be driven where he wills, but men and women with minds and wills of your own, and rights to be respected." He had stopped shouting now and was speaking earnestly, tensely, and there was no doubt that he had the attention of all. "If you had fought before this, you might still be in your crofts, but as it is you may still be able to get these terrible conditions improved. You can hardly lose by struggling, since he can do little worse to you than he has done already. You will most probably gain. John Dunn is taking big risks. It is fairly certain that he is going considerably further than Lord Alcaster's instructions. Trouble, resistance, will be the last thing he wants. If it is widespread, he will not be able to put it down with his own resources. He will have to compromise or call in outside aid— which he cannot wish to do. Humility is what he wants, meek acceptance of his orders—not rebellion. Surely, if it does nothing else, your resistance would give you the satisfaction of making things difficult for him. Support each other, so that it is not one man, or two, that he can single out, but all of you. Use your judgement, and try to keep as far as possible on the right

165

side of the law, but make yourselves such a nuisance that he will wonder whether results are worth all the trouble." He paused, and from somewhere amongst the crowd a voice was lifted in a high-pitched, skirling cry, significantly a woman's voice. It produced a thrill of emotion that raised a sibilant indrawn sigh from the company. Adam was not unaffected himself.

"All the world has heard of the fierce wild spirit of the Highlanders, of the proud traditions of your race," he cried. "Even now your husbands and sons and brothers are upholding that tradition gloriously on all the battlefields of Europe. Always the cry is for Highlanders, more Highlanders. They cannot do without them. Will you not show them that that spirit is not dead in the hills where it was born?"

He stepped down amidst a confused babble of noise, enthusiastic, critical, enquiring, till one of the pipers put his soul into his chanter and burst into fierce music, wild and challenging, that clinched the matter. In the uproar, Michael O'Brien gripped his hand. "'Tis eloquence you have, man Metcalfe—a gift and nothing else," he shouted. "That was the very word they wanted." His blue eyes were dancing. "For sure, I couldn't have done it better myself!"

Alison just touched his arm. "Good, Adam," she said softly.

It was a little later, when Adam Metcalfe was taking his leave of them, that Donald MacVarish added his comment. "Fine words those were, my friend, and true, never a doubt," he said. "It was brave talking—the best we have heard for many a day." He paused, and looked away over the grey water that was ribbed with white. "I am just hoping you do not have to pay the big price for them—nor us either!"

The younger man looked at him soberly. "I have thought of that, too," he answered him. "Mine I am prepared to pay, if need be. Yours you have paid already."

In that spirit he left them, to seek John Dunn.

The shroud of smoke that had covered Strathmoraig had fled before a freshening easterly breeze, but the stale, ominous smell of burning tainted every breath of wind, as Adam made for

Menardmore. And on the same wind, long ere he reached there, came a wailing sound that rose and fell and never ceased, that was indeed the logical complement of the reek of the smoke, the vociferous clamour of many sheep. As he approached the vicinity of the House, the noise became deafening, an unrelenting uproar that beat against the brain with its idiotic repetition. All the infields, that had been made sorely out of the pasture of the Menard crofts, were filled to overflowing with milling, bawling sheep. A large consignment of Bullough's new stock had arrived.

Adam picked out Bullough, and Dunn with him, at one of the great fanks, superintending the labours of many men, who strove with ruddle and pitch at the branding of protesting animals. Towards them he made his way, bracing himself for what was to come. He had need to.

Bullough observed him first, and spoke a word to the factor. Dunn looked up, stared, and jerking his head to his companion, strode forward, kicking a yelping dog and two flouncing sheep out of his way to do so.

It was not so much a meeting, this, as a clash, an impact. Many workers lifted their heads to watch. Bullough, as ever, followed just behind the factor. The younger man knew, not for the first time, a sense not so much of loneliness as of isolation. That was part of his burden. He had come to realise that he had a burden to bear in this place.

All around, the din continued.

John Dunn got in the first word. "Where have *you* been?" he shouted. He had halted close to his deputy, close enough to be menacing, but he had to shout, nevertheless, to be heard. He might well have shouted anyway.

Adam did not give ground, either in word or in person. "I have been down seeing your handiwork at Bay of Tarve," he answered him, steadily. "I have come here to protest . . . and to warn you."

"What?"

Adam did not repeat what he had said. It had been heard, he knew.

167

Dunn thrust his face close. "Did I hear ye say protest?"

"Yes—and warn!"

"Warn . . . !" The man's hand shot out and gripped the other's arm like a vice. "You! You'd warn *me*? My God . . . ?"

Metcalfe did not move. He knew that he could not twist his arm out of that grasp. He knew that he had not a half of this man's muscular strength. He had only his tongue to fight with. "Take your hand off me, Dunn," he said quietly, almost whispered, yet so tensely that his words cut clearly through the baa-ing. "Try and control your oafish habits when you are dealing with a gentleman!"

He heard the factor actually gulp. "Christ . . . !" he muttered thickly. The hold on Adam's arm tightened till it was almost unbearable, and there was a significant quiver behind the grip. He watched the colour suffuse the other's features, and almost, it seemed, his eyes, and waited.

What he had said was absurd, childish, crude—but only on the face of it. John Dunn came of lowly peasant stock, imbued with an irradicable respect for the gentry and their manners. It was his weakness, that he could not live it down. He tried, he was always trying. Adam had known it since the first words he had had with the man; the frequent jeers at 'the parson's son', the slighting but dareful references to Alcaster, the hatred of Ewan MacVarish, whose breeding was the most intangible and quietly apparent of all, that of a Highland gentleman, all pointed to it. So, below the surface, Adam's crudity was not crude at all. But it was dangerous. It could have only one of two results.

That it had the result it had, could have been due in part to a factor of which Metcalfe knew nothing. For the man suddenly broke into a laugh, a mirthless bellow that all but choked him. "Rich, burn me," he gasped, and he loosed the other's arm, but loosed it with a wrench that gave the lie to his laughing. "Harry, d'ye hear that? We're dealing with a gentleman! I say d'ye hear that . . . ? My God, let's get out o' this hellish row!" and thrusting round, he stamped and kicked his way through the press of sheep, toward the road. Adam followed, with Bullough bringing up the rear.

At a dip in the road about half-way up the hill towards the House, Dunn turned about and stood, his hands clasped at his back, his head forward, his eyes narrowed. He might have been before his own fireplace. "There be one or two things I've got to say to you, young man," he snapped. "Just one or two. But I think we'll hear your protest . . . and your warning, first." He shot a grin at Bullough. "Happen we might not have the privilege of hearing them afterwards—eh, Harry? And that would be a pity, lad, a pity." He was very confident now, and entirely at his ease, rocking a little back and forwards on toes and heels, and smiling. But, as the other said no word, the smile switched off. "Well, man—speak up," he rasped.

Adam chose his words carefully—he did not like Dunn's assurance. "I have seen what you have done to Glen Luie and the rest, while I have been away, and I have heard how it was done," he said, "—and I cannot congratulate you on your wisdom or your humanity. But, leaving that aside for the moment, what I must protest against are the conditions you have deliberately imposed down at the coast. They are unbelievable, shameful—and a disgrace to any estate. By your decrees and restraints you have made it impossible for these people to live there. The ground you have given them in exchange for their crofts is worthless, absolutely useless—as well you know. I blame myself that I should ever have accepted your word that the alternative holdings would be suitable. I should have gone to see. I might have known! Of a set cold-blooded purpose you are working to destroy a well-doing inoffensive people, for the sake of private gain. I cannot imagine that Lord Alcaster will thank you. He has a personal connection with these people—he is their Chief . . ."

Dunn raised a hoot of a laugh. "Hark at him!" he cried. "Alcaster . . . ! D'ye hear that, Harry?"

"And as to warning," Adam went on steadily, "I tell you that you will have trouble, serious trouble, if you do not improve conditions down there—and quickly. The people are roused, justifiably . . ."

"Trouble—I like trouble. If there's any trouble here, I'll make it, sink me! And if I do, they'd better look out, same as yourself, my cock."

"You may like trouble, Dunn, but does the Earl?"

"The Earl—Alcaster!" he shouted. "Always Alcaster!" He beat the heavy dog-whip that he was apt to carry on the stone dyke of the roadside. "Enough o' this, b'God. Here, you—see this," and fumbling in his skirts-pocket, he produced a paper, two sheets of a letter, obviously. The first page he retained, and the second he thrust at Adam. "Read that," he commanded.

The younger man took the paper with a sinking heart. There was an elaborate design of coronet and crest at the top. Beneath, he read:

. . . and shall be glad to observe your progress. I am informed that mutton and wool prices are rising steadily.

As to your inquiry regarding Metcalfe, I can assure you that he was sent up to Strathmoraig in no other capacity than that of assistant to yourself, and certainly not as any personal friend of mine. If he has given you to understand otherwise then he has done so without warrant, and you will know what steps to take, no doubt. He is quite an able youth, but headstrong—a weakness contributed to, foolishly, I am afraid by the attentions of certain members of my family in the past, a state of affairs that is not my intention should continue. I suggest a strong hand, such as, I understand, you are well able to wield.

As regards the expenditure on shepherds' houses, this seems rather an excessive charge . . .

Adam read no more—he had read enough. Desperately he sought to marshal his thoughts. Only as he read had it come to him how much he had built, in his relations with Dunn, on this spurious foundation of Alcaster's friendship. It had been his one card, and he had used it to the full, come to rely on it—not for his own sake, to be sure—and now his bluff was called, and he had no other card to play . . . except maybe? Precipitately his mind worked. He started reading the letter again to give him time to try and think out a course of action—but back his thoughts went, to Humphrey Augustus that had been his friend once, closer than brothers ... they had played together, schooled together, hunted together, wenched together, and ...

But the factor was giving him no time for consideration. He reached out and snatched the letter. "Well," he gibed, "how's the fine gentleman now, the friend of Lord Alcaster? Ye see what your lord says?" Then, as so often, fury swept over him. "God, I'll make ye pay for this, you damned jackanapes, you! Did ye think ye could fool John Dunn? Blind me, ye'll be sorry for this. Ye made a bad mistake, there, and now it's out it'll break ye ..."

Swift as a rapier-stroke Adam's voice thrust in. "Like your's— your double game, factor and sheep-speculator!"

"What do ye mean?" Each word stood by itself.

"I mean that I know you are deeply involved in Bullough's ventures—that your money is in it—that you are working hand-in-glove with him, at the estate's cost." And as Dunn took a step closer. "And others know it, besides myself, so you need not think that you can ..."

Adam saw the factor's whip-hand lift, and Bullough stumble forward, arm outstretched. Throwing up his own arm instinctively, he was aware of an agonising pain, a blinding flash, yellow to red, a violent persistent red ... and nothing more.

17

JUST as a thunderstorm, that has loomed oppressively, after the sudden violence of its breaking may leave the air clearer and fresher for its fury, and the waiting for violence frequently be harder to bear than the violence itself, so Adam Metcalfe found himself in the days that followed to some extent released from the dread of violence, that, barely acknowledged, had dwelt with him for many days. He had tasted of it, and found himself by no means daunted.

He had come to himself, that day, some time later, lying on a couch within the House of Menardmore, with a splitting head, a throbbing arm, and a comprehensive sickness. Bullough had been standing watching him—of Dunn there was no sign—a blandly solicitous Bullough, who had offered cold water or brandy, and the affable suggestion that Mr Metcalfe should really be more careful—accidents will happen, and stone walls apt to be hard on the head. He had had only a tumble this time, he could assure him, but a little circumspection in future might be advisable, he thought. It would be a pity if, through not watching where he was going, he should trip up again, with possible more serious results . . . Was Mr Metcalfe sure that he could walk well enough? There was no hurry to leave . . .

Adam, dizzy, supporting a swollen wrist, that turned out to be fractured, and with a contusion on his brow where the whip-handle had struck him, had made his unsteady way back to Achroy. His anger had been more definite than his alarm.

He did not go near Menardmore for the next few days, deeming an arm in a sling all the excuse necessary—especially in the circumstances—and no one came from the House to ask for his health. He did make his way, however, more than once, to the Manse, where a young woman, with eyes that were clear as well as soft, was not even momentarily deceived by his talk of an unfortunate accident, and bravely refrained from giving him urgent advice with her sympathy. He did not encounter the minister on his first visit, but on the second occasion Andrew Hardie intercepted him on his way round to the farmery behind the house, and had made his attitude quite clear, and that briefly. Mr Metcalfe would oblige him by refraining from calling at the Manse in future. That was all. Alison, overtaking him afterwards, explained that her uncle had heard from Dunn of Adam's true relationship with Alcaster, and had been deeply moved. He had forbidden her to have anything further to do with a fellow who had only been tolerated hitherto owing to his supposed connection with an Earl. She suggested that they meet in future in the wood just across the hanging-bridge, where, where . . . he knew! He knew.

From Alison also, he learned that conditions were by no means improving down at Bay of Tarve. She had not been down again herself—her uncle disapproved—but she had heard from Art Munro the packman. They could not get on with the house-building at all without timber, try as they would, and the rain and exposure was producing much sickness. There had been some trouble too, disturbances—his advice was not being ignored. Some of them had cut down one or two rowan trees and small birches that they had found growing in a ravine, and when one of the factor's men had interfered, he had been turned on, decried, and finally driven off. Another party had gone back over the hills to Glen Luie to try to recover some of their property—more than one had gone before, alone, and been turned back and assaulted—and when they had threatened them, the watchers had come in for some quite rough handling. And one of the rangers that had been set to see that the crofters' cattle did not stray off their own miserable pasture on to better ground, and who had attempted to molest a young woman, was thrown into a burn to cool his ardour. The Highland spirit appeared to be reviving.

All this was confirmed by Ian MacErlich, who visited Achroy dramatically every now and then, inserting himself through a window—even when the door stood open—or creeping stealthily along the walls after making elaborate signals and dartings from the garden shrubberies, as was his nature. He told of night raids into the hills after deer and hares, for food—not all of which passed off without a clash with the estate's minions; of a spirited protest against the factor's new edict that a percentage of all fish caught must go to the estate in exchange for the laird's mussels which were being used as bait; and of the occasion when Hopkins, searching the croft-houses at Invermoraig for some old folk from the cleared glens whom he suspected had taken refuge there, had been quite decisively manhandled. Though he did not say so in as many words, Ian implied that he himself had been fairly prominent in all these gallant affairs—as well as in others that he was too modest to mention. Ian More MacErlich was a natural-born actor.

Things came to a head presently. An evening or two after these tidings came his way, Adam received a curt note from Dunn requiring him to report at Menardmore for duty next morning. The man Colin, who brought the message, indicated, fearfully, that the factor was in a terrible great rage, whatever.

Adam sought out Ewan MacVarish's pistol from his bedroom upstairs. Ewan would have been wiser to have had it with him always.

On a still grey morning, her oars splintering the glassy surface of the water, Mairi MacErlich rowed him across the loch, with Ian Beg towing a toy boat in their wake. It was all idyllic, peaceful.

Up at the House, Adam found that the factor's party had not waited for him. There were instructions for him to follow them down the strath-road. Astride a pony, he came up with them not far from the Manse. Dunn ignored preliminaries. After a sustained and pointed stare at the other's brow and arm, he spoke. "If it isn't asking too much, *Mister* Metcalfe, to expect you to attend to your duties once in a while, I'll be obliged if you'll accompany us down to the coast. Your precious friends there seem to be needing a lesson."

"I told you you would have trouble," Adam retorted.

"And *I* told you that *I* would make the trouble, didn't I? Aye—if it's trouble they seek, happen they're going to find it! Curse me, d'ye know what they've had the damned insolence to do, the scum? They've started stealing the deer, they've tried to stop my men carrying out their instructions—they've even threatened and attacked them. And now, they've tried to make a fool of me—of Harry Bullough. They even laughed in his face. B'God, this is going to stop."

Adam had to smile slightly. "Perhaps Mr Bullough may have been annoying them ... all unwittingly, of course," he suggested mildly. "It is strange. Normally they are so very polite, almost unnaturally so."

"I was only warning them to keep their beasts off my land— a thing I have every right to do," Bullough asserted.

"Your land ... ?"

"The land I have rented."

"Ah!" Adam nodded. "Perhaps their cattle have not yet learned to recognise your land—it is unfenced as yet, you will remember ... ?"

"Bah!" John Dunn roared, and marched on down the road. The others followed him, one man and a constable leading ponies, and Bullough mounted. Dunn himself would never put his legs across one of the despised Highland garrons. Soon he turned round again. "I'll teach them," he proclaimed definitely. "I'll make them sorry."

"Would it not be simpler to make them happy—to improve their conditions?"

He got no answer. That last had been a final statement.

They moved down with the rock-bound river, a small party, silent and awkward. Adam was surprised at the smallness of the party, taking into account its apparent errand, till he considered; with all the glens and the grazings and the fishings to be watched, the factor's man-power was being taxed to the utmost. The flood of Dunn's prohibitions and decrees entailed a widespread system of enforcement. There conceivably might come a time when John Dunn would find that he had bitten off rather more than he readily could chew.

The factor and his assistant had but the one further bout of conversation during all the rest of the long journey. Adam it was who started it. "I understand that you are forcing the crofters to purchase the timber they need for their houses?"

"I am not forcing anybody to purchase anything," Dunn snapped.

"They cannot build new houses *without* wood."

"Then they should have used the wood from their old hovels."

"You burned it."

"Not without warning them—you it was who gave them the warning, wasn't it! Maybe ye didn't do it properly."

"You did not give them a chance."

"I gave them weeks of notice. Not one of them moved a stick. After term-day they had no rights on the property. If they were too lazy to remove their stuff, they've just got to buy new, that's all."

Adam did not speak for a moment or two. Then, "What price are you charging?" he asked coldly.

"A crown for young fir poles, a half for birch—to be cut by themselves, under supervision."

"You do not underestimate their value."

The man grinned, in the way he had. "I do not," he said.

Adam made a brief calculation. "I will buy fifty fir and one hundred birch."

"You . . . ?"

"Yes. You cannot object to that, can you?"

"Object!" Dunn barked. "Not likely. If ye're fool enough, I'll take your money. It'll be the first good the estate's had out o' ye since ever ye came, curse me." And then, violently, "Ye're a damned obstinate young fool, Metcalfe!"

The other pulled his pony back, and silence descended again on the party.

At Invermoraig, where the river joined the sea, they halted while Dunn made arrangements for their accommodation for the night in an empty cot-house amongst the crofts. Then they moved on up the coast.

The factor's party must have been observed some time before it reached Bay of Tarve, for, by the time they topped the headland, with the encampment below them, a large crowd had gathered. As they went towards it, Adam's feelings were chaotic.

In complete silence they drew close, and the crowd opened to admit them, and then, still wordless, closed in again at their backs. The factor's man and the constable glanced swiftly around, and their eyes were uneasy. John Dunn strode straight on, looking right ahead of him. Bullough was just at his elbow, dismounted now, preoccupied apparently—but not quite exclusively—with the clouds above. Metcalfe came just a little way behind.

Suddenly the factor halted, and slowly turning, his glare swept the circle of faces. His jaw, prominent, aggressive, worked steadily.

From behind him, a voice spoke quietly, mild-seeming for the occasion. "We are glad to see you here, Mr Dunn—though in honesty I cannot give you welcome to the place."

Dunn whirled round. "Ah—the other MacVarish!" he cried. "That was a lie, too. You are not glad to see me, I'll wager."

"I tell no lie, John Dunn." Donald Bàn had stepped a little way out from the press, and two others just behind him, a big white-haired man whom Adam did not know, and Ian More MacErlich. "There are things that we are wanting to tell you— things that we are wanting you to see, here. It is because we have complaints to make, that I said we were glad to see you."

"Complaints! Good God, d'ye think I came all this way to hear your damned complaints? If ye've any complaints, ye can come up and make them at the proper time at the estate office . . . and they'd better be genuine, or believe me, it'll be a sorry man that brings them." His little eyes gleamed, darting to either side, and narrowed in a sudden decision. He spoke slowly. "And somehow, Mister MacVarish, I don't think there may *be* so many complaints in the end, after all." He swung round in a half-circle, and his stubby finger, jabbing at random, pointed to a certain middle-aged crofter. "You!" he shouted. "Have you any complaints to make—legal ones, mind?"

The man gaped, stepped back a pace, and his lips moved silently.

"Well?" Dunn demanded.

The crofter shook his head bewilderedly, and muttered a few words in Gaelic.

"No complaints!" the factor jeered, and, as his glance swept the circle, everywhere there was just the least movement backwards. His hand shot out towards another. "You, then. Have you anything to say?"

This man, a toothless ancient, grinned foolishly, and turned to either side to seek the help of his neighbours. He was beginning to shake his head likewise, when a woman spoke in his ear. Fear, indecision, and then a desperate resolve, was apparent in his old red-rimmed eyes. "*Mo mart*, my cow," he faltered, "she is taken, held by your men."

"In the pound for straying, eh? You should not let her stray."

"But there is no holding them. The land you gave us has no *feur*, no pasture to it. The beasts will stray where they will be finding the good grazing."

"Then hobble them."

The old man stared, not understanding. Someone translated for him. "That we did try, too, sir. But on the steep brae-side that is all that you have given us, the beasts just do be falling and their legs breaking. Many are dead."

"Then appoint herds to watch them. Build a wall; there's plenty stone. Your brutes must keep off the ground that Mr Bullough has rented for sheep grazing. And if you are too damned lazy to do it, you must pay your fines to get your cattle back, that's all."

"It is not lazy I am," the ancient quavered. "All day I am at the fishing . . . I am trying to make a house . . . I have no money for the fine . . ."

"That's enough." Dunn stopped him. "I said complaints, not snivelling whimpers at the results of your own idleness. You sit on your bottoms all day, and call the estate responsible. Now, you—" he pointed at the woman who had prompted the old man, "—you, that were so quick at telling the old fool what to say. Have you anything to say *now*?"

The woman looked him in the eye. She did not attempt to counter him in the unfamiliar English. But she addressed him forcefully, fluently, in a stream of Gaelic and gesture whose import required no interpreting. Condemnation, fierce and scornful, was apparent in every word, and as she spoke, from the crowd a murmur rose and swelled.

John Dunn did not like it. "Stop it!" he roared. "Enough o' that jabber." Quickly he went on, "If ye've no complaints, I have—plenty. Only, I'm not complaining—I'm acting. I'm making sure there'll be no more complaints." His voice grated. "Now, first, I want the men who attacked this man, Richards, in the performance of his duty. He tried to stop them, three of them, deer-poaching, and they set on him. Who was it?"

Once again complete silence held the company.

Dunn waited, his eyes busy. "Come on—out with you," he cried, ". . . or it will be the worse for you when I *do* lay hands on you—as I will, b'God!"

The people stood, mutely hostile.

"All right." The factor turned. "Richards, you said you would know these men again. D'ye see them here?"

The man gulped. "Can't say as 'ow I do, sir. I can't see that many o' their faces."

"Go amongst them and look, then—and when ye've found them, bring 'em here." And when the fellow hesitated, "Go on, man, blast you—what are ye waiting for? I want those men."

Richards, with faltering step, moved round the ring of impassive figures, found a gap, looked backwards doubtfully, and was swallowed up in the crowd.

"Now," Dunn resumed deliberately, "we'll have the men that went skulking back to Glen Luie and attacked this constable and another of my men. Five o' them, there were."

Apart from the slight ripple set up by the man Richards' halting progress, there was no movement from the watching throng, hardly so much as the flicker of an eyelid. It might have

179

been stricken to immobility.

The factor's frown became a glare. He appeared to be having some difficulty with his breathing. "Are ye all deaf?" he demanded. "Ye heard what I said? Come here the men who attacked this constable in Glen Luie."

He waited through perhaps half a strained minute, and then, striding across, he confronted Donald Bàn. "You, MacVarish—who are those men?"

The Highlandman shook his head silently.

"God damn you, you'll tell me! I demand an answer, in the Name of the Law. You, who boast of your honesty—do you know these men?"

Donald Bàn spoke then, slowly, quietly, as ever. "Yes, I know them, John Dunn . . . but I could not be telling you."

"You could not . . . !" The man's voice rose nearly to a scream. Adam, behind him, saw the thick neck change from red almost to black above his neckcloth. Bullough took a hasty pace forward, and his hand plunged into the skirts of his coat, where an ominous bulge was evident. Adam, too, stepping forward, reached for his pocket, and his hand closed on the butt of his pistol. He was past considering questions of conduct and responsibility; only essentials mattered now.

Dunn's great fists were lifting slowly, the circle of tense-faced crofter-folk drew imperceptibly closer, and Bullough's left hand was already at the other's shoulder, when MacErlich made his gesture. Stepping quickly in front of MacVarish, he drew himself up to his full height, one hand thrust within his plaid. "Keep you your distance, John Dunn," he cried. "You are not going to treat Donald MacVarish as you treated Ewan!"

It was extremely dramatic, shamelessly ostentatious, but by no means an empty show, with John Dunn the man he was facing.

That man reacted quickly. Both his hands shot out, gripped the other's arms just above the elbows, and jerked him violently forward. At the same time, Dunn's knee came up viciously and caught the Highlandman full in the pit of the stomach. And as, with a gasp and a groan combined, MacErlich doubled-up, he

180

was hurled backwards. He was not a small man, nor light, but he was thrown a matter of yards back amongst the press, where he fell to the ground writhing. It was all done in a couple of moments. Dunn spared him no further glance. He turned back to Donald MacVarish. "Now, you!" he said.

Adam drew a deep breath, and came nearer, but before he could speak another voice was lifted. "'Tis not one man you have to be dealing with, Dunn, it is all of us, whatever." It was the big elderly man at MacVarish's elbow, a stooping bearded figure that had been a giant once. His words drew a murmur of approval from the crowd. He was the smith of Glen Evoch, and a man of importance amongst them.

It looked for a moment as though the factor would deal with him as he had done with Ian More, but he seemed to change his mind. "Are you going to tell me those names, MacVarish?" he demanded.

"I am not, then," Donald Bàn gave back steadily. "You heard Angus, here?"

"So be it, then." Dunn's brief spell of action appeared to have done him good, restored his poise. "If ye are all collectively responsible, so much the better—so much the easier for me." He turned round. "Constable—arrest five men, any five ye like . . . and ye can include that fool MacErlich amongst them."

The constable, like the man Richards, now disappeared, was not too happy about the situation. They were not quite men of Dunn's calibre. Looking round the circle of faces, he decided in his prudence, to make a start with one who was a casualty already. He advanced on MacErlich.

Ian More was on his feet now, his breathing partly recovered. Wild-eyed, he backed before the oncoming constable, one hand outstretched as though to ward him off. "Keep your hands off me," he cried, his voice breaking as it rose. "*Iosa Criosd*, don't you be touching me." Around him the crofters closed.

The constable wavered, and glanced back at the factor. Dunn exploded into an oath, and stamped forward. "Sink me, must I do everything?" he exclaimed. He came up to MacErlich. "You, blast you—you're arrested, in the King's name!"

The other still shrank back. "You will not take me, I tell you. You will not."

"Will I not!" Grinning, the factor raised his hand.

"No, my God!" Incredibly swift, Ian More's hand darted within his plaid and flashed out again. Desperate, at bay, he crouched, and a long slender-bladed knife gleamed evilly within his fist.

The sequence of events thereafter was rapid and confused. The constable, in his anxiety to get out of harm's way, blundered back into John Dunn, and was thereupon hurled violently aside. Bullough, some distance in the rear, tugged out his pistol, glanced at the priming, and advanced to his friend's aid. Adam Metcalfe grabbed his own weapon, and then thought better of it. Quick as his thought he came up behind Bullough, and brought down the edge of his hand, with all his might, on the other's wrist. "Drop that, you fool!" he cried, "Do you want a riot? You haven't a chance with that—there's hundreds against you."

The pistol dropped, and he stooped to pick it up and pocket it, heedless of the big man's urgent protest. Together they moved toward the factor.

But, though they had not realised it, the whole situation had changed. John Dunn, swearing and blaspheming horribly, his red face suddenly strangely pale, was edging back foot by foot, and Ian More, still crouching and full of menace, was following, the wicked blade of his *sgian dubh* weaving and quivering. He was speaking too, a sibilant murmur beneath his breath, not English, that was only occasionally to be distinguished through the flood of the other's fury. Stuttering curses, threatening a terrible vengeance, incoherent, malignant, the factor gave ground, his eyes fixed unwaveringly on that flickering knife. Most obviously, John Dunn had a horror of cold steel.

At his elbow, Bullough started to speak, but Dunn cut him short with an oath. He started pushing his friend away with his left hand, while he himself edged away over to the right. Soon his object was apparent. He wanted Bullough to get over to the

182

flank, so that MacErlich could not give undivided attention to himself. Ian More saw it too, stopped, and straightened up, his dagger still very evident.

"I have a mind just to cut out the foul black heart of you, John Dunn," he cried. "Likely never will I be having a better chance. You have done so much hurt in your time that God could not but be forgiving me for ridding the world of you. You are a coarse, ill-mannered cur, with the heart of a weasel and the breeding of a rat." Ian More was enjoying himself.

"Where's that pistol?" The words were hissed across from the factor to Bullough. It was the measure of his defeat that he, who had declared to his assistant that he never carried a weapon, that his own strong arm was all that was required, should thus call for the help of firearms.

"Metcalfe's got it."

Dunn just had time to shoot a glance of sheerest malice at Adam, when MacErlich, on the crest of the wave now, started forward. "Pistol, is it!" he cried. "Thunder of God, is that the way of it!" and his dagger-hand flashed upward.

John Dunn had seen and heard enough. Backing again, quickly, he shouted to Bullough, "Come on, we'll get out o' this," and to Adam, "Metcalfe, since you love them, you can deal with this accursed rabble," took a deep breath, and turning about, plunged back through the crowd. And as the crowd parted before him, somebody laughed, and quickly, all around, the laughter was taken up and spread—not just jeers and mockery, but the laughter of relief and sheer amusement. The factor was apparent, for the first time, minus his power and his dignity, a short-legged squat man in a great hurry to be away from that place. They found it funny. And Ian More MacErlich, head back, tossed his *sgian dubh* into the air, a whirling, glittering living thing, and deftly caught it again, and his laughing was the loudest of all.

At the patiently-waiting ponies John Dunn seized the first, and, for wonder, hurled himself on to its back, dug it viciously with his heels, and clattered off. The constable made a good second, and Bullough followed on, rather less hurriedly. Then another great shout of laughter rose from the throng. The man Richards, shouting his anxiety, had broken from the crowd and was running like a hare after his master, pursued joyously by a yelping, lanky young sheep-collie, that, tied by a string to the wrist of an aged woman, perforce dragged her after it, spindle-legged and screeching, in apparently furious chase. The gathering howled its appreciation.

Presently, a little way off, Dunn reined-in and turned his garron, and waited for the others to come up with him. He sat, while they came around him and passed him, staring back at the crofters in an attitude of what can only be described as brooding hate. Then, suddenly, he raised his clenched fist above his head, and shook it, wordlessly, viciously. And the mirth and talk of the crowd failed and stilled before the sheer concentrated malevolence of the gesture. Wheeling his beast, he moved on in the wake of the others.

Adam Metcalfe turned round. "You are a terrible man, Ian MacErlich," he said. "I wonder what Mrs. MacErlich will have to say about all this?"

Ian More threw up his chin. "Mairi MacErlich will say the word that a woman should," he proclaimed. "She does be knowing her place." Then relaxing, and speaking confidentially in Adam's ear, "Just the same, it might be the kind thing not to be troubling her with it, Mr Metcalfe. You know the women."

"Kindness and prudence," came Donald MacVarish's musing murmur, "'Tis not every day you find them hand in hand."

Adam spent that night at Invermoraig, as arranged—but alone. The factor's party had passed through, going hard, but had not even paused to say that they were not stopping. In the morning, he started off on his long walk up Strathmoraig—it was his pony that Dunn had commandeered in his need. He took his time. He was not over-anxious to reach the end of his journey. Passing the Manse in the afternoon, happily if not entirely fortuitously, he had a meeting with Alison. He had much to say to her, not all of it relevant to this chronicle.

It was evening, then, before he arrived back at Achroy. He

found a bored lieutenant in sole charge.

"Thank God you've come," Seton greeted him. "I have not had a soul to speak to all day—except that MacErlich woman. And you know, Metcalfe . . . sometimes I think that female is laughing at me."

"Never!" Adam proclaimed incredulously. "And the Manse is so far away, of course!"

"Well . . . I had a notion . . . You see, Miss Alison gave me a kind of hint." He looked uncomfortable. "Well, anyway," he blurted, "I'm no poacher."

"Um!" Adam said. "Ah . . . and—er—where is your uncle?"

"He's gone. The factor arrived over here last night late—we were just going to bed. He was in a bit of a state—in fact he was in the very devil of a rage, I thought, about something or other. He had a long discussion with my uncle—I don't know what about—and the upshot of it all was that they all left for Dingwall first thing this morning, Mr Dunn, Mr Bullough, and my uncle. Deuced queer."

"Dingwall!" Adam stared. "Now why should Dunn dash off to Dingwall . . . and take the Colonel?"

"I haven't a notion," Seton admitted. "They did not tell me a thing. I'm afraid Uncle Ronald is a bit of a clam at times. It is a long way to Dingwall."

"Yes," Adam agreed slowly. "And I would very much like to know why they went."

18

THEY had a full week to wait before they discovered why John Dunn went to Dingwall—the county town being over fifty long miles distant, across the wildest country in all Scotland. During that time Adam found himself in undisputed control of the estate—or nearly undisputed, since Hopkins was the complete obstructionist, and Bullough's head-shepherd made what trouble he could.

The deputy-commissioner made hay while the brief and unexpected sun shone. He got the crofters' roof-trees cut, and, since it was to be done only under estate supervision, he dutifully supervised it himself, and provided ponies to assist at the timber's transport. He emptied the pound of the crofters' straying cattle, commuting the fines—they could be paid out of his own not very full pocket if the worst came to the worst. He authorised the evicted tenants to repair to the Invermoraig peat-bog, and cut as much peat as would solve the fuel problem for the meantime at least. The Invermoraig people promptly joined in the good work, and for days, all those who were not wood-cutting or house-building, men, women and children, were cutting and carting and stacking peat. He arranged that volunteers from the crofting areas that had not yet been evicted, should go to Bay of Tarve and assist with the construction work to be done there, and he even sent a message, by Ian MacErlich, up to a coastal village that he had come across in one of his northern surveys, asking one or two of the men to come down and teach the art of sea-fishing, at which they were expert, to the evicted. Other things he did too, that John Dunn would not have thanked him for—but which he had not expressly prohibited. He made men work hard, and he worked hard himself, knowing the time short.

It was a strange thing, that Adam, preoccupied as he was with the prospect of the factor's return, dreading it hourly indeed, should, in the event, remain so long ignorant of his arrival and his subsequent actions, which all the rest of Strathmoraig learned only too soon. It was Saturday night, eight days after Dunn's departure, and Adam, just finished his supervision of the last day's tree-felling, was heading up Moraig-side for Achroy, when just across the suspension-bridge he found Alison Hardie waiting for him. His smile of pleasure at finding her there—not so unusual a thing, indeed—faded before her expression.

"Oh, Adam!" she cried. "Have you heard? I have been to Achroy, and came back here, hoping I'd catch you. It is terrible . . ."

"Yes, my dear," he soothed. "Is it Dunn again?"

"Yes—have you heard? He's back—and he has brought the soldiers with him."

"Soldiers . . . ! Good Lord!"

"And the Sheriff, too. They've arrested ten of the crofters as hostages already, and they are threatening terrible things. It is awful . . . What are we to do now?"

The man stared straight in front of him, unseeing. "Soldiers," he repeated. "—I never thought. My God, I never thought of that!"

There was no doubt that Adam Metcalfe had miscalculated. He had reckoned on John Dunn being anxious that his troubles in Strathmoraig should not be noised abroad, that the unorthodoxy of some of his activities should receive a minimum of publicity, and accordingly he had advised resistance. An extra constable or two, assistance from neighbouring estates, even some sort of pressure from the legal authorities, he had been prepared for. But not the military. He had underestimated both the man's boldness and his ruthlessness; most evidently he was prepared to go to all lengths in support of his interests, to take all risks—as perhaps was only consistent, since no doubt his all was at stake. Yes, Adam Metcalfe had miscalculated—his dread now, was the price that others might have to pay for his error.

Dunn wasted no time. The very next morning the word went out that there would be a meeting the day following, Monday, at Menardmore, to be attended by the crofters, not only from Bay of Tarve, but from all Strathmoraig. Every tenant and able-bodied man must be present, and distance from the venue would not be accepted as an excuse for non-attendance. The Sheriff's authority, it appeared, was behind the summons, and half a company of the garrison of Fort George was behind the Sheriff, and it would be a foolhardy crofter indeed who stayed away.

Adam, beyond making a brief report at Menardmore, and being pointedly ignored in front of the Sheriff and the officers in charge of the troops, had no further contact with the factor prior to the meeting. No doubt Dunn was well-informed as to his junior's activities during his absence by Hopkins.

He made his way early to the meeting, which was to be held on level ground near the loch-shore—very convenient for the promotors, if a long day's journey for the evicted tenants—and timed for late afternoon, in the hope of conferring with Donald MacVarish. But though Donald Bàn had come early too, he had no speech with him. He came, along with nine others, including Angus Ross the smith, their hands tied behind their backs, in charge of a platoon of soldiers, an exhibit and a warning.

Eyeing the people as they assembled in that place, in twos and threes and large parties, Adam saw them silent and seemingly cowed and apprehensive. He found himself to be avoided, even by men with whom he had been tree-felling only two days ago, not in enmity or reproach so much as in embarrassment, and perhaps a mannerliness that would not look at a man in his eclipse. Of Ian MacErlich there was no sign.

John Dunn made an impressive arrival, preceded by the rest of the troops and followed by the Sheriff, Andrew Hardie, and a bevy of constables. Presumably it was the Sheriff's entrance, but it was the factor who dominated the scene. They took up their position on a little knoll crowned by a single pine tree, and the soldiers shepherded the crowd around them. John Dunn held up his hand.

"Quiet!" he shouted—unnecessarily as far as the crofters were concerned. "The Sheriff here has something to say to you. It will be to your advantage to listen carefully. He has come a long way, and he is not going to waste his time." He turned and bowed briefly to the undistinguished-looking little man at his side.

The Sheriff had a high-pitched squeaky voice that went aptly with his appearance, noticeably unimpressive after the factor's broad North-country harshness. "People of Strathmoraig," he began, "as His Majesty's principal Law Officer for these parts, I am here to inform you—to *demonstrate* to you—that that Law cannot be flouted, as you have flouted it." He spoke with the clipped pedantry of the Edinburgh lawyer. "Order must and will prevail, if not by conviction, then by, ahem, constraint. My purpose here is twofold—firstly, to restore law and order permanently, and secondly, to apprehend and duly punish those who have been responsible for these reprehensible disturbances. With these ends in view I have selected some ten of your number,"—he produced a paper and read in a dry and creaky voice the names of the ten hostages—"who, having refused to divulge the persons of the real culprits, I have arrested as accessories after the fact. These men will be held in custody till such time as the prime offenders are delivered up, and due recognisance produced regarding your future conduct. I trust that I make myself clear?"

It is safe to say that not one in ten of his listeners understood even the gist of his wordiness. But from the densest throng a voice answered him. "And what is to be the fate of these hostages should your methods not achieve the results desired, Mr Sheriff?"

Adam thought that he recognised that voice, despite the impression gained that the speaker was trying to disguise it. It looked as though John Dunn had done so, also. He turned quickly to Andrew Hardie and said a few words, and then to the captain in charge of the soldiers, who with Colonel Dunbar and Alexander Seton, stood nearby. They all looked in the direction from which the query had come.

The Sheriff answered at some length. It seemed that, in the circumstances, he would be justified in ordering the severest measures, in view of the recalcitrant attitude of the district and the perilous state of the country—in the well-being of which they appeared to have no interest. He went on to elaborate this theme of their obvious lack of love for and sense of duty towards their country.

Adam felt a touch at his elbow. He looked round to find Ian More there, a bonnet pulled well-down to his eyes, and an ancient patched cloak thrown about him, looking thoroughly conspiratorial. He put a finger to his lips. "Hush!" he whispered. "'Tis just myself—Ian MacErlich. The mannie there must not see me."

Despite himself Adam had to smile.

"Myself and Michael O'Brien have a ploy, a plan," he went on. "Be you ready for anything, Mr Metcalfe," and nodding mysteriously, he disappeared back into the ranks of the crofters.

The Sheriff had got to the end of his reply, ". . . and whether it will be to transportation or defence works or just to gaol, they will be sent South under escort. The remedy lies in your own hands," he concluded. "It is my duty to see that the law is enforced, and I will do my duty—to the utmost."

He moved back a little into the knot of his supporters, but John Dunn spoke a word in his ear, nodding towards a segment of the crowd. The Sheriff stepped forward again.

But before he could speak another voice was raised, Adam Metcalfe's voice. "Mr Sheriff!" he called. "You say that it is your duty to see that the law is enforced. Is it not, even more typically, your duty to see that justice is done?"

The other started, cleared his throat, and turned to Dunn. That man shrugged and tossed a contemptuous word. The Sheriff spoke, frowning. "That goes without saying. It is justice I seek—the punishment of the guilty, the putting-down of violence, the re-establishment of authority, without which all talk of justice is a mockery."

The man's smugness incensed Adam Metcalfe—and he was roused already. "Is not the burning of these people's homes and the driving them down to a barren coast devoid of shelter or food—is that not violence?" he cried. "Would not the putting-down of a totally illegal system of fines and prohibitions by the estate, seizures and destruction of tenant's personal belongings—would not that be the establishment of authority? And who is most guilty, the tenants who at long last have protested against a reign of cruelty, brutality and intimidation, or the man who is responsible for it all—whether he calls himself factor and magistrate or not?"

Affront, uneasiness, and even alarm, showed themselves on the Sheriff's face. He sought his snuff-box and consideration. "Young man," he said pompously, "I cannot imagine that you are serious in your preposterous charges, but I would warn you that this is no time for unconsidered talk . . ."

Adam interrupted. "I can assure you, sir, that I am deadly serious . . . and are charges preposterous that a hundred witnesses can substantiate?"

The Sheriff was visibly shaken. He looked behind him. The factor spoke to him urgently, impatiently, almost commandingly. Andrew Hardie, too, appeared to produce very definite advice.

Adam, all caution cast aside, went on. "As for unconsidered talk, sir, will you record that I, Adam Metcalfe, Deputy-Commissioner to Lord Alcaster, before yourself as Sheriff and this gathering as witness, hereby charge John Dunn with robbery, grand larceny, and assault, and I request . . ."

The Sheriff produced a laugh—not a very good one. "Preserve us from the havers of an hysterical youth!" he exclaimed. "B'Gad, Mr Dunn, I doubt that your assistant is suffering from a touch of the sun."

"Or over-work," Dunn suggested humorously, to Bullough's shout of laughter.

But Andrew Hardie did not laugh—nor ever did, for that matter. "He is a dangerous man, a scoffer and a Jacobin, I do believe. Your honour should not suffer his insolence."

Adam proceeded, as steadily as his wrath would allow, on his chosen course—his boats were burned, anyway. "I suggest, sir—I request—that you take official action appropriate to my charge."

"Silence, fool!" The little man's voice rose to a squeak. "If you can't keep quiet, I'll have to take means to make you, damme. It is outrageous, insupportable, that I should be interrupted in this manner. Now," he turned half-away from Metcalfe, studiedly addressing himself to the crofters, "there is another matter. The man Ian MacErlich, a scoundrel of the worst type, and the renegade priest O'Brien, must be apprehended. We have reason to believe that they may be here, even amongst this assembly, in their impudent effrontery. They must be handed over to the Law. The soldiers will see to it that they do not escape. Every man take a look at his neighbour. Anyone found to be shielding them will pay dearly for his folly. In them I believe we shall have laid hands on the instigators of this rebellious outbreak."

"And that is where you are wrong!" Adam's cry was like a bugle-note. "I it was who advised resistance."

"You . . . ? What's this madness?"

"Yes, I urged them to it—so that their plight might at least be made public. I reasoned that Dunn would not wish his activities published abroad, and that if they were, no legal authorities worthy of the name would permit the conditions he has imposed on the crofters to continue. Perhaps I was wrong . . ."

"Arrest that man!"

It was John Dunn's voice, vibrant and dominant, but the Sheriff's men moved to obey it without question, thrusting their way through the people. But before they had gone more than a yard or two, a wild uproar arose in the midst of the crowd at the farther side, yells, thuds, and then a couple of shots, and more shouting. Thereupon, pandemonium broke loose. It all seemed to centre about the spot where a number of the crofters' ponies had been standing. These were now charging about wildly, their accustomed stolidity forgotten, careering around in circles with their legs apparently hobbled, and only urged to further efforts by the cries directed at them. From all points the soldiers were pressing towards the maelstrom of the disturbance, and the crowd, milling and bunching, did nothing to assist their progress. And threats, orders, and directions hurled from every side, the

barking of dogs, and a wild skirling that could be only deliberate, completed the confusion. The name MacErlich could be
made out fairly frequently above the general din.

Adam, like so many others, was staring in astonishment,
when his arm was tugged again. It was Father O'Brien this time,
enfolded in an old tartan plaid and a Highland bonnet. "Follow
me quickly," he said, "—and keep your head down."

The younger man hesitated. "But . . . where . . . ?"

"Don't worry about that. This shindy wasn't started for your
benefit, but it's you would be a fool not to profit by it. Come on,
man—and hurry."

It is possible that, had Adam been given time for consideration, he might have decided that to fly now was folly, and that
much more might be gained by allowing himself to be arrested
and tried—or, on the other hand, he might just have decided to
do exactly what he did. He glanced about him swiftly, nodded,
and ducking his head, followed the priest. Willing hands patted
and helped him on his way, and the ranks closed after him. The
urge for freedom, to escape out of the hands of one's enemies,
is strong and irradicable.

Edging and sidling their way through the press, O'Brien
brought him quickly to the rim of the crowd; only fifty yards
away was the loch-shore. At their back the hullabaloo continued. "Wait you there one moment," the priest directed. "Face
inwards. Ian More is doing finely, God bless him. I'll see to the
others. If anything goes wrong, bolt for those alders at the
water-side. Your own boat is lying behind them. But I'll be back
for sure, in two shakes," and, grinning cheerfully, if unclerically,
he was gone.

Adam, filled with a sudden wild excitement that he had not
known since childhood, turned about, feeling terribly con-
spicuous. The hubbub, far from abating, seemed to have grown
worse in the few moments that had passed. If Ian MacErlich was
responsible for it all, he was working hard. No doubt a large part
of the crowd was co-operating, at least to the length of obstructionist tactics. And even as he waited, another storm-centre
developed over to his left, with an out-break of cries and curses

and scuffling. It was a large crowd, fully three hundred strong—John Dunn's doing, that—and in an apparently stupid passive fashion, for a time, could be extraordinarily difficult to handle, even for half a company of soldiers, widely scattered.

Dunn had left his knoll and was striding furiously through the throng towards the first disturbance, supported by two of the officers, each holding a pistol, when Adam found Michael O'Brien beside him again, and more than O'Brien—Donald MacVarish, Angus Ross, and two or three others of the hostages, their hands still tied behind them. He gripped Donald Bàn's arm in silence, and then, with a knife the Irishman gave him, helped to cut their bonds.

The priest spoke quickly. "We'll be moving round the edge of the crowd till we're opposite those alders. When I give the word, make a dash for the boat. Don't all go in a bunch, and jink about as you run. When you get to the boat, lie as low as you can—likely they'll be shooting at us. Come on, now, and the good God be with us."

Warily, furtively, they slipped round, just within the outer fringe of the crowd, the crofters passing them on with straight faces and muttered encouragements. O'Brien led, Adam was just at his shoulder, and the rest close behind. One or two of the soldiers must have seen them, but, widely-spaced, with many of their number pushing their way towards the disturbances in answer to their officer's shouts, they did nothing. Undoubtedly many of them were Highlanders themselves.

Then, with the alders no more than eighty yards away, the priest turned round and pointed. Adam, crouching low, stepped forward on his toes, ready for a sprint, and then halted abruptly. A few yards away, Lieutenant Seton was staring straight at him, and quite close a corporal and another soldier stood, their muskets at the ready.

For a moment or so the two men looked into each other's eyes, and behind, the other fugitives held their breaths. Then Seton spoke, to the soldiers, not to Adam. "Go on, you fools!" he cried. "Did you not hear Captain Brough ordering you all to close in on him? Does the Eighty-first have to give its orders twice?"

The two soldiers stiffened, swung on heel and toe, and marched off as if on parade, their faces expressionless.

Alexander Seton stepped aside. "Good luck, Metcalfe," he murmured.

"Thank you, Seton. Tell Alison not to worry," and, in answer to a prod from O'Brien, Adam started to run.

He was the youngest of the runners and reached the alders first, but even before he got there, there was a volley of shouts behind. There were more soldiers than the two Seton had misdirected, and there was nothing wrong with their eyes. But they had not had orders to shoot.

The boat was not tied, only hitched to a tree-trunk, and Adam had it loosed in a moment, and held it steady for the others to clamber in. Seven of them, there was, including the priest, and they splashed up and tumbled aboard in a heap. They had the oars out, and Adam, up to his thighs in water, was pushing off, when the first shots rang out. O'Brien grabbed him by the collar and actually dragged him aboard, with surprising strength. "Down, everybody," he shouted. "Work the oars from the bottom of the boat." He himself, however, stood up and shook his fist at the pursuit. "Bah!" he cried. "Woman-fighters, house-burners—you can't even shoot straight!" With a grunt he collapsed on the floor-boards as Adam pulled him down amongst them.

"What about MacErlich?"

"Och, Ian will be fine," the priest assured. "His own plans he has—he can look after himself, Ian." He chuckled. "A grand rumpus he's made today, and no mistake . . . Mother o' God, that was a close one!"

Bullets were flying about them thick and fast now, splashing into the water, and chipping and splintering the gunwale. Rowing from below was an unhandy and irksome business, and the progress it made halting and erratic. They were moving out from the shore, but painfully slowly, and already some of the soldiers were in the water within twenty yards of them.

Adam shook his head. "As well be hanged for a sheep as a

lamb," he muttered, and from his pocket produced Ewan MacVarish's pistol, adjusted the lock and the priming, peered over the stern, and fired. The bullet threw up a spout of water between the two foremost soldiers, who stopped abruptly, cursed, and began to back.

"Good for you—give them a fright," Father O'Brien crowed. Almost, he appeared to be enjoying himself.

A shower of orders rained from the shore, but above them all, John Dunn's voice rose. "Aim for the boat, you fools—sink her," he roared.

"Pull, Angus man—pull," the priest urged. "Keep her stern to them—'tis the smallest target." He raised a hand to help pull an oar, let out a cry, and drew it in again, clutching it to himself. A splinter, torn by a bullet from the oar itself, had scored a long cut up wrist and forearm. "Saints of Glory," he complained, "'tis as well I am a poor rower, to be sure."

Almost simultaneously two more shots struck the boat, one well above the water-line, but the other below. Fortunately the lower ball made a clean hole, not a rent like that above, and a man's hand held over it stopped the flow while he made a plug to fit.

"Keep at it," O'Brien commanded. "Another hundred yards and we're quit of them. We can be across at the other side long before they can."

"What about the factor's boat?" Adam reminded.

Sucking his wrist, the Irishman grinned. "Stove in," he said. "Wicked work, but necessary. And there's not another boat on the loch. They'll have to go round, unless it's a regiment of swimmers they are."

Another volley of shots collapsed Angus Ross with a bullet in his shoulder, and a second hole appeared below the water-line. Adam was just in time to catch the smith's oar before it slipped into the water. He found rowing in this inverted position tiring in the extreme, and not noticeably effective. With the westerly breeze in their favour they were moving away from the shore, but desperately slowly and on no consistent course. Obviously, by the way the bullets were striking them, they were as often broadside on to the beach as stern-first. If only . . .

Suddenly he began to wriggle about in the huddle of men on the floor-boards. "Take this oar, somebody," he urged. "And help me off with my coat—quick."

"Are you hit, Mr Metcalfe?" That was Donald MacVarish.

"No. We must get away more quickly, and we must keep endways on, or we'll be riddled. And there is only one way to do it. Pull off those boots, will you, down there . . ."

"Ah—swim, is it?" the priest cried. "Sure, that's the thing—grand, if you can manage it."

"I'll be all right—and the boat will shield me." Swiftly he tied the boat's painter about him, and worked his way up to the bows. "Stop rowing till I give the word," he directed, and clad only in shirt and breeches, he rolled himself over the side and into the water. He swam below the surface till the painter brought him up short, and then, swinging the boat's prow round, he struck out towards mid-loch. A bullet or two passed over his head, but none fell near him.

At first he found the going extremely heavy, and his powerful breast-stroke making little way with the squat heavy boat. Then, glancing round, he saw that they had started rowing again, and actually were pulling away from him, negativing his efforts. Shouting for them to desist, he strove on, and soon the slap-slap of wavelets against the prow behind him told of his success. The shooting was still going on, in regular volleys now, and he could hear a thud or two amongst the many splashes as a ball struck the boat. After a bit, a look behind him revealed an arm baling out water with his, Adam's, hat. "Try the oars again," he gasped, "now there's some way on her. I'll tell you if it's no good."

"A board I've got out at the stern acting as rudder," O'Brien called back. "You are doing finely, my son."

So, Adam pulling, two men rowing, two baling, and the priest steering, they moved steadily away from the shore. And presently the firing stopped, and in a little the fugitives ventured to sit up. The crowd was dispersing and parties of soldiers were hurrying along the loch-shore at both sides.

"Belay, there," the priest shouted, "and we'll take the pilot aboard. Rowing as men were meant to row, we'll be across this water before any of these gentry are half-way round—if God is good and the craft doesn't sink under us! And once we are in those woods there, I'll defy all the red-coats in Scotland to catch us." And as he helped to pull Adam aboard, "The saints be praised for your good wits and your thews and your lungs, Metcalfe man," he cried. "You're the darlingest fine factor ever I saw."

The younger man, panting, smiled grimly. "I am afraid that I am a factor no longer, Mr O'Brien. I have burned my boats."

The other's eyes were suddenly grave. "Yes, you have paid a price for others, that others will not forget—nor God Almighty either. But," he looked at Adam keenly, "—it was bound to come to this in the end, you know, my son."

"I know!" Adam agreed quietly. "I have known it in my heart since the first day I came here."

They turned to face all the wooded slopes of Achroy. "I will lift up mine eyes unto the hills, from whence cometh my help," the priest intoned.

19

HIGH above the lonely valley wherein Ewan MacVarish had been darkly buried, a vast moor rose in great waves and ridges to an ultimate barrenness that was no summit nor hilltop, but a bald table-land, lofty as many a neighbouring peak, windswept, bare and sterile, Càrn na Muinc of the eagles. And scoring this stony desert and running down into the billowing heather breasts of the moor a number of small corries cut their way, narrow green fissures out of whose loins white burns were born, which, joining lower, formed the river that made the glen. In one of these corries, neither greater nor smaller than its fellows, and with no approach either from above or below that was not obvious and open to observation, Michael O'Brien had his retreat, his hermitage as he named it. Here, near the corrie's head, beneath the spreading roots of a giant and jagged tree-stump from which the earth had receded, he had made a den for himself—not the only one in his wide 'parish', but, if not the most convenient, certainly the most secure. And here, circuitously, he had brought Adam Metcalfe and the escaped hostages two nights before, and, finding the party too much for his little eyrie, had spread them out beneath adjacent roots, for all those high slopes were dotted with the great stumps of ancient trees, black and iron-hard and fully a thousand feet above the present tree-level, relic of the days when Scotland's clime was softer, or her trees like her men were of hardier breed.

The priest had the place astonishingly well-provisioned in a simple way, for the labourer is worthy of his hire, and the flock, though poor, saw that its shepherd did not want. Oatmeal and flour and salt, he had, and cheese and honey and smoked mutton and kippered salmon, not to mention a little tea and a noble jar of amber whisky. And around were ptarmigan and blue hares and the red deer of the hills, and below grouse and rabbits and roes, and fish in all the lochans and burns. Even if O'Brien's store was not calculated to support a company such as that he was now saddled with for long, they would not go hungry. An active man with a quick eye and hand need not starve in that country.

In a superficial way, Adam Metcalfe had enjoyed his two days in that high sanctuary. His position clarified, his doubts resolved, relieved of the ever-present nightmare of bearing with and resisting John Dunn, with no immediate decisions demanded of him, and in company he found to be excellent, he knew something of the short-range freedom of the outlaw, with no responsibilities and little left to lose. Care indeed, was unseemly and rather ridiculous in that quiet place of sunlight and fleeting cloud-shadows and wandering winds, where the thin whisper of young burns and the sigh of air over heather were the only sounds and disturbed the hush of it not at all. Something of the eternal peace of the high places enfolded him, and he did try to fight against it. There were problems in plenty that would require his attention, but for the moment he could do nothing about them—Alison, Alcaster, his belongings, his work, his whole future. They must wait on events. Meantime, he could discuss theology, mythology, or sheer rubbish with Michael O'Brien, tempt Donald Bàn to sing the haunting songs and talk the great talk of his people, lie on his back and watch the speck that was an eagle or a buzzard suspended in the vault of heaven, or seek, with Ian MacErlich and with varying success, to supplement the menu. Ian More had arrived at their retreat, that night of the flight from Menardmore, only some two hours after the other fugitives, highly delighted with the day's work, and his own share in particular. After creating his diversion with an old pistol, his good lungs, and the hobbled ponies—he had inserted thistles under some of their tails—the commotion of the hostage's release and flight had drawn away attention from himself, and with the co-operation of the crowd he had had little difficulty in making his escape. There had been some small attempt at a chase thereafter, but what red-coat or Sassenach or any other party at all could lay hands on Ian MacErlich in his own heather! It had been child's-play, it seemed, just child's-play.

It was late afternoon of the second day, and a discussion on which would likely be more profitable, an expedition against the stags of the high-tops or the roe-deer of the foot-hills, was interrupted by Ian More coming to tell them that two people had come out of the head of the glen and were climbing up towards them. There were no more than two, as far as he could see. The priest went for his old telescope, and followed the others to the lip of the corrie.

At first it was difficult to pick out anything amongst the hummocks and peat-hags of the shelving moor, but presently movement revealed two figures that climbed slowly, heavily. "I think . . . yes, I am sure—one of them is a woman," O'Brien reported. "The other is hidden by a heather-clump. I think it is your wife, Ian. This glass is not all it once was. So Mairi knows our little secret, does she?"

"Och, I was just mentioning the place one time to her," MacErlich answered hurriedly. "A woman likes to be knowing where her man is. But," he frowned blackly, "she never should be after climbing the hill there, and her the way she is, at all."

"You'll have to be speaking to her," Angus Ross suggested mildly. He had his arm in a sling, but seemed little the worse for his wound.

"I will so. Some meal or the like she'll be after taking us."

The priest shut his glass with a click. "Like enough, Ian—but why is she bringing Alison Hardie with her?"

In a silence that was not altogether comfortable the men awaited the women's arrival. Michael O'Brien would not allow anyone to go out and meet them; it might well be that they were being watched, followed, and the inviolability of the hiding-place was more important than any display of chivalry or fine manners. The priest did not say so, but it sounded as though he considered women to be redundant and out of place on a mountain top.

But when, reaching the foot of the corrie, the climbers changed direction, proceeding along the face of the hill, and Ian More assured the others that his wife knew the place fine and

201

that they were just making their approach indirect for the sake of secrecy, the Irishman allowed himself a word of commendation. Nevertheless, he was still against any deputation of welcome. Why spoil the ladies' good work for them, he reasoned. Adam always had heard that Irishmen were impetuous.

Clambering wearily over the rocky spine of granite and quartz that was the corrie's easternmost barrier, Alison Hardie and Mairi MacErlich stopped, and stood looking down at the men who came up towards them. Each carried a fair-sized bundle, Alison's the larger—Mairi MacErlich had enough to carry without that. Their expressions were very different, but each had something in common behind them, a quality almost of defiance. What other emotions were represented between them, it would take a bold man to say—though Alison Hardie had expressive eyes, and one man at least searched them intently.

For all the looking, it was Father O'Brien who spoke first, as was proper enough. "'Tis an unexpected pleasure, to be sure, seeing you here, ladies," he greeted them elaborately. "A long and hard road it is that you've come, and 'tis us that's honoured."

"Thank you," was all Alison said. It was not the priest that she was looking at.

Adam Metcalfe was strangely tongue-tied before her. "You must be tired," he said.

"Yes, I am tired."

"It was good of you to come. But it was too much—too far. You should not have done it."

"I had to come, Adam." There was a hint of pleading in her voice to go with the suggestion of defiance.

"You need not—you ought not to have taken the risk . . ." He did not know why he spoke as he did; it was the wrong things that he was saying. He wanted to take her in his arms, and kiss away the tired lines about her eyes, the droop at the corner of her mouth.

"We were not followed," Mairi MacErlich assured him. "We met in the big wood, and came not straightly at all. Always we

202

were watching . . ."

"I did not mean that—I mean the risk to yourselves. You must not get involved in this trouble."

Ian More put in his word. "It is not suitable for you to be after tramping the hills the way you are, woman," he told his wife severely, with glances right and left. "It's an injury you will be taking. And where is Ian Beg and the baby . . . ?"

"Och, quiet you," she told him, but not crossly. "Ian Beg is all right, and the baby, too. Morag MacKinnon has them."

Alison Hardie sat down suddenly on her bundle, biting her lip, obviously near to tears. All the men standing there, it is safe to say, felt themselves to be louts and oafs. Donald MacVarish took charge. "Come you down to our fox's den, *nighean*—both of you. A bite and a sup we all need, and our evening meal on the way—porridge and a stew of hares and ptarmigan. 'Tis just concerned we are for you. Come, now."

Adam picked up Alison's bundle, and found it fairly heavy. He sought to take her arm, but she drew slightly away. "You have come a long way to visit a boor," he managed to whisper. "Do not think me ungrateful, my dear."

She did not answer him. There seemed to be some absurd barrier between them.

Donald Bàn got busy at the little fire amongst the roots, blowing up the smouldering peats. "The porridge is gone off the boil, and . . . my-o-my, yes, there's lumps to it an' all. Plain fare, I doubt, but wholesome . . ."

"Give me that, Donald MacVarish," Mairi MacErlich commanded, taking the spurtle and not awaiting his obedience. "'Tis a woman you need here."

Her husband grinned.

Father O'Brien emerged from his cave carrying a little horn beaker with golden spirit. "Take you that, Mistress Alison," he directed. "A little *aqua-vitæ* will put new life into you—but not till you've had a mouthful or so of food. 'Tis not just the thing for a lady's empty stomach."

The girl shook her head. "No, thank you, Mr O'Brien. I am all right."

203

"Come on, girleen. 'Tis just what's needed to set you up."

"I'd rather not." She actually drew away from the out-stretched hand. "I hate the stuff." Adam thought that he understood the reason for her repugnance.

The priest was persistent. "Maybe, but it collects your strength, the stuff—and you will require all the strength that you can gather, for your journey back."

"But I am not going back."

In the silence that followed, the only sound was Mairi MacErlich's gentle crooning as she stirred the porridge.

"You will have your reasons for saying that," Donald Bàn said at length, vaguely.

She nodded. "I have my reasons."

"I cannot think that they can justify such a decision, my child." The priest's voice was grave. "This is no place for a woman, a girl gently nurtured like yourself. We are broken men, fugitives, at war with the law. This may seem an adventure to you, but its consequences are serious. A young woman's repu-tation is a precious thing, but kittle—and, my sorrow, always there are idle tongues to discuss it."

"My reputation!" She was finely scornful. "What time is this to think of reputations? Anyway, my reputation is my own, sir, and I am not concerned for it."

"Perhaps not today, but you have your life to live—and our road is not your road."

"But it is—that is why I am here. Anyway," with a shake of her head, as though to finish with argument, "I cannot go back."

"Does Andrew Hardie—does your uncle know about this?"

"He will by now. I left him a note." Her voice dropped. "I told him that . . ." She paused, as if for breath, and her glance rested on each for a second, save only on Adam. "I told him that, that, I had gone to the hills to marry Adam Metcalfe, and that I would never come back." A laugh, unsteady and unconvincing. "The last is no lie, anyways."

At length her eyes were lifted to the man's. He had not spoken. He did not speak even yet, Adam Metcalfe who was not a man unready with his tongue. He had been sitting on a granite

204

outcrop, but now he was on his feet, and, with a pace that was swift and yet deliberate, was beside her. Deep into her eyes he looked, and taking her hand, he raised it to his lips in a gesture that was fervent, almost reverent, and more eloquent than any words. Then, with her hand still clasped in his, he turned, and standing upright at her side, faced the little company of onlookers, unspeaking still. But his eyes were shining.

The priest it was who spoke. "'Tis no liar at all you are, my daughter," he said, in his deepest voice. "Praise be to God."

"Amen," she breathed.

It might be, that in the sight of God, they were wed in that same hour.

20

TO attempt to describe the rapture of the days that followed would be an impertinence. They were married the very next morning, before an altar in the wilderness and beneath the vault of heaven itself, an Episcopalean and a Presbyterian wed by a Romish priest, and no one thought to call it incongruous. Thereafter, they retired into a world of their own, a world of happiness unalloyed, and well-being physical and spiritual. Seldom can two people have found their bridal days more free from things mundane and from the everyday cares of life. In that airy world of light and mist and silence they achieved a pre-occupation with bliss and a release from care that only such circumstances could have made possible. That it could be only an oasis of delight in a desert of trouble, both were well aware. Deserving it all, let us leave them to it.

The little community on Càrn na Moine, though isolated, was not entirely cut-off from other men. Michael O'Brien had his channels of supply and intelligence, and Ian MacErlich, a restless man and avid for both gaining and dispensing information, was very active. They learned that John Dunn's fury was a thing approaching near to madness, with him raging about the country like a wild beast, and even the Sheriff, it was rumoured, advising restraint before prudently removing himself back to Dingwall. Hardie too, was unapproachable, and the few who had attended church on Sunday had had a grim time. The Colonel and Lieutenant Seton had gone, but the other military remained, and its hand was heavy. More than a score of new hostages had been arrested, and reprisals were the order of the day. All the old decrees, with new ones in addition, were more rigorously applied. Fines were stepped-up unmercifully, and impounded beasts, unless redeemed within a very short time, were driven off and declared forfeit. And the timber that Adam Metcalfe had had cut for the people at Bay of Tarve was confiscated—on the grounds that the bond of a fugitive from justice was worthless—even the wood already built into new houses was pulled out and taken, demolishing everything, unless the occupant could pay cash for it. And assaults on man, woman and beast were becoming commonplace, and redress unobtainable. And if all this was not enough, word began to come in to the effect that the evicted crofters were facing something of internal as well as external collapse. Morals were not what they had been. The stills on the hillsides were busy, and sorrows were being drowned in their products. Dissensions were apt to become violent, and self-interest was a growing force. The people, torn from their roots and hopeless, were becoming desperate, furtively desperate. In a landslide, other things slide besides land. The priest and Donald MacVarish became increasingly anxious.

Then, one day, the outlook changed. Ian MacErlich, big with news, brought the information. Things would be different now, by God. The chief, the laird, Lord Alcaster himself, had arrived. A MacVarish he was himself, through his grandmother. Poor chief as he might be, he would not have come all this way for nothing. He had started already. There was to be another meeting—everyone was to go. There would be changes now. Maybe Mr Metcalfe's letter had done its work!

It was the night of the meeting, and Adam Metcalfe had slipped down early through the woods of Achroy and round the far eastern end of the loch, and so, by way of the birches and junipers and knowes of Menard, to the back-quarters of the House. Here, awaiting his chance, he reached the back door unobserved, and thereafter the kitchen, where he found the man Colin's wife, something of a friend of his, and possessed of considerably more spirit than her husband. From her he learned, amid urgent appeals that he fly back whence he had come, that Lord Alcaster had finished his meal and was now up in his room with his valet—the big room at the head of the stairs. But surely to God Mr Metcalfe would not be doing anything so foolish as to go up there? If John Dunn caught him in this house, he'd be the death of him, whatever. She shook her head over him as, cautiously, he made for the stairway.

At the door above, he paused only long enough to recognise the earl's languid voice within, whipped it open, and was inside with his back to its panels, all with a minimum of fuss.

"What the devil . . . ? Good God, it's you!" Alcaster had been lounging at ease upon a couch, one silk-stockinged leg outstretched for the polished Hessians that his valet was holding. He sat up with a jerk at Adam's abrupt entry, and then allowed himself to sink back gracefully. Almost automatically he felt for, found, and raised his quizzing-glass. "Adam Metcalfe, 'pon my soul. And sink me—what an apparition!" The glass roved. "Where have you sprung from—a ditch?"

"It could be. When rogues ride, honest men must take to the ditches."

"Indeed!" The other's voice was cold. He waved a hand. "You can leave us, Symons. Come back in five minutes." And when the man had gone. "Well—you have been a great success up here, haven't you?"

"I have sought to serve your interests to the best of my ability."

"E'gad, you have your own conception of my interests. Does raising riots, shooting at the military, assaulting my servants, and resisting my representative, all come under that heading?"

Adam did not attempt to counter that. "Nevertheless, I have not spared myself in your service," he insisted. "All that has been forced upon me by circumstances—and the biggest scoundrel it has been my misfortune to meet."

"Meaning . . . ?"

"Your factor!"

Alcaster examined the set of his cravat in a hand-mirror, with some thoroughness. "I am afraid that I cannot accept your valuation, Adam," he said. "John Dunn is an unpolished diamond, of course, but an efficient factor. His methods may be rough and ready, but he gets results. And you do not. Baldly speaking, y'know, you are a complete failure . . . and I do not like failures, Adam." He put down the mirror, apparently satisfied.

208

"I sent you up here as assistant to Dunn—nothing else. From the first you appear to have presumed on past relations with my family to pass yourself off as something considerably more—a sort of personal ambassador of mine—whether for reasons of your own or for sheer vanity, I do not know. You took up an independent, or rather, antagonistic, attitude to your superior right away, and if he has had to deal fairly strongly with you, there is no one to blame but yourself. In fact, I think he has been very patient, for a man of his temperament. And look where you have landed yourself! A fugitive, wanted by the law, hunted by the soldiery, companion of rogues and broken men, and mixed-up in some barn-door affair with the parson's niece—the man I gave the chance of a life time!" It was not often that Humphrey Augustus permitted himself any display of emotion, but this time, obviously, he was sorely tried. His voice actually quivered. "And so, by your folly, I have had to come all this way up here, make the damnable ever-lasting journey to this God-forsaken country, to try and clear up the mess that you have made ... and at the height of the Season, too, damme. So you need not come to me seeking sympathy—if I do my duty, I shall hand you over to the constables right away."

Adam sought to control his temper. He had not come here on his own business. "I do not want your sympathy. It is on your tenants' behalf that I am here," he said tersely. "You have heard John Dunn's story. I came here to catch you before the meeting, in order that you should hear something of the other side's—as no doubt you will wish to do?"

The earl's eyebrows rose. "And what makes you think that?" he wondered. "I did not come all the way to this accursed place to hear stories. I judge by results. And John Dunn produces results beneficial to me, and you do not."

"Beneficial? I wonder. Is it to your benefit to have a formerly contented tenantry now execrate your name—the man they look on as their chief? Is it to your benefit to have the country roused, with every man's hand against the estate—how secure are your sheep-runs going to be in these circumstances? And is it to your benefit to help Bullough—and Dunn, too—make fortunes at your expense?"

"What do you mean?"

Adam left his stance at the door. "Tell me," he said, "—when I left Lakingham, I understood that you intended the estate to do the sheep-rearing. Now the land is all being let to Bullough. Why did you change your plans? Was it on Dunn's advice?"

"It was." Alcaster was no longer languid, and his glass had dropped. "Why?"

"What reasons did he give?"

"He had found out that the wintering of large numbers of sheep up here had its risks and advised that the estate leave the risks to tenant farmers, and content itself with clearing the ground and raising the rents. It seems sound advice."

"Sound for Bullough—and for Dunn," Adam agreed. "Does it surprise you to hear that your factor, while advising you against sinking your money in sheep, has sunk all his own in them, and become Bullough's partner?"

The earl got to his feet and moved over to the window, an elegant figure only slightly marred by the curiously-formed shoulders—if a little incongruous in stocking-soles. "You know, you interest me, Adam," he said softly, without turning round.

"I am glad of that," Metcalfe said briefly. "One more question, if I may." This was purely rhetorical, since he knew the answer, had seen it in Alcaster's letter to Dunn. "Has the new tenant begun making demands on the estate, backed by the factor—new houses for his shepherds, roads, drainage?"

The other coughed slightly. "Something of the sort, perhaps. Not on a big scale."

"Not yet. It is a very convenient arrangement, don't you see? Bullough chooses the ground, Dunn has it cleared and decides the rent they will pay. Bullough asks for this or that, and Dunn passes it—at your expense—buildings, fences, bridges. They will bleed the estate white. You are making them a present of the place, a whole province."

Alcaster still stared out of the window, his eyes on the drifting curtain of rain that veiled the hillsides. He did not speak.

Adam waited.

A knock sounded at the door, and the valet looked in. "Is your lordship ready for me?" he enquired. "It is half-past the hour."

Adam heard the other take a deep breath as he turned to face into the room. "All right, all right, Symons—come in, man. B'gad, you're always so damnably concerned about the time." He was all the languid elegant again, for the valet's benefit apparently, and Adam, knowing it to be a pose assumed with effort, wondered the more at the man that had been his friend.

Symons closed the door behind him, and cleared his throat. "Mr Dunn is out there, m'lord," he mentioned, but it was not at the earl he looked. His father had been gardener at Lakingham Vicarage. "I gather that he is, er, looking for somebody."

"Indeed?" Alcaster let himself down on the couch again with a sigh. "My boots," he demanded. Then, idly, "I rather think friend Dunn may be looking for you, Adam."

"I shouldn't wonder."

"Perhaps you ought not to keep him waiting?"

Adam was stiff. "Perhaps not. Perhaps you should have him in here and challenge him with the matter I have just mentioned?"

The other barely frowned, but his look was hard. "I think not. You always were an impetuous creature, Adam. You should try and counteract it, you know, for your own good." He took snuff leisurely. "A little caution, restraint, is an excellent thing."

Adam permitted himself the suggestion of a bow. "In the interests of caution and restraint then, I would suggest that you get me out of here without a scene."

The earl pretended to look startled, and rose with surprisingly alacrity. "A scene! Sink me, no scenes. I won't abide scenes. My hat, Symons," and he opened the door.

Out on the stair-head John Dunn waited, blocking the passage. Alcaster did not so much as glance at him. The factor took a step forward. "That man . . ." he rasped.

The quizzing-glass rose. "You spoke, Dunn . . . ?"

"My lord—I have a warrant for Metcalfe's arrest."

"Indeed!" Alcaster paused in front of him and stared, as

211

though at something interesting if mildly distasteful. "Then keep it, man, keep it. A handy thing to have, b'Gad." With Adam passing behind and on to the stairs, he took a couple of steps after him. "You will have to do your arresting another time," he said, turning back. "I will not have scenes in my house. I have just been telling Metcalfe that—I detest scenes."

John Dunn's expression was not a pretty thing as he watched the two proceed downstairs.

Out on the rough terrace, Adam halted. "I have to thank you, sir, for your . . . escort," he said, with the formality that was the politest reaction the man inspired in him.

"You have . . . but perhaps, if what you told me upstairs is the case, I may owe you some small appreciation."

Adam's voice grew urgent. "Then—is it too much to hope that your appreciation may be reflected in what you have to say to the crofters tonight?"

"You are deuced interested in these folk of a sudden?"

"I have found them fine people, woefully exploited."

"Exploited? I don't like your choice of words!"

"Yet exploited is the word, and worse than that—though I cannot imagine that you could condone what has been done in your name. But—this would be an excellent opportunity to undo some of it!"

Lord Alcaster seemed as if he stifled a yawn. "You are a queer fish, Adam—and devilish officious," he said. "But you can compose yourself—I have made adequate arrangements for your barbarians, entirely adequate," and turning about, he strolled back to the house.

Adam Metcalfe made his way down through the junipers, sombre-eyed. He had played his hand. He could only await the decision.

Lord Alcaster addressed his tenants and clans-people from the terrace before the House, a natural platform up to which those thronging the slope beneath most properly must look. He stood alone, with John Dunn only hovering in the background and no sign of military or constables. There had been an undercurrent of excitement evident amongst the people, which had come to the surface in an audible indrawn sigh as the earl's sauntering person had emerged from the doorway; whatever his reputation, he was still in this country a man apart, a figure to which clung the vestiges of an ancient glory and a legendary tradition. He was all they had for a chief, the heir of MacVarish, and this was Strathmoraig's first sight of him.

Seemingly more concerned with the weather than with the importance of the occasion, he kept glancing upward and around. Indeed, throughout his address, the possibility of rain seemed to preoccupy him, and may have been partly responsible for the brevity of the proceedings. He dispensed with preamble.

"I understand that there has been a deal of trouble up here of late," he began, "—discontent, ill-feeling, and lately, lawlessness, which in its turn has given rise to counter measures of some severity, necessary but unfortunate. In normal times I should leave this matter to the parties duly concerned, my factor and the proper legal authorities. But the times are not normal. This country is at present passing through a period of trial and danger, grave danger, and I feel a certain responsibility to make sure that my property up here plays its due part in the national effort—a feeling occasioned, no doubt, by the long period ancestors of mine have held this estate. In a time such as this, when Bonaparte is threatening imminent invasion of our land, and at the same time endeavouring to starve us into submission by means of his blockade, personal and sectional interests must bow before the nation's need. It is a grief to me that, so far, the tenants of this property have shown so little appreciation of the true state of affairs, that they have resisted all attempts at the improvements of the estate. The country needs meat and wool. We can, and shall, provide it here. Surely I should not require to tell you where your duty lies? Crofting, such as the majority of you pursue, is a most wasteful and uneconomic way of using the land—well enough in the past perhaps, but quite out of date today. The upland pastures and the glens, ideal ground for the sheep the country requires, must be cleared and made productive. The estate has endeavoured to make available alternative

213

land—which it was in no way bound to do—and at the same time to introduce to you a further means of livelihood in sea-fishing. But in all this it has had no assistance from the tenants, who, it is apparent, have done everything in their power to make the change difficult and unsuccessful. I have instructed my factor to continue with this experiment, uneconomical as it is from my point of view, but I must point out that suitable land for crofting purposes is very limited, and it is quite out of the question to replace every tenant in a new holding. The fact of the matter is—experts all agree on this—that this Highland country is quite unsuited for the support of a large population. Nature has not intended it, and, ahem, man cannot fly in the face of God." His glance, which had remained fixed for some time somewhere near the summit of the hillside opposite, swept quickly over the silent company, faltered for a moment when it met Adam's, right below him and near the front, and then moved on. "Fortunately, however, the situation has its brighter side." He spoke more quickly. "There is no need for any to go either hungry or idle. There is a great demand for labour in the South. The country has never needed so many workers, in agriculture, in the new manufactories, on defence works, and at the sea-ports. Then there is the Army, crying out for more men. I understand that lately you have had two officers here conducting a recruiting campaign, which met with a most disappointing reception. It should not require strangers to point out to you the duty of every man fit to bear a musket when your country and your king need you. I am determined that Strathmoraig shall not be backward in this respect—I trust it will not be necessary for me to bring pressure to bear!" He paused significantly. "Lastly, there is a matter into which I have put much thought. His gracious Majesty has vast territories across the seas, rich, fertile, empty lands, awaiting only the labour of men's hands to make them yield abundantly, lands which make this island of ours seem only a barren rock. At considerable trouble and no little expense, with your future well-being in view, I have arranged with my friend Lord Berwick to share the cost of chartering and fitting-out a ship to take as many of you as is possible out to his

214

new colony of New Berwick in the Canadas, where there is room for all, land for all, and to spare. This vessel will be at Kinlochardoch approximately three weeks from now. I hope a large number of you will take advantage of this opportunity to start a new life under these favourable circumstances. I may say that my arrangement with Lord Berwick requires that a minimum of one hundred and twenty settlers will go. This number must sail. In this connection, to make the offer available to all, and in response to the entreaties of someone who has your interests very much at heart,"—his eyes searched for Adam's— "I am prepared to use my influence with the Sheriff to cancel the charges against all those who have been arrested or whose arrest is sought. I trust that this gesture will be understood. It is necessary that the problems of this estate be solved swiftly and satisfactorily. It is my intention that they shall be solved in the manner I have indicated." He took out his snuff-box, and tapped it deliberately. "That is all," he said, and walked away.

That was Lord Alcaster's meeting.

From the stricken silence of the gathering, Adam Metcalfe ran in pursuit of the speaker. There was no veneer of deference about him now, as he clutched the other's arm and swung him round. "So that is the best you could do—those are your adequate arrangements!" he charged.

Alcaster withdrew his arm coldly. "Yes—are you not satisfied? I have been generous. You are a free man again—and all your strange friends likewise."

"Generous!" Adam snorted. "That cost you nothing. None of us have done you hurt. But, setting yourself up as a patriot, you have condemned your people to exile—for your own base profit."

"I would advise you to select your words more carefully, sir."

He was ignored. "And what about Dunn? You are going to let him remain in charge up here?"

"Naturally. I told you he was an efficient factor."

"Knowing that he is defrauding you . . . ?"

"Knowing what I do, he is more valuable to me than ever.

215

Why kill the goose that lays the golden eggs, when you can squeeze even bigger eggs out of it? I will raise the rents and raise them again, and though Bullough, through him will protest, they will have to pay. And I will make them pay for their improvements. With the information I have, I hold them in a cleft stick. I will make them enrich this estate for me, at no cost to myself—indeed, they will pay me well for the privilege. No, my friend, I shall not dispense with John Dunn yet awhile—as long as there is a screw still to turn!"

Adam was staring at the man. "My God, Humphrey," he said, almost in a whisper. "I believe you are the biggest knave of them all!"

The Earl of Alcaster swung on his heel and made for the doorway. After a few paces he turned his head. "I said you were a free man, Metcalfe," he jerked. "But I advise you to go, nevertheless, and as far away as you can. You understand me— as far away as you can!"

Later, Adam, with the others, set his face and his feet for the hills and Càrn na Moine. They were talking, angrily, bitterly, or hopelessly. But Adam did not talk. His face was set. He had made his decision, and was schooling his mind to accept the consequences.

21

THE *Charlotte's* timbers scraped shudderingly against the wooden jetty as she lifted gently to the incoming tide, and now and again the whole vessel swayed, to a long-drawn creaking, when some weary echo of the long Atlantic swell reached the head of the loch. Overhead, the stripling wind of evening whistled fitfully through the cordage, a thin sound, mournful as the others, to which the sorrowing circling gulls added their endless collect. Below, the people who stood or sat about the decks amongst the ropes and baggage, though silent, were in tune with the general refrain. There was no wailing, no keening, only the quiet that spoke loudly as either. Even the crew was out of evidence, with cargo and stores already stowed, and the captain only awaiting full tide to make sail. The noise and demonstration was over; only the reflection of it all remained.

Near the gangway that still linked with the shore, a little group sitting on multi-shaped bundles and packages, spoke together in the undertone that the occasion imposed.

"He will be here." Father O'Brien was assuring. "That one always turns up. 'Tis a last minute entry he'll be making, the way he has."

"Mairi should have come with us," Alison said anxiously. "She should not have waited for him. She is in no state for hurrying." Her eyes swept the road where it ran back along the loch-shore till it was swallowed in the blue waves of heather. "There is no sign of them, at all. Ian More is so absurd. Why can't he do things sensibly, properly, like other people?"

Her husband smiled at her. "He would not be Ian More if he did, my dear." He stooped and patted the small head at her knee. "If this young man grows up as good a man as his father, he will not do badly."

Ian Beg did not look up. Playing with a toy boat that Donald MacVarish had whittled for him, he was crooning contentedly.

That his young sister was crying fretfully in the arms of Anna Bain nearby, worried him no whit.

Alison Metcalfe sat on the heap of her worldly belongings, a tartan plaid thrown around her shoulders—for the evening air had a chill to it—and the setting sun made a halo about her wind-blown hair. Her eyes were clear as she looked back at the land she was leaving—it had been her home but not her cradle. "You can see the smoke even from here," she pointed out quietly.

"That is Glen Guish," Donald Bàn nodded. "They are not wasting their time, at all, and the folk scarce out of the houses."

"Better treatment than we had, our own selves," Angus Ross commented. "But it is hard, hard, whatever."

"Yes, it is hard," the priest agreed. "The evil flourish, and God's ways are inscrutable. But sure as there is a Heaven above, the time will come that those responsible will regret what they are doing today."

None answered him—save only the wheeling birds.

Presently a voice hailed them. "Hey, Mister—it's near deep water," the skipper shouted aft. "I won't be able to wait long for your late-comers. The channel's shallow enough at full-tide, s'help me."

Adam nodded. "Give them as long as you can, Captain," he pleaded.

Michael O'Brien stood up. "Time it is for me to be on my way, my friends," he declared. "As it is, 'twill be near tomorrow before I am at Càrn na Moine tonight."

Adam took hold of his arm. "Will you not change your mind and come with us?" he urged. "Start a new parish in the New World. The people need you."

The priest shook his head. "Not so much as those that are left, my son," he said. "I cannot leave them. This is where I was sent, and here I must remain, meantime. Someday, perhaps, I shall follow you, with the others, and leave this land to the sheep."

His goodbyes said, he moved to the gangway, and at its head turned, and, lifted his hand. And all the hundred and fifty souls that thronged the deck and faced the unknown, Catholic and

Protestant alike, sank to their knees, while he blessed them, first in the Gaelic then in English, comprehensively, their bodies, souls, and spirits, their voyaging, their land-fall, their homes to be, the flocks and herds they would raise, the crops they would grow, their future freedom and prosperity and the fine land they would make of the country they sought, and their everlasting peace. His strong rich voice broke as he finished, and wheeling abruptly, he strode down to the pier without a backward glance.

They watched him as his figure diminished and grew indistinct among the shadows of the halting track that threaded the rolling moors, till, in a stray level beam of the setting sun he was etched for a moment clearly, on the summit of a knoll, small and infinitely lonely, before he plunged down into the purple gloom, and was gone.

It was only a minute or two after the priest had vanished, that another figure came into sight on the same sunlit knoll, hastening in the opposite direction. "Here they come, thank Heaven," Adam cried. "I was afraid that they were going to be too late."

Alison shook her head. "There is only one there—and it is Mairi. Ian More is a terrible man. He has no thought for her, worrying her like this. How much longer will the captain wait?"

The men were silent, watching.

Mairi MacErlich came hurrying, and her trial was apparent to all. Panting, her heavy bosom heaving, she reached the gangway, and two sailors, loosing the cables preparatory to casting-off, found the spectacle amusing in the extreme. Alison went to her, and taking her plaid and her bundle, brought her in.

"Is that the lot, then?" the captain shouted.

"No—there is one to come still," Adam called back . "This woman's husband." And to Mairi MacErlich, "Will Ian More be long now?"

She stood before them in her distress, for she was seven months gone, and she had come fast and far, and her son, running to her, clung to her thigh and began to cry. But, though her breathing was difficult, she looked at them steadily and her expression was composed, as it always was. "Ian More will not

219

be coming," she said, then, quietly. "He will not be coming at all."

"But, Mairi . . . !"

"Ian More is dead. John Dunn is dead, too. Ian More killed him with his *sgian dubh*, his little knife. It was the thing he had to do. The soldiers shot him, running. Wheesht you, Ian Beg, wheesht you, now, *mo graidh* . . ."

Slowly the vessel's bows swung round into the sunset, to the flapping of canvas and the thrumming of the rigging, and somewhere forward a woman threw her apron over her head, and her wail of sorrow lifted up and endured. Alison shivered, and Adam's hand pressed her shoulder. He remembered Andrew Hardie's words, ". . . just women's easy tears; the least thing will set them off at it. What they need is faith in God . . ." Then, from the stern rose up a sound that pierced and stilled the woman's keening, as a piper took his reeds and put his soul and all the suffering of the world into a lament, that rose and fell and rose again, and fused all other sounds of wind and gulls and tears into one antiphon of sorrow, inexpressible, exquisite.

Alison turned up her face, and great tears welled into her eyes. "Oh, Adam . . ." she choked. "I am afraid . . ."

His arms enfolded her. "Courage, my dear," he whispered. "There is nothing to fear. The fear is behind us. Look at it," and he turned her head towards the north-east and Strathmoraig and the darkening hills, where a murky glow was growing to tinge the clouds of night. "There is fear—all past and done with, consumed in fire. And there," he directed her back to face the glory of golden light into which they sailed, where sea and sky met in a blaze of colour, "—there is the future, there is our road." He paused. "Listen—do you hear the piper now?"

Strangely, almost imperceptibly, the lilt was changing. The notes were shortening, the undertones were rising, the tempo was quickening. Sorrow was in it still, but not the lost despairing sorrow it had held before; there was hope in it now, courage and resolve. It was not a lament that the piper played any more, it was a challenge, MacVarish Mor's Challenge, as the *Charlotte* sailed out into the West.